BEAUTIFUL MIDNIGHT

FRANÇOIS HOULE

DRB

Dawn Rainbow Books

OTTAWA, ONTARIO

This is a work of fiction. Names, characters, places, and incidents either are a product of the author's imagination or are used fictitiously, and any resemblance to actual people, living or dead, or to businesses, establishments, events, institutions, or locales is completely coincidental.

For permission requests, please email: francois@francoisghoule.com

www.francoisghoule.com

Beautiful Midnight/François Houle. -- 1st ed.

ISBN: 978-1-7750490-2-9

Published by Dawn Rainbow Books

Cover Design: KD Design

Cover Art Image: lightpoet©123RF.com

Editor: Ethan James Clark, SilverJay Editing

For Mom

ONE

~ September 2001 ~

I should have been dead long ago.

Midnight Madison looked at herself in the bathroom mirror, her wet body, skeleton-scrawny and lacking curves, dripped on the cold, cream-coloured ceramic tiles. She noticed a pimple on her forehead and sighed. Seemed she couldn't keep up with them lately and frankly she didn't care. Her short brown hair, which was almost dry, wouldn't help her hide this small blemish. Everyone at school would notice. Again, she didn't really care. It really didn't matter. Maybe once it would have, but lately it seemed like these things so many kids her age stressed about meant so little to her. Even her hair. It had been long most of her life, but last year she'd decided it was time for a change and cut it. A move her friend Samantha had questioned.

I was tired of taking care of it, she'd told Samantha.

Apparently not the only thing, Samantha had said.

Samantha just didn't understand. They'd been friends since grade one, but as sophomores in high school, their differences had become more and more apparent over the last three years and were now taking them in opposite directions. Midnight didn't think they were going to remain friends, let alone best friends, much longer. Life had a way of making that happen.

Midnight grabbed the plush purple bath towel off the rack and dried herself.

Why did He spare me?

It wasn't the first time the thought had crossed her mind. She wasn't anyone special. Hadn't done anything really great or mindful or caring in the last fifteen years. She was just another teenage girl trying to fit into a world she didn't understand and which seemed to be going to hell anyway. Just yesterday, two planes had crashed into the World Trade Center and now everyone waited for the world to end.

God spared me for this bullshit?

Midnight gave her reflection in the mirror the middle finger, walked out of the bathroom with the towel wrapped around her, and crossed the hallway to her room. She could hear her dad snoring in his bed. He'd probably been up late, as he normally was, either working on his writing or working on a bottle.

She hoped it had been his writing this time.

She pulled on a pair of low-rise blue jeans and a short-sleeved black t-shirt and headed to the kitchen to grab a piece of toast with blueberry jam. She made a pot of coffee, not so much for her but for her dad, hoping the smell would get his butt out of bed. If he'd actually hit the bottle last night, he would need his black java.

Midnight poured herself a cup as well and drank it black, just like her old man. She sort of hated it, but figured if she was making it, she might as well get addicted to it too. After she'd finished eating her breakfast, she put the dirty dishes in the dishwasher, brushed her teeth, grabbed her backpack, and headed for the door.

"What, you don't have a kiss for your old man?"

"Hey Dad," she said and kissed his cheek. "Guess the black java tickled your nostrils."

"Yes, thanks for making it."

"Headache?"

"A little."

"Told you not to drink so much."

"Have I told you how much I love you?"

Midnight grinned. "I know. Got to go. Love you too."

"Have a wonderful day at school," he said. "Make someone happy."

She closed the door behind her and didn't look back. Sometimes, her dad worried her. It had been twelve years since his dream life had ended, but he still bled it every single day. Funny how he felt it was her Christian duty to make someone happy, yet she couldn't make him happy. Not that he was unhappy with her—she was a straight-A student, didn't get into trouble, took care of him best she could. But he was such a mess most of the time. His heart was so full of love and goodness and Midnight hated to see him wasting away like he was. She would even welcome a stepmom if that pulled him out of his lifelong misery.

He deserved that much after everything he'd done for her. After everything he'd given up for her. Midnight stopped and glanced back at the old house she'd called home since the day she was born. The roof shingles had needed replacing for years, but still they'd managed to get through one more winter. The heat of last summer had made more of them curl at the corners. She knew they didn't really have the money, but eventually the roof would get damaged and they'd be looking at a whole lot more money to fix that.

Her gaze shifted to the living room window, where she could see the shadow of her father looking out at her, a cup of coffee in his hand. She resisted the urge to wave, letting him think that she couldn't see him. She knew he worried about her, probably felt guilty about the state of their lives. She had never complained. He'd done his best to raise her and Octavia, her older sister. He'd figured a way to work from home and be there for them. Being a freelance writer had meant spells where assignments didn't come and money had to be stretched, but they'd never gone without life's basic necessities. Sure, some of the kids at school nowadays were showing up with cell phones, but she didn't see the need for one. They had basic cable at home, which was fine and kept her TV-watching to a minimum, and their groceries fit within a tight budget, but she'd never gone hungry.

Midnight didn't let these trivial things bother her.

It's just the way her life was and she was fine with that. Some might think she were poor, especially by twenty-first-century standards, but she had a roof over her head, clothes on her back that Octavia had passed down to her, and maybe they weren't as fashionable as when her sister had worn them, but Midnight didn't really care. She liked the retro style. For the most part, she was happy. Not somersault-and-backflip happy, but by her definition of the word, she was. All that really mattered was that her dad was there for her, that she never had to worry that he wouldn't be there when she came home after school, that he would never abandon her.

And she would never abandon him.

He needed her probably more than she needed him now. The drinking was bothering her, though. It was a demon he struggled with—had been for a long time—and sometimes he seemed to be winning, but most times it owned him.

Midnight pulled her lower lip between her teeth. She wondered what would happen to her father if she weren't there to take care of him.

Maybe that's why He spared me.

☙ ❧

Samantha Carmichael sat at the beautifully crafted cherry makeup table in her bedroom where she went through her morning ritual, applying black eye shadow, black eyeliner, and black mascara—the look she preferred lately. She pulled it all together with glossy pink lipstick that made her already full lips look that more delicious.

Samantha smiled, but there was venom in that smile, cobra-venom, like she owned you if you stared at her for too long. That smile bordered on a sneer. *Careful what you wish for*, it seemed to taunt.

A few unfortunate past boyfriends—four, to be exact, in the last twelve months—walked wide circles to avoid her now.

With broken hearts.

Samantha braided her long golden blond hair, then changed her mind and combed it out a dozen times, until all the knots were gone. She let it fall over her shoulders, down the middle of her back. Satisfied, she stepped into a pair of skin-tight, low-rise blue jeans and donned an antique white blouse, untucked, sleeves rolled up, the top three buttons undone. She knew it would tease the boys at school as they tried to get a good look.

Samantha admired herself.

Perfect.

Totally BBM.

Beautiful.

Blonde.

Money.

A lethal combination, she knew, but so what? So what if her daddy had made his money in the stock market? So what that most of her friends were her friends because she now had money? So what if all the boys wanted to get into her pants?

Let them think they could.

She was just a teenage girl, and this was what teenage life was about. A time to screw up and not care because it didn't really matter. Teenage years were the audition for the rest of your life, and you weren't expected to get it right. It was a time for foolishness and experimentation, and that was exactly what Samantha Carmichael was doing. Sure, she felt like a fraud at times, but weren't they all at that age? Most of her friends, she wouldn't trust to turn her back to, but then again, most of them wouldn't dare cross her. Samantha was it-girl, the in-girl, the one they all wanted to be seen with.

And she relished it.

Why shouldn't she?

But all good things had to have a bad side, and as popular as she was at school, home life wasn't like the facade she wore at school. No, home life was full of tension, anxiety, and high expectations.

"Your grades slipped last year," her mother had reminded her last week when school started. "You had better pull it together this year if you want to get the grades for university. You've got opportunities I never had."

Samantha was so bored of that conversation. At least her dad didn't bitch at her all the time. Then again, she rarely saw him. He came home late, when he came home at all, and was gone before she woke. She actually didn't really know what he did, had never cared to ask. They had moved to this five-bedroom mansion last summer, a far cry from the tiny three-bedroom townhome they'd lived in. Now her room was more than twice the size as before, she and her younger sister Emily shared an ensuite, one of the spare bedrooms was a gym for her mom, and the fifth bedroom was for when visitors stayed over; the kitchen was the size of the first floor of their old house, and the backyard had a gigantic in-ground pool that looked tiny in the expanse of the entire yard.

All because her daddy had become rich in stocks. At least, that's what they were told. She didn't care. It was nice to live in a house big enough that if she wanted to avoid her mother, she could do so easily. It was nice not to hear her parents fighting because their room wasn't adjacent to hers anymore. It was on the other side of the house, at the end of the hallway, separated by three other bedrooms and the ensuite. It was nice to wear designer clothes, and to have straight teeth—her braces had come off last September, which is when her popularity had climbed to new heights. She'd started to blossom two years ago and now she was absolutely gorgeous.

And she knew it.

And she used it.

And to hell with those who didn't like it.

But she wasn't all bravado. She knew how quickly everything had changed for the better and when she was alone in her room, lying in bed with the lights turned off, she worried that all her good luck could evaporate as quickly as it had come. At those times, she pulled the blankets over her head and cried quietly so that Emily didn't hear her, and she cried until exhaustion dragged her into troubled sleep.

Her parents fought a lot. Too much to be happy. Too much to be in love. It had been that way at the old house, mostly fighting about money and the lack of, but now it was about Dad never being home, Dad always working and leaving Mom alone, and well, where the hell did the money come from if it wasn't because he was working his ass off, so cut him some slack. Samantha had no idea if one had to work hard to make money in the stock market, barely understood what the stock market was, and she'd heard that yesterday's attack on the U.S. could be disastrous for the stock market. She just hoped her dad didn't lose all their money, and if he needed to work like a dog to make sure they didn't lose it all, then her mom should just shut up about it and let him work.

Samantha had always thought her mom to be somewhat needy and she often wondered what had brought her parents together. They seemed so different.

"Samantha, we've got to go," her mother shouted from the bottom of the stairs. "Come on or you'll be late for school, which means Emily will be late too."

Samantha took one last look at herself in the mirror, nodded, grabbed her backpack that was sitting on her bed, and hurried down to the foyer where her beautiful mother waited with the patience and grace of a rabid Dalmatian.

☙ ❧

Midnight decided to wave to her dad after all and then started to walk away. Out of habit, she glanced at the neighbour's house, an identical home to hers built some thirty years ago. It seemed that builders lacked imagination back then, as they'd built the same model with just slight variations in elevation, siding or brick colours, and window offerings. An older couple with a Shih Tzu—her name was Snow, which was appropriate because she was mostly white with a few blazes of light chocolate running across her back and belly, and she always ran up to Midnight with her tail wagging—lived there now. They were a nice couple of Russian origin and had thick accents. Now that she was older, Midnight chatted with them on occasion, mostly about Snow, who had been a five-month-old puppy when they'd bought the house from the Murphys. Tyler Murphy had lived there.

Her first and only boyfriend.

His family had moved away when she was five and she hadn't seen him since. Every morning, as she walked by his old house, she wondered if he ever thought of her or even remembered her. It had been ten years, and he was a boy, so she doubted he ever gave her a passing thought.

Midnight crossed the street and glanced at the park where they used to play soccer, football, tag, and any other games they could think of. She had kissed him, full on the lips, behind the spruce that now stood twenty feet or more but back then had been half the size and width. The park looked really old now.

And empty.

Seemed all the little kids in the area had grown up and barely ever came to the park now, except late at night to drink and smoke behind that row of spruces close to the fence that stood between the park and the next row of backyards.

Midnight picked up the pace. She didn't want to be late. Being late was a sign of disrespect—another thing Samantha didn't quite grasp. She believed everyone should be waiting for her, that the whole damn world should pause until she showed up.

It truly irritated Midnight.

The friendship had been in a slow decline, it seemed forever. Somehow, they'd managed to remain friends. For now. She should feel sad about that, and there were times, mostly when she was home alone, that she did, but when the two of them were together, it just made Midnight's vein in the middle of her forehead throb. She reached the end of her street and waited for Samantha's mom to pick her up. Midnight was more than willing to walk to school even though it took her thirty minutes, but Mrs. Carmichael said she didn't mind, that it was on her way. Not exactly true, as she had to get off the main road, but come winter Midnight would be grateful for the ride. Her dad could drive her, but he couldn't always be depended on.

Less than five minutes later, the beige minivan pulled up.

"Need a ride, mister?" Samantha said and laughed. "Oh sorry, you're not a boy after all."

"That joke was old months ago and now it just reeks of decay," Midnight said and climbed in to take a seat beside Emily.

"Hey Em."

"I have no idea why you're friends with my stupid sister," Emily said.

"I often wonder that too," Midnight said. "Morning, Mrs. Carmichael."

"Morning, honey. Hope we didn't keep you waiting too long. Had to wait for Miss Princess to put herself together. How's your dad?"

"He was just getting ready for work when I left," she said.

"He's still doing that writing thing?"

"I think you asked Midnight that just last week," Samantha said. "It's his job, so why wouldn't he still be doing it?"

Midnight felt the temperature dip ten degrees so she quickly jumped in. "He likes it. And I like it that he's there when I come home."

Her father had converted Octavia's bedroom to an office after she'd moved out, which had been better than being stuck in a cold damp basement like he'd been all the years before that. Octavia was seven years older and had moved in with her boyfriend Mark last year. Midnight missed her sister and often visited, although it took her two buses and nearly an hour to get to her place.

"I'm glad to hear that," Mrs. Carmichael said. "You guys doing okay?"

"We're fine," Midnight said. She knew Mrs. Carmichael worried about her and even though Midnight had never told Samantha's mom, she *was* grateful. It was nice that someone other than her dad cared. "We are."

Midnight saw Samantha's mom look at her in the front

mirror, and if she didn't quite believe Midnight, she didn't call her out on it.

"Okay, so let's drop Emily first and then the big girls."

"Ugh," Samantha said. "I really hate it when you call us that."

"Better than being called a tramp," Mrs. Carmichael said. "Or worse."

"Seriously, Mom."

"Guess next year when I'm in grade seven, I'll be one of you," Emily said.

"Fantastic! You can be the big girl in my place. I'll gladly give up the moniker."

"Wow! Did you hurt yourself?" Emily said. "You don't usually use *big* words. Oops! There's that word again."

"Shut up."

"Make me."

"Girls."

Midnight looked out the side window and tuned out the nonsense that was going on with the Carmichaels. She couldn't remember ever bickering with Octavia. Maybe the age difference had something to do with that. Or maybe it was because she loved her sister. Maybe Samantha and Emily *did* love each other and this was their way of showing it.

Midnight shrugged. The minivan moved away from the curb and instinctively she tried to look down the street, but she couldn't see her house, nor Tyler's old house.

☙ ❧

Midnight always enjoyed Art Class, except that today she simply sat there staring at a blank piece of paper, a frown on her brow.

So much had happened yesterday, and the world had become a little uglier.

Last night, she and her dad had watched the news, which kept showing the planes flying into the towers over and over again, and he had looked completely devastated.

"This is so close to home," Midnight said.

"New York city doesn't seem that far from Ottawa," Jim said.

"Will we have a war?"

"I don't know," he said after downing the last of his third beer. "Terrorism has no borders. It's not like a specific country can be blamed. These people are almost impossible to find."

It was during that conversation that she really noticed that her dad had grown older over the past year, the crow's feet around his eyes deeper, and his hair thinner and greyer, as if this latest world tragedy was his burden to bear alone. He was a man of deep feelings, something that made him a wonderful man, but also a tormented man. He seemed unable to let go of things he couldn't change.

He'd had too much to drink again last night and her thoughts drifted to two years ago, when out of desperation and anger, she had gotten rid of all the booze in the house, pouring it down the kitchen sink while he took a nap—well, he'd passed out, to be truthful—but when he'd woken up, it had been an ugly sight.

"Why did you do that?" he'd yelled. "D'you have any idea how much that stuff cost? I can take care of myself; I don't need you to look after me."

Midnight had never seen her dad so hot, his anger exploding behind his eyes and pinning her with such ferocity that she'd started to cry and had run to her room and had hid under her blankets, shaking, a hole in her heart so big she could have fallen into it.

"Can I come in?" her dad had said after knocking gently on her door a few minutes later. "I'm . . . I'm sorry, honey. I totally overreacted."

She'd pulled the blankets over her head and remained silent. She'd heard the door open and then felt her dad sit on the edge of the bed.

"I know you meant well," he'd said. "And I'm an ass for blowing up like that. I drink way too much, I know. I know. I'll join AA. I will. I need to." He'd sat quiet for a moment. "I'll never yell at you again. That's a promise."

He had joined AA.

But his loneliness and emptiness had needed solace and he'd lapsed with the AA meetings, and a six-pack had started to come home with him with regularity, and even though he drank most nights, he had been true to his words and had never yelled nor gotten angry with her again.

Midnight hated to see him so damn broken.

But what was she supposed to do? All she could do was look out for him and love him. Because he really was a great guy and when she saw what her mother leaving had done to him, it made her hate the woman that she barely knew even more. On more than one occasion, Midnight had hoped that her mom was dead, that she had died a horrible death because what she had done to the man she had vowed to love forever, through good and bad, until death, was unforgivable.

The bell rang, class ended, and Midnight made her way to her locker where she grabbed her gym clothes and headed toward the change room. She hated gym. Not because she wasn't any good—in fact, she was better than all the girls in her class. No, what she hated was seeing every other girl with boobs and curves while she remained boyishly shapeless, puberty seemingly bypassing her or playing a cruel joke on her.

So she put up a front, one that showed indifference, but she was still just a teenage girl with feelings, and as hard as she tried to stifle them, it still hurt to hear what the other girls said, murmurs behind her back, murmurs that she was weird, murmurs that her mom hadn't loved her enough to stay.

Her armour wasn't impervious.

Maybe Samantha was right about her haircut and maybe she should let her hair grow back. It's just that she'd heard her dad compliment her too many times how like her mother she looked before she'd cut it.

Midnight changed as fast as she could and headed out to the soccer field where she did her best not to kill anyone when she pounded the ball—an outlet that helped her unleash the frustration bottled up inside of her.

☙ ❧

When Midnight got back to her locker after gym, Samantha was waiting for her. No matter what might be happening between them, whether their friendship was really slowly burning itself out or not, the two friends always ate lunch together and Samantha always waited for Midnight at her locker. It was like Samantha cut class a couple minutes early to make sure she was there when Midnight showed up.

For a moment, when Midnight saw her friend standing there

all beautiful and sexy and having it all, a surge of hot blood rushed through her veins and she wanted to scratch Samantha's perfect skin off her face, dig deep painful and scarring grooves that would make her invisible to the world like Midnight was.

She loved Samantha and her heart felt like a tiny aching fist inside of her chest. How could she have these thoughts about her best friend? Midnight knew Samantha had never asked to be born so beautiful and lucky, just like she herself had never asked to be born so ugly and unlucky.

Okay, until a year ago Samantha hadn't been that pretty. She'd worn glasses and had braces on her teeth, and lived in a tiny house down the street from Midnight, but Samantha's luck had changed.

Midnight frowned. What was getting into her today? She felt out of sorts, angry and lost and feeling a bit sorry for herself.

So not Midnight Madison.

"Hey girl," Samantha said. "Gym, huh?"

"My favourite," she said and any ill thoughts she'd had disappeared.

"Next year we don't have to take it, so look forward to that."

"I am, believe me." Midnight stuffed her sweaty gym clothes into her locker and grabbed her lunch bag. "I'm starving."

"Why do you still bring a lunch bag? You can buy food here."

"I'm not eating that crap. Full of refined sugars and who knows what. Not a chance." Her body might not be the body of a goddess, but Midnight respected it. She was afraid of what might happen if she didn't. It had once turned on her and she was doing her best not to let that happen again. "I like to know what I ingest."

"Who says *ingest*? You're so weird sometimes."

"It's really not such a difficult word to say. And it is what we do with food."

"Whatever," Samantha said. "Let's just go *ingest* our lunch."

"Shut up!"

"You shut up!"

The two girls walked away, and all eyes followed Samantha—the boys wanted to be with her, and the girls wanted to be just like her—and all the mean-spirited whispers were aimed at her geeky freaky friend Midnight.

What if He'd spared me so stupid teenagers could torment me?

The thought slammed into her like a fist out of darkness, but it wasn't the first time it had crossed her mind. Lately, her thoughts seemed twisted, morose, self-deprecating.

"Hey, Night-Night, you with me?" Samantha said.

Midnight pulled a fake smile out of the depth of her darkness and plastered it onto her face. Samantha had given her that nickname back in grade one, and she used it occasionally, usually to get Midnight's attention. "Yeah, I'm with you."

Samantha stopped her with a hand on her forearm. "You okay? You seem off today, more than usual. Your dad okay?"

Midnight nodded. "Yeah, we both are. I mean, he's drinking again, but it's not too bad. It's not that, really. It's . . . what happened yesterday."

"The towers."

"Doesn't it bother you that people died for no reason?"

Samantha looked uncomfortable. "It does. It's unbelievable. But what are we supposed to do? I mean, we're just teenagers living in another country."

"I know," Midnight said. "It would just be nice to do something, you know, to make the world better."

The two girls started walking again. "I'm not sure we can change the world. It's so messed up."

"Maybe not the whole world," Midnight said as they reached the cafeteria doors and Samantha pulled on the left one. "But maybe we can do something here. We do have to fulfill our forty hours of community work and I haven't put in a single hour yet. Have you?"

Samantha shook her head. "Please don't go all nuclear on this like the time they found that girl's body in the woods."

Just last year, Jordan Lachance had disappeared and three weeks later her body had been discovered by a jogger over at the pit. Jordan had been a senior at their school and lived just three streets over from Midnight. She had volunteered for Jordan's search, and the longer the search turned out empty, the more freaked out Midnight had become, to the point that her dad had had to insist she stop helping.

The week that followed the discovery of Jordan's body, Midnight had been haunted by extremely violent nightmares where she woke up screaming so loud it left her throat sore and raw for days.

"I just want to do something," she said, but her words where swallowed by the cacophony that filled the cafeteria, a noise that could only be generated by two hundred teenagers controlled by raging adolescent hormones.

Midnight followed Samantha, who led her to their table on the other side of the room where some of Samantha's friends waited. Midnight was sure they only tolerated her and on days that Samantha wasn't at school, Midnight normally skipped lunch or took it outside where she'd find a quiet spot and eat alone with her notebook. She sometimes drew, sometimes wrote her thoughts. On the front of the notebook she had written *Make Someone Happy*.

Maybe she could *make someone happy* like her dad told her every morning when she left for school, like he truly believed that she had the power to do such a thing.

Maybe she did, if she'd try.

☙ ❧

Samantha saw Kim and Julie sitting at their table and sort of forgot about Midnight. Those two were her audience; she could manipulate them as she pleased and Samantha loved the rush it gave her. Knowing that Kim and Julie idolized her was an incredible high and right now she needed that. Midnight, as much as she loved her, could exhaust Samantha. Right now, she just wanted light and fluffy.

Kim and Julie were light and fluffy.

Sure, she tired of them quickly. Intellectually, she and Midnight were a better match, which was why she was still friends with Midnight, but the bad girl in her, the one that wanted to have fun and not feel guilty about it, tended to gravitate towards her other friends. Besides, Kim's older brother Derek, a senior now, was really hot and Samantha was ready to move on from the guys in her grade to an older boy.

"Does she have to sit here?" Julie said. "She's like mosquito repellent."

"That makes no sense," Samantha said. "Besides, Midnight is

cooler than you'll ever be."

"I think not," Julie said. "But whatever."

"SO-ooo, my parents are away this weekend," Kim said, "and Derek is throwing a party."

"I thought you and Derek were throwing a party," Julie said, sounding a bit confused. "I thought—"

Kim gave her the *duh* face. "Sounds better if I say he's having the party, that way he's the one getting in trouble if my parents find out. I'll just happen to stay home that night and have a few girlfriends over."

"Brilliant," Samantha said. "So, how many girlfriends are you having over?"

"Well, the two of you, of course—"

"And Midnight too," Samantha said.

Kim and Julie looked like they'd rather run naked through the cafeteria right now than invite Midnight.

"Yeah, sure," Kim said. "You can come too, Midnight. If you want."

"I think I'll pass," Midnight said.

Samantha turned to her friend. "Why? It'll be fun. You need to loosen up."

"Not my style," Midnight said and popped a baby carrot into her mouth. "I'm sure you'll all have more fun without me there."

Julie didn't even try to hide her relief. "Yeah, probably—"

"Shut up," Samantha said. "If I say Midnight is coming, then she's coming."

"I really don't want to," Midnight said. "It's not my thing."

"What *is* your thing?" Kim said.

Julie was about to add something but Samantha shut her

down with a glare. "Don't bother."

"It's okay, Sam. I know they don't want me there and I don't *want* to be there. I don't need to be Carrie."

Samantha saw the lost look in Julie's eyes. God, she really was dumb. "You won't be."

"Because I won't be there," Midnight said. "Please Sam, just let it be."

Samantha turned her back on Kim and Julie. She looked at Midnight, hating that her friend was purposely cutting herself out. It wasn't right. They were fifteen and this was supposed to be the best time of their lives. Why couldn't Midnight just go with it for once?

"Why?"

"Because I'm asking you," Midnight said and popped another baby carrot into her mouth. "And I really don't want to go. They don't want me there either. So just let it be."

Samantha held out her hand and Midnight dropped a few carrots into her palm. She ate them all. She was starving and should get something to eat before lunch was over.

"I just hate to see you not want to be part of us."

"I'm *not* part of you, Sam. I'm just your friend. And I sometimes don't even know why we're friends."

Samantha got up, grabbed Midnight's hand, and pulled her along as she headed for the line-up. She'd grab one of those sawdust burgers and greasy fries.

"Don't do that," she said to Midnight.

"What? Say I don't want to go to a stupid party?"

"Embarrass me in front of them," Samantha said. "If they see you saying no to me, maybe they'll think *they* can say no to me, and then all the lines will be blurred."

"What are you talking about? What lines?"

"The line that separates me from them. The line that says I'm the alpha."

Midnight looked at Samantha just like Julie had earlier. "You did not just spit that shit out of your mouth."

Samantha stared back. "You don't get it, do you? I used to be just like you. Don't you remember when I wore those stupid thick glasses and my teeth were all crooked and my face was full of pimples? I was a real leper."

"Is that what you think of me?"

"No," Samantha said, shifting into damage control mode. "Don't put words in my mouth."

"You put them there yourself."

"It's not what I meant."

"So what did you mean?"

"I just meant that I wasn't always popular, and now that I am, I really like it. And I can help you."

"Maybe I don't want your help. Maybe I'm just fine being who I really am."

"What is that supposed to mean?"

"Yes, you're pretty. Yes, your dad's got money. And yes, you're now popular and I'm just the same old Midnight. We used to make fun of girls like that and now . . ."

"And now I'm one of them."

"You're trying to be."

Samantha took a step back and the two friends stared at each other, cold glares that left little room for maneuvering. Kids tired of waiting for them to move up the line just went around them.

"I'm the only friend you have."

"I never asked you to be."

"So you don't care about our friendship?"

"I didn't say that."

Samantha crossed her arms and poked her cheek with her tongue. "You know, when everyone makes fun of you, I stick up for you. I tell them they have no idea what it's like to have your mom walk out on you when you're barely three just because you got sick. I mean, I have no idea either. Most times I can't stand my mom, she *so* annoys me. But at least she's there. I know it must suck for you to take care of your dad instead of the other way around. I'm just trying to make you happy. You know, include you."

"I don't need you to feel sorry for me."

"That's not what I'm doing. We've been friends forever."

"And maybe forever just arrived."

Midnight turned to go but Samantha grabbed her arm.

"You don't mean that."

Midnight pulled her arm free. "Even long-term friendships can wither away. We've been growing apart since the end of grade six."

"You're throwing this away?"

"We're not the same, you and me. Not anymore." Midnight pointed at Kim and Julie. "Maybe those aren't true friends, but that's where you belong now."

"Then go," Samantha said. "Don't let me hold you back from being miserable."

Midnight left and Samantha watched her childhood friend walk away, leaving her feeling a little less important, a little less self-righteous, a little less whole.

She wouldn't go after Midnight to beg, though. Maybe, hopefully, Midnight just needed some time to herself, to sort things out. Maybe. Hopefully. When she couldn't see Midnight any longer, Samantha turned and saw Kim and Julie watching her, and she knew that they'd seen it all, and she knew that the only thing she could do was go and join them.

Someone important had possibly walked out of her life, someone she knew could never be replaced, but she couldn't let her new fake friends see her bleed. No, she couldn't. That would have to wait until later, when she was home alone in her room.

Samantha got her lunch and returned to her table, the smile on her face showing every penny of the seven thousand dollars her orthodontist had charged her daddy for those perfect pearly whites.

☙ ❧

Midnight let herself into the house and locked the front door. The drive home had been icy and quiet, uncomfortable really. Midnight hadn't wanted the ride home, but Mrs. Carmichael hadn't known what had happened earlier and Midnight hadn't wanted to seem rude. Maybe tonight Samantha would tell her mom and starting tomorrow, Midnight would need to walk to school.

She would wait and see.

Midnight heard the television playing and poked her head into the living room to find her dad asleep on the couch. There were five empty bottles of beer on the coffee table. She should be angry with him, but what use would it be? She switched the television off and pulled a blanket from the linen closet to cover him.

She kissed his forehead and whispered, "Oh Daddy."

She headed to her room to do her homework, but had trouble concentrating. She lay on her bed and stared at the ceiling. There was a dusty spider's web going from her light to the corner that she should wipe, but she couldn't be bothered. Instead, she lay there and worried about her dad, worried about Samantha, worried about the world. So much ugliness everywhere. How could she make a difference? Who was she really? The thought rolled around in her head like a pinball being bounced in all directions, the answers crushed before they formed. Life—*her* life—just seemed to be getting more complicated. She'd hoped, as she grew older, that it would finally start to make sense, but the opposite seemed to be happening.

Life is a gift, her dad had told her more than once. *How many people's lives you can better is really what it's all about,* he'd also said often.

She couldn't change the entire world. That just wasn't possible. But what if she could change the life of one person? Her father would be her first choice. He needed help in the worst of ways. Samantha was another. Midnight saw trouble ahead for her friend, but after today, she didn't think Samantha would listen to anything she said.

So who could she help? Maybe it had to be a stranger.

Volunteering.

Where could she volunteer that would satisfy her school curriculum obligations and also make a difference for someone?

Make someone happy.

The answer became obvious.

TWO

~ June 1991 ~

"I don't like you anymore!"

Midnight stood at the edge of Tyler Murphy's driveway, arms crossed, eyes narrowed, her lips pressed together into a tight line. The setting sun cast her long shadow across the narrow single-car driveway and onto the front lawn where a dormant sprinkler waited to be resuscitated. The last few days had been hot, humid, and sticky—a sign that summer had arrived. Everyone predicted that this one would be the hottest on record and after the harsh and long winter, no one was complaining.

Yet.

At the park across the street, the sound of kids hollering and laughing echoed throughout the small neighborhood, a hundred hyenas drowning out everything from the drone of lawnmowers to the distant endless flow of traffic on Greenfield Road. Over the rooftops on the other side of the park, the sun was slowly being pulled into the horizon, but dusk was still an hour away. Today had been the last day of school and all the children were taking advantage of staying out a little longer after dinner, the long June days pushing darkness past 9:30 p.m. and providing plenty of extra play time. Everyone had big smiles across their faces.

Almost everyone.

Midnight's angry stare bore holes right through Tyler while her face became a darker shade of red. She fought back tears, determined not to show her breaking heart.

"You're not ever my boyfriend again."

Tyler stood at the top of the driveway, the evening breeze ruffling his longish and unruly copper-coloured hair, confusion in his blue eyes, his lips pulled into an uncertain smile. He scratched the bridge of his freckled nose and then stared at his running shoes.

"I don't want to be your boyfriend anyway," he said while still staring at his feet. "I'm only five."

Midnight felt hot tears escape and run down her cheeks, and then her murderous glare shifted from Tyler to the other boy. Everything had been fine until *he* had showed up. Everything was always fine until *he* showed up.

That boy.

Midnight's nemesis.

Bradley Eriksson.

Midnight looked back at Tyler and wiped her nose with the back of her hand. "You're being mean, just because of him," she said and pointed a finger toward Bradley.

"You're mean," Bradley said in a baby voice, his fists going up to his eyes, pretending to wipe invisible tears. He laughed a mean-spirited sort of cackle. "Tyler doesn't want to be your *boy-friend*, so there. He doesn't even like you."

Midnight shot daggers Bradley's way. "I hate you."

"I hate you," Bradley mimicked. "I hate you sooooo much." He laughed.

Midnight's normally bright green eyes were bloodshot and stung from salty tears. Tyler never behaved that way when it was just the two of them playing. He had always been kind and fun and her friend. Right now he was behaving like he didn't want her around, like he was ashamed of her.

She covered her face with her hands.

"Go home," Bradley said. "We don't want you here. You're just a dumb girl."

Midnight looked at Tyler, begging him to stand up to Bradley, but he just kept staring at his feet. This was too much to bear and she stormed off and headed home, her breathing coming in big hiccup sobs. She let the front screen door slam, ran up to her bedroom, and threw herself on her bed, flopping face first into her pillow.

Boys were impossible to understand. Why didn't Tyler come to her rescue? Why did he pretend he didn't like her? Why couldn't he tell Bradley to go away?

Midnight screamed into her pillow.

"Hey Munchkin," her dad said as he walked into her room and sat down on the edge of her bed. "What's wrong?"

"Tyler is not my boyfriend anymore," Midnight said, her words muffled by her pillow.

"Want to tell me about it?"

She sat up beside her father. "Because when Bradley comes to play with him," she said and wiped away the last of her tears, "all they want to do is play rough games and not play with me.

Tyler always wants to play with me when Bradley is not there. It's not fair. Tyler is my friend, not Bradley's friend. I hate Bradley."

"I know Bradley isn't your favorite person, but honey, boys will be boys," Jim told her. "You know Tyler behaves differently when it's just the two of you."

Midnight snorted back phlegm, making Jim grimace.

"Here, blow your nose," he said, handing her a tissue.

Midnight and Tyler had been best friends since they were infants, born just three days apart at the same hospital. They'd been side by side for most of the last five years—in their swings, their saucers, the playpen. They'd always played together, sharing their toys, their games, their food. They really were best friends.

"Honey," Jim said and ran a hand over Midnight's beautiful, long, silky dark hair, just like her mother's. "Sometimes, boys just need to play with other boys. That way they can get their aggression out."

Midnight stared up at her father. "What's *gression*?"

Jim took a deep breath. "Aggression is when people behave sort of . . . unfriendly. Sometimes they don't mean to, but they get so caught up in what they're doing that they become almost mean. Boys, especially, seem to have this need to play rough games, to fight. Everything is a competition to see who is stronger."

"Tyler is not mean or unfriendly when Bradley is not there," Midnight said. She took another tissue from the box on her night table and blew her nose. "It's always Bradley's fault. I hate him."

"Hate is a pretty strong word, honey," Jim said. "I think maybe you dislike the games Bradley plays—"

Midnight shook her head almost violently. "No. I *hate* him.

He's a big bully and I don't want him to live here. I wish he'd move away."

Jim hugged her. "Well, it's getting late anyway. You have a whole summer ahead of you, and I'm sure you and Tyler will spend plenty of time playing together. Let's forget about Bradley for tonight. okay?"

Midnight nodded, but didn't smile.

"How about a nice bath?"

She nodded again.

Midnight followed her dad into the bathroom, where she poured a capful of bubble soap into the hot water that was filling the tub. She threw a few toys in to play with—a boat, an old Barbie, some plastic animals—and waited for her dad to leave before undressing and getting into the tub. Thirty minutes later, the water was cold, her fingers and toes where shrivelled prunes, and she was getting tired, so she pulled the plug and got out.

By the time her dad tucked her in after her milk and cookies, dusk had chased the last of the day's light and had also taken her anger along with it. She'd just about forgotten about Bradley Eriksson.

She couldn't wait to play with Tyler tomorrow. Maybe he could be her boyfriend again.

"Night Daddy."

"Night honey," Jim said and turned off her bedside lamp.

☙ ❧

Tyler was alone. Bradley had left soon after Midnight had stormed off, and now Tyler had no one to play with. Still, he wasn't ready to go in yet, so he tried to skateboard down the driveway. Not being very good, he fell and scraped his hands and knees. Having enough of that, Tyler put the skateboard into the garage and grabbed a basketball. The ball got away from him and bounced until it hit his father's red sedan parked on the street at the end of the driveway.

Tyler sighed and took the ball into his arms. He couldn't concentrate.

After a moment, he turned, his eyes wandering toward the house next door. He should have stuck up for Midnight, he knew. But if he had, Bradley would have given him a hard time, made his life miserable. It was easier to tell Midnight he was sorry later.

If he remembered.

Which he probably wouldn't.

But Midnight wasn't just a girl. She was his best friend. They always played together and not just sissy girl games. She played football with him, threw a baseball with him . . . any game he wanted to play. She was fun.

Not like Bradley.

Bradley always wanted to play *his* games, and as soon as *his* games weren't going *his* way, he would change them. Tyler didn't like that. But Bradley was much bigger—he was a year older and at school he often bullied the smaller kids, and that's why Tyler played with him when he came over—because he didn't want to be bullied. He didn't particularly like Bradley, but he liked being picked on even less.

Tyler looked up at Midnight's room again.

Why was it important to her that he be her boyfriend? He wasn't really sure what that meant anyway. They were friends, so why wasn't that good enough? He liked her. A lot. Did that make them girlfriend and boyfriend? That was sort of yucky. He liked her because she was fun to play with.

It was getting pretty dark so he flipped the light on in the garage so he could see. He dribbled the ball a few times and threw it at the basket. It sank right in, not touching the rim. When it bounced back to him he grabbed it and held it. He saw the light turn off in Midnight's room.

"What're you doing, bud?" his dad said, coming back from the park holding Tyler's younger brother Jake in his arms. "Your brother is totally worn out. Sort of lost track of time and then it was dark. Just like that."

"Yeah, I guess it is." Tyler didn't tell his dad what had happened. He didn't think grownups would understand what being five was like. So confusing. "I was just shooting hoops."

"Guess Midnight went home?"

Tyler nodded.

"Time to go in and wash up before bed."

Tyler didn't say anything.

"Everything all right, champ?"

Tyler looked up at his dad and shrugged. "Yeah. I'm just tired I guess."

"Well . . . summer is just starting, so you don't have to get everything done in just one day. There's plenty of time left. Your brother is getting heavy, so how about we call it a night."

"Sure, Dad." Tyler threw the basketball into the garage, where it bounced off the skateboard, hit a bike, shifted and knocked a shovel off the wall, bounced against the old fridge his dad kept his beer in, and finally came to rest, stopped by a bundle of hockey sticks lying on the floor. "Oops! Sorry Dad."

"Maybe tomorrow you can clean up that mess. Turn off the garage light and push the button to close the door."

"Okay."

They went into the house.

☙ ❧

Jim looked at the clock on the bedside table and closed his book. It was nearly midnight, the time when Midnight normally woke—sometimes screaming—from a bad dream. The nightmares had been reoccurring most nights over the last two years, ever since Midnight's mother had walked out of their lives. Jim felt certain that Midnight didn't really have many memories of her mother, but the ones she did have came back at night and tormented her.

She wasn't the only one.

He met his wife in high school, in detention of all places. It was his first offence for being late for class—an unavoidable Mother Nature call that he'd been too embarrassed to tell his teacher about, but she'd kept insisting to know and he'd mumbled something that had sounded like she was being stupid and that was that—but apparently Karen Phillips was a regular attendee at detention: a drop-dead gorgeous brunette with mischievous hazel eyes and lips that begged to be kissed.

She was trouble with a capital T.

The youngest of three kids from a broken marriage, her mother had no time for her, nor did her older siblings, and her father was completely out of the picture. Karen Phillips had attitude, anger, and lots of sex appeal. Jim had heard of her. Her name was permanently engraved in the bathroom stalls—you can guess the rest—but this had been his first actual encounter with her. There were only ten seats in the room and all but one was left, right beside Karen.

"What're you in for?"

"Being late for science class," he said.

"That's lame," she said. "I was smoking in the girl's bathroom."

Jim had been about to ask her why she'd do a thing like that but the teacher in charge of detention cleared her throat and reminded them that this was detention, that there was to be no interaction, that they could do homework or just sit there quietly and think about what had landed them here in the first place so they wouldn't repeat the offence.

"Don't worry about her," Karen whispered. "I'm here almost every day."

Jim turned sideways, disbelief on his face. "Why would you do that?"

"Do what?"

"Whatever it is that gets you in trouble every day."

Karen grinned. "Oh, we are *so* gonna have fun together."

"I don't think so."

"Oh, but *I* do."

And before he understood what was going on, Jim Madison was caught in Karen Phillips's web, a web he was still trying to escape from two years after she had left them.

At first he thought she would forget about him as soon as detention was over, but she started to show up at his locker. He was just a sophomore and she was a junior so he couldn't understand why she hung around with him. But then all the guys in his grade started talking, saying how lucky he was to have the hottest girl in school be his girlfriend—she wasn't, yet—and why she'd want him when there were so many better-looking guys. After about three weeks, he didn't care why she'd chosen him. He had fallen for her, and fallen hard.

And so had his Johnny-be-good persona.

Grades started to slip, detention happened more frequently, as did cutting class. Smoking came next, drinking, pot, and sex. Lots of sex. Karen was amazing. He had no idea people could do that with each other.

And then near the end of his junior year, after they'd been dating over a year, Karen got pregnant.

Jim's parents, being devout Catholics, insisted that he do the right thing and marry Karen and take care of his child. They let them live in the basement while Jim finished high school and since Karen graduated before the baby was born, his parents accepted that she stay home and embrace her motherhood role. Jim's mother had been just nineteen herself when Jim's older brother Darrel was born, the difference being that Jim's parents were already married—common for people of that generation—when she got pregnant.

Jim noticed Karen change during her pregnancy, seeming to accept her new role of becoming a mother. She'd told him a few times she was actually looking forward to the baby's birth, probably because she'd grown tired of being so big and uncomfortable, and then insisted they give the baby a name that was different, meaningful, and not so goddamned boring.

During his junior year, Jim read *Antony and Cleopatra* for English class, and Karen remembered reading it too the previous year, and even though she hadn't cared for the story, she had loved the name Octavia.

Had the baby been a boy, his name would have been Octavius.

Jim's parents weren't exactly thrilled with the idea of their grandchild having such an unorthodox name, but Jim had never been able to say no to Karen, and after the baby was born, everyone got used to Octavia. It was sort of cool and unique.

Karen insisted their second daughter be named for the hour she'd been born on, and Jim often joked he was grateful Midnight hadn't been born at any other time.

Their marriage worked for a while, but Karen never quite seemed entirely at ease with being a mother, a normal boring couple, a suburban family.

And then Midnight got sick.

Jim heard his bedroom door open slowly as it made an annoying squeal that sounded ten times louder at this time of night than it did during the day, and watched a sleepy little girl hugging a teddy come toward him.

"You okay?"

Midnight stood by his side. Jim pulled her into his arms.

"A bad dream?"

Midnight nodded.

"It was just a dream, you know that, right?"

Another nod.

"How about I tuck you in?"

"Can I sleep in your bed?" she said, her voice tiny and her eyes pleading.

He sighed. She'd keep him up all night with her tossing and turning. Last time he'd let her, he'd woken up when he got a foot in the eye. Not a pleasant way to wake up.

"You'll sleep better in your own bed," he said.

"No I won't," Midnight said with a whine. "I'll have the bad dream again."

"I'm sure you won't. You never have it twice in the same night. Come. I'll rub your back until you get back to sleep."

He walked her back to her room and helped her climb into bed.

"Daddy?"

"Yes honey?

"Do you think Tyler gets bad dreams too?"

"I'm pretty sure he does. We all do at times."

Jim pulled the blankets over Midnight and sat beside her. He rubbed her back. She didn't say anything for a few minutes and he assumed she'd fallen asleep. He got up and walked out of the room.

"Daddy?"

"Yes honey?" He turned back in the doorway.

"Is Tavia home?"

Midnight had had a difficult time saying Octavia when she'd started to speak, and still preferred to use the short name.

"She came home just after you went to bed. Why?"

"No reason. I just didn't get to say goodnight to her."

"I'm sure she came in and kissed you." Jim didn't know whether Octavia still did that or not. He would have to ask her in the morning. It was important to Midnight. "Good night, sweetie."

"Night Daddy."

☙ ❧

A few minutes later, Midnight walked into Octavia's room, slipped under the covers, and snuggled up to her sister.

She slept dreamlessly until morning.

THREE

~ September 2001 ~

Midnight came down about an hour later to find her dad still asleep on the couch. She grabbed the empty bottles of beer and put them in the garage, and then headed into the kitchen to make dinner. She pulled a container of homemade spaghetti sauce—her dad was actually a really good cook and every few weeks he made a big pot of sauce that they froze in serving-size containers—and put it in the microwave to defrost. She put a pot of water on the gas stove and fired it up, and then prepared a Caesar salad.

Fifteen minutes later, dinner was ready and she went to wake her father.

"Hey honey," he said while sitting up and rubbing the sleep from his eyes. "Why didn't you wake me when you came home?"

Midnight shrugged. "You seemed to need it."

Jim stretched and yawned. "I didn't sleep well last night."

Midnight knew better than to ask. She already knew the answer. It hadn't changed in twelve years. "Maybe you can go to bed early tonight."

Jim nodded. "Is that spaghetti I smell?"

"Let's go eat before it gets cold."

Midnight watched as her father pulled a beer out of the fridge and then thought better of it and filled a glass with iced water. She let go of the breath she hadn't realized she'd been holding. Hopefully, he was done drinking for today.

"How was your day?" she said.

"Not so good." He sat down across from her. They shared a small round table in the kitchen. The dining room table was rarely used. "The words weren't flowing. I'm supposed to write copy for this new financial letter my client is launching, but honestly, my track record when it comes to finance isn't really stellar."

"You'll get it done. You always do."

Jim shoved a mountain of spaghetti into his mouth and then tried to talk.

"What?"

He swallowed. "I said I'm not so sure this time. I'm not feeling it. Probably why I had a beer, hoping to get inspired, you know, but one didn't work and before I knew it, I'd had five and needed a nap. I'm sorry, honey. I really am."

"It's fine," she said, swallowing the lie. There was little point berating her dad over his choices. He beat himself up enough already, and it was not helping him, obviously. "Maybe tomorrow will be better."

"I hope so," he said and stuffed more spaghetti into his mouth. "What about you? Did you make someone happy?"

Midnight held her fork close to her mouth, backwards, like she was about to hit him. "Samantha and I had a fight."

"What happened?"

Midnight put her fork down and told her dad the events of her day.

"Why don't you go to the party?"

"Because it's not my thing."

"Don't use me for an excuse. Honey, don't miss out on your teenage years because of me. I don't want you to resent me."

"I won't." The crayon drawing of her mother on the fridge caught her eye and her demeanour stiffened. After a moment, she stood and began to clear the table, put the dirty dishes in the dishwasher, wiped down the counter, and filled one of the sinks with soapy water to wash the pots.

"Midnight?"

She turned around slowly.

"Please be a kid. Go to that party and have fun. You can't continue to punish yourself because your mother left. It's not doing you any good. It wasn't your fault."

"YES IT WAS!" she yelled and started to cry. "M-mom left us because of me. I got sick and she couldn't handle it so she ditched us. What kind of mother does that? I *hate* her."

"Oh honey," Jim said and went to hold her. "Don't blame yourself. Your mom . . . she just wasn't cut out for the family life. I knew she wasn't. She knew she wasn't. But you know, she tried, she really did."

"Stop defending her," Midnight said and pulled away. She grabbed the picture from the fridge and ripped it up. "Why is this stupid picture still here?"

"I thought you wanted it there to remind you—"

"I don't need to be reminded that my mom didn't love me."

"Of course she loved you."

"Dad! She abandoned us. That's not love. She doesn't love us and we don't love her. She doesn't deserve our love. It's time we moved on, like Tavia did. She never talks about Mom, and maybe it's time we both did the same. We need to let her go."

Jim ran a hand through his thinning grey hair and looked at his daughter. "I wish it were that easy."

"It is, Dad. Just let her go. She's been gone twelve years. I don't think she's walking through the front door any time soon. Why do you still hope she will?"

His face crumpled. "Because if I stop, I'm afraid I'll . . ."

"Maybe I've been afraid to live because I've been afraid to get hurt. Maybe I'm pushing Samantha away because I'm afraid to get hurt. I'm tired of hurting, Dad. Aren't you?"

Midnight didn't wait for an answer. She let the ripped pieces of paper fall to the floor and stormed off to her room.

ᘓ ᘐ

Jim picked up the torn drawing and reassembled the pieces on the laminated kitchen counter. The stick picture of Karen no longer had the power it had held before Midnight had torn it. Maybe it never had any power except for the power that Jim had allowed it to have.

Midnight was right. But—

Jim ran a shaking hand across his face and then grabbed a beer from the fridge. He gulped half of it. "Damn it!"

He poured the rest of the beer down the sink, balled up the torn picture, and tossed it in the trashcan. He had two beautiful daughters that meant the world to him, and they had given him years of memories he would cherish forever, yet his heart haunted him.

His heart yearned for her.

Jim remembered a Saturday night at her place. Karen's mom was never there, out with a different guy almost every night, looking for a savior probably. Jim and Karen had gotten stoned and made love and Octavia was born some nine months later. On that night, he'd been so deeply in love with her, like he couldn't let her go after they'd climaxed, afraid that none of it was real, that she wasn't real, and if he let her go, he'd wake up in his bed at home, alone and lonely.

He ran his fingers over his lips.

Too bad he'd just poured his last beer down the drain.

Slowly, he walked out of the kitchen, and stood in the middle of the living room, looking towards the front door as if it held the answer to the question he'd been asking for the last twelve years, the answer that would finally liberate him.

☙ ❧

Samantha slammed her bedroom door and screamed. Her mom had been into her, wanting to know what had happened between her and Midnight, picking at her, gnawing like a dog on a bone. The woman could be relentless.

There was a knock on her door.

"Go away."

"Honey, please, can we talk?"

"I'm done talking to you."

"Samantha Carmichael," her mother said as she pushed the door open and stepped in, "you'd better keep that tone out of your voice. You keep it up and you'll be grounded all weekend."

"Great, I'll be a loser too."

"I really hope that's not what you think of Midnight."

Samantha clenched her jaw. "What happened between Midnight and me isn't your business. She's *my* friend."

"And I care about her and her family," Tracy said. "I've known Jim my whole life, and he was such a wonderful young man . . ."

Samantha sat up on her bed, her annoyance replaced by curiosity. She eyed her mother. She had never heard her mom speak so caringly about someone else, certainly not about Samantha's dad. "What does that mean?"

"Nothing," Tracy said too quickly. "It's just nothing. I just feel bad for them, especially Midnight, so I don't want you to make her life harder than it already is."

"I'm not," Samantha said. "She's the one who never wants to join in. I've been her friend a long time, but Mom, maybe we no longer should be. I don't know, friendships come and go. How many high school friends do you stay in touch with?"

Tracy shook her head. "None, I guess. But it's different once you become an adult. People move around, start families, life gets busy. Too busy. And people change."

"That's what I'm saying. Midnight and I, we've changed. I don't think we know each other that well anymore. Doesn't seem like it, anyway."

"Don't cut her out too fast. Give her a chance."

Samantha pinned her mother with a glare. "You didn't, like, date Midnight's dad or something in high school, did you?"

Tracy seemed lost in thought for a second. "No, I didn't. He was just a very good boy . . . and then he changed."

"You had a crush on him!"

Tracy pulled on her long hair. "Don't be absurd. He was just a boy I went to school with."

"You're so lying, Mom," Samantha said, glee in her eyes. "Wait till I tell Midnight."

Tracy came to sit beside her daughter. "Maybe I did have a little crush on Jim. He was cute with his long hair and those few freckles on his nose. He was so smart. In class, he always seemed to have the answers. Teachers loved him. Everyone loved him. He was so easygoing, easy to talk to, always willing to help. But all of that disappeared when—"

Tracy turned to her daughter, tucked Samantha's hair behind her left ear. "Just don't give up on your friendship. You're important to her."

"She's told you that?"

Tracy smiled. "Pay attention and you'll see it." She stood and walked to the bedroom door, turned, and looked at her daughter. "Not everything is said with words."

Samantha watched her mother leave, wondering if her mom could be right that maybe she was so engrossed in her selfish pursuit of popularity that she simply didn't hear what Midnight was saying.

☙ ❧

Midnight pulled her journal from her desk drawer, sat on her bed, and wrote: *Today is the last day I'll allow my mother to torture me.*

She put the end of the pen in her mouth and read the sentence over and over. Her eyes narrowed, focused, assimilated the words she'd put to paper. She said them out loud one at a time to make sure they carried the weight she'd intended them to carry. Slowly, her head moved up and down.

Yes, these words felt right, liberating, like a caress on her soul. She felt energised as she discarded this burden that she had lugged along for a lifetime.

Could it be this easy?

Maybe it could be this easy. A stroke of pen and Midnight's mother was finally put away for good—no hesitation, no regrets, just the right decision.

Goodbye, mother.

Goodbye. Mother.

GOODBYE MOTHER!

God, it felt good. So good. It was like eating a double chocolate mousse ice cream cone on a hot summer's day. It was like satisfying a craving that had hounded her all her life. It was like she'd found freedom.

But then a finger of doubt wrapped itself around her heart, which became a cold hand—a cold, *strong* hand—and she felt it squeeze and squeeze and squeeze.

Always a price to pay, it seemed.

A knock on her door. Her dad poked his head into her room.

"Can I come in?"

"Sure," she said and closed her journal.

"You still writing?"

"When I feel inspired."

"Talking about your mother inspires us all."

"No, Dad, it doesn't. It pisses me off. And don't bother commenting on my choice of word. I'm done with her. She doesn't exist to me anymore, just like we don't exist to her. She made her choice long ago and we're the fools waiting for her to come back to us and tell us she is sorry. That day of me taking her back is gone. Mom isn't coming back. Not for you. Not for me. Not for us."

"Falling in love with her was like finding air in a vacuum."

"And little old me got sick and ruined everything. If it wasn't for me, maybe Mom would still be here and you wouldn't be so broken."

"You are the most precious thing in the world to me. I would never give you up, not even if it meant your mother was still here. I couldn't imagine my life without you. I'd rather be broken than to never have had you."

"But Dad—"

"Midnight, stop," he said and inched toward her. "You're not the reason she left."

"She doesn't deserve your love. Or mine."

"You're probably right, but . . ."

"So let her go," she said. "Start dating. Meet new women. Find happiness. I want you to be happy."

"I've got you."

"Someday, I'll move out too and then you'll be alone. I don't want you to be alone."

Jim sat beside her and pulled her into his arms. He kissed the top of her head. "I just don't know how to let go of her."

"Just like a Band-Aid. Pull it fast and be done with it."

Jim chuckled. "If only it were that simple."

"You have to make it that easy. Maybe you should start by getting rid of all the clothes she left behind. They're so out of style now anyway. Maybe get rid of her pictures. They're already all boxed up in the back of your closet anyway."

"We can't pretend she never existed, erase her from our lives."

"She did."

Jim let go of Midnight. He held his face in both hands and stared at the carpet. "You're more like your mother than you realize."

"I wouldn't know."

"But I do," he said, looking at her. "She wasn't all bad. She loved you and your sister."

Midnight scoffed. "Well, she sure had a funny way of showing it."

"Midnight."

"I'm tired. And I have homework."

Jim nodded. "All right."

"Sorry. I don't mean to take it out on you."

"I know, honey. I know. This isn't something that we're going to solve in one night. You do what you need to do, and I'll try and do the same." Jim started to leave.

"Dad?"

He turned. "Yes."

"I know she meant a lot to you. But maybe there's someone else out there that could mean just as much. Or more. And be better for you."

Jim nodded and left her room.

Midnight felt this ache in the pit of her stomach, like something heavy and moving. She hated fighting with her dad. She knew deep down he hurt and was fragile, but she also knew that he was part of the problem. Midnight really believed that there was someone out there for him, someone good for him, but he was too damn scared to let himself be found.

She wrote in her journal: *I need to help Dad find happiness.*

FOUR

~ June 1991 ~

On the first day of summer vacation, Jim woke up too early and made his way down the hall to Midnight's bedroom and saw that her bed was empty. He poked his head into Octavia's room, and there they were, his two girls, sleeping, Midnight wrapped in her sister's protective arms.

Jim watched them for a moment, a knot in the back of his throat.

His mother—God rest her soul, six years passed away—had told him that one day, when he had kids, he would understand why she choked up so easily at the most mundane things they did.

Like share a bed.

Jim closed the door and headed down to his office in the basement, and tried to work on a brochure for a client, but he gave up when Midnight came to find him around eight thirty, Bugs trailing behind her.

The cat, Karen's cat, had lasted longer than their marriage. And had stayed.

A sad smile tugged the corners of Jim's mouth.

"Hi Daddy." Midnight came to him and he pulled her into his lap. He wrapped his arms around her and for a moment he felt like the luckiest man alive, a man who knew his daughter had cheated death two years ago.

"Hungry?"

Midnight nodded.

"Let's go make waffles," he said.

While he made breakfast, Octavia dragged herself into the kitchen, sleepy-eyed with a mop of short strawberry blond hair on her head that was in desperate need of a brushing.

"My cooking was too much for you to sleep through?"

Octavia plunked herself down on a chair, holding her head with both hands. "I suppose." She then got up and poured herself a cup of coffee.

"Since when do you drink coffee?"

"*Really*, Dad," she said. "I'm not a kid anymore."

Twelve going on twenty, Jim thought. Octavia had become a woman in the last few months and her moods had been somewhat unpredictable. There were days he needed to walk wide circles around her and some arguments about nothing had gotten pretty hot.

"No, you're not," he said and kissed her forehead. "You've had to grow up a little faster than you should have."

☙ ❧

Right after breakfast, Midnight scooted up to her bedroom to make her bed and get dressed, anticipating Tyler to come and ask her to play at any time. He didn't disappoint, knocking on the front door a few minutes shy of ten o'clock.

"Want to play hockey?" Tyler said when Midnight stepped out of the house. "I got the net all ready."

"Sure," Midnight said. She looked around.

"What's you looking for?"

"Bradley."

"He's not here," Tyler said and shoved his hands into his pockets and stared at his feet. He sort of swayed back and forth, biting his lower lip. "He was mean to you yesterday and I should have told him to stop."

"Yes, you should have."

Tyler looked at Midnight. "Huh! Are you mad at me?"

"A little," Midnight said. "Why do you play with him?"

"He plays with me," Tyler said, looking away. "If I tell him I don't want to play with him, he'll probably beat me up."

"He won't beat you up here. You can call your dad."

"Maybe not here," Tyler said in agreement. "But at school. I see him do it to other kids."

"He's such a bully."

"Yeah. A big bully."

They stood side by side for a moment, Tyler looking away and Midnight looking at Tyler looking away. When nothing more was said, she went and grabbed one of his hockey sticks.

"You play goalie," she said.

Midnight could shoot the ball, but she wasn't good at stopping it. They played for a little while and then Jake came out to join them. At first, Tyler whined about it, until his mother told him that if he kept whining, he would end up in his room, with no one to play with. That put an end to his complaints. An hour went by while the three kids played T-ball, threw the football and ran around tackling each other, and played golf with Tyler's Easy Hit Golf Set.

"I'm thirsty," Midnight said.

"Me too," Jake said.

"I'll go ask my mom for some Kool-Aid."

Tyler dashed into the house while Jake and Midnight sat on the grass in the front yard, quietly watching cars go by. Across the street, at the park, a group of older boys were playing a game of soccer.

"I don't feel good," Midnight said.

"Me too," Jake said.

Midnight collapsed to the ground. Jake imitated her. Tyler came back with three cups of Kool-Aid. Jake jumped up and grabbed a cup and drank it in one long gulp.

"Midnight?" Tyler said. "Here's your drink."

Midnight didn't move. Tyler looked at Jake, a wrinkle in his brow.

"I pretended. Like her," Jake said, a red moustache on his upper lip from the Kool-Aid. "Why is Midnight still pretending?"

Tyler kneeled beside Midnight, put the two cups on the lawn and made sure they didn't tip over, and shook her shoulder.

"Midnight? I have your drink."

"Maybe she's really sleeping," Jake said.

Tyler wasn't sure. He thought it was sort of strange for Midnight to pretend for this long. He didn't like this.

"Go get mom," he said. "Now!"

"Why?" Jake said.

"Because I said so!"

൬ ഌ

Jim washed the last pan and stacked it against the other clean dishes in the left sink to dry. He put the dish towel on his shoulder, something his mother had done, and leaned against the counter, waiting.

"Midnight was really agitated last night," Octavia finally said. She was staring out the patio doors into their backyard. "She tossed like she had bees in her pants."

"I know that quite well," he said. "Did you end up with a foot in the eye?"

"I guess I was lucky."

"She had a bad dream around midnight, and she wanted to sleep in my bed but I wasn't up for that," he said. "When I put her back to bed, she asked if you were home. Must have sneaked into your bed when I got back to my room."

"She's having a lot of bad dreams."

"Almost every night."

"*She* did that to her."

A pained look flashed across Jim's face.

"It's true, Dad, so don't look at me that way. Midnight was so sick when she left, as if she didn't care what happened."

"Your mother wasn't—"

"If she was here, I wouldn't have to play mother to my own sister." Octavia's ears were turning bright red. "She only cared about herself."

"Honey," Jim said and walked toward her.

"Please don't," Octavia said, putting out a hand, palm up. "I'm only twelve, Dad. Twelve."

"I know," he said. "And I appreciate everything you do."

"I love Midnight and would do anything for her," she said and turned away. "But sometimes I have no idea what I'm doing. Most times."

"You're doing great."

"I shouldn't have to," she said, the tears she'd been fighting back becoming too much to hold. "What if I do the wrong thing and hurt Midnight? It's so hard."

"Come here," he said. "I forget how much you've taken on, and I'm sorry. You're doing great, trust me. Someday you'll be a wonderful mother."

"I'm so afraid to mess up," Octavia said and fell into his arms, her cheeks streaked with tears. "I don't want to mess up."

Jim stroked his daughter's hair. She had cut it just a few weeks ago after sporting it long, very long, for so many years. He'd thought it was because of all the dancing she did, easier to handle, and maybe it was, but he also figured it was a statement.

"I wouldn't worry," he said in a whisper. "You're doing better than I am."

That pulled a smile out of her. "That's sad."

"I guess it is," he said. "You and your sister are so precious. I remember when I first heard you cry. I was holding you so awkwardly and you wiggled and I thought I was going to drop you, but I didn't. Looking into those beautiful eyes of yours when you finally opened them was magical. I fell in love with you instantly."

Octavia pulled away and looked up at her dad. "You were so young. You could have given me up. Your life would be different, and maybe . . . maybe she wouldn't have left you."

"Giving you up was never a thought that crossed my mind,"

he said. "I knew that being your dad was going to be what I was meant to be. Not a moment of regret."

They stood at arm's length from each other, a father trying to do his best by his children, an elder daughter feeling her way toward adulthood.

"We'll be fine," he said. "You'll be fine."

She raised herself on her toes and kissed his cheek, something she hadn't done in quite some time. "I'm going to take a shower."

"I'll be in my office."

ଓ ଓ

"Dad!" Octavia shouted from the top of the basement stairs. "Something's wrong with Midnight. Come now. NOW!"

Jim and Octavia rushed out of the house, following Tyler. Jim felt pressure in his chest, invisible hands squeezing his lungs. His temples throbbed. Fear filled his mind with phantoms, the same sort of fear he'd experienced two years ago when Midnight had gone through chemo. She'd been so little and vulnerable, or so he'd thought, but she'd surprised him with her toughness.

Had his daughter's fight all been for nothing?

The doctors had said she'd beaten the cancer, that she was in remission, and that chances were good—not *very* good, not *super* good, but still good—that it would not return. The cancer had been caught very early. She'd been one of the lucky kids at the hospital, unlike so many others who were terminally ill.

Midnight had beaten her cancer.

Beaten it.

Damn it, she had beaten it!

"We called 911," Veronica Murphy said. "Jake came to get me

and Roger. Said Midnight was sleeping on the lawn. That didn't sound good. I rushed out and then told Roger to go call 911. Hope you don't mind?"

"God no! Thank you. Thank you."

Jim kneeled beside his unconscious daughter, feeling for a pulse and getting one, a nice steady strong one. She was warm—hot really—but then again, the day was humid and the kids had been playing, running, exerting themselves. Could her body still be weak from all those treatments? It had been just over a year now since the doctors had said she was healthy, that she could be a kid again, that she could live a normal life.

Had they been wrong?

Damn them. Had they been wrong?

"Is she okay?" Octavia said, sounding small and scared.

"I don't know," Jim said. "She's breathing. Maybe she passed out because of the heat."

"It is kind of hot," Octavia said.

"Maybe . . ." He scratched his forehead as if trying to dig out a thought that would tell him what to do. "Maybe we should just take her to the hospital."

"The paramedics should be here shortly," Veronica said.

Jim looked at his neighbour, a pretty woman in a plain sort of way. She'd go unnoticed in a crowd, but she'd give you her right arm if you needed it more than she did.

"Right," he said, trying to keep his voice steady. "I can't . . . you know . . . think. What if—"

"I hear sirens," Octavia said. She kneeled beside her sister and took her hand. "I'm here, Midnight. We're all here for you."

Jim nodded and looked at Octavia. "Yes, we are."

"She opened her eyes," Tyler said.

They all stared down at Midnight.

"You okay, honey?" Jim said.

"I guess," Midnight said and tried to sit up. "Why are you all looking at me? Did I do something wrong?"

Jim pulled her into his arms. "No, you didn't do anything wrong. We were just worried when you fainted."

"I fainted?"

"I think so," Jim said.

"I don't remember," Midnight said.

"Ambulance!" Jake said and rushed to it. "Ambulance!"

"Jake, stay back," Veronica said. "Let the paramedics check Midnight."

A man and woman approached.

"Daddy, I don't want them to put needles in me," Midnight said and held on to her father. "I don't ever want needles in me again."

"They won't," Jim said, looking at the paramedics.

"We just want to take your blood pressure," the male paramedic said. "Look into your eyes, listen to your heart. No needles."

Midnight wrapped her arms around Jim's neck.

"It'll be fine, honey."

Midnight looked into her father's eyes. "Promise?"

"Yes, promise."

Jim carried Midnight into the back of the ambulance, and they emerged a few minutes later, Midnight running to stand beside Tyler.

"No needles," she said with obvious relief in her voice. "I was brave, right Daddy?"

"Yes, you were very brave."

"She checks out all right," the female paramedic told Jim. "But with her background, I'd recommend you take her in to see her doctor. To be safe."

"I will," Jim said. "She really had us scared."

ɞ ʚ

Later that afternoon, Midnight was outside again, running and screaming and having a ball. Jim had insisted she come inside and rest for a while, and then had made lunch and they'd watched a movie, but then she'd gotten restless and bugged him to go play with Tyler.

Jim found yard work to do—the lawn did need mowing—so he could keep an eye on Midnight. He wondered, as he took the trimmer around the flower bed where in the early spring beautiful tulips and azaleas brought vibrant colours to the front of the house, whether Midnight had simply passed out from low blood sugar. He had worked with an older gentleman, before going out on his own, who had simply passed out one day in the middle of the office. One minute they were talking, and the next minute this man was falling. Luckily, Jim had reacted and caught him before the man smacked his head on the corner of the desk. His co-worker had been diabetic and he'd been so busy that morning that he'd neglected to test his blood sugar level.

Jim would make an appointment on Monday with Midnight's doctor, to be on the safe side. Not that being diabetic was all that great, but he'd take that over the alternative anytime.

He stopped and watched his daughter play. That year, 1989,

had been a living hell, and the thought of Midnight's cancer coming back gave him an uneasy feeling. He'd lost his marriage last time. Would he lose his daughter the next time?

He didn't want to think that, but how could he not? He had learned long ago that God didn't always play fair, that innocent people died, that children died, and the shattered lives their absence left for those that survived them was like living inside four empty walls with no exit door. The grief, the loneliness, the unanswered questions never left you alone.

Jim sighed.

No, he told himself. The cancer wasn't back. It simply couldn't have returned. The doctors had been very confident that Midnight was one of the lucky ones. Jim wanted to believe that, needed to believe that she was going to be just fine.

"Dad?"

"Huh?" he said, turning to Octavia.

"I'm going to my ballet lessons," she said. "Are you okay?"

Jim looked long and hard at his eldest daughter, seeing hints of Karen's features in her chin and nose. She was going to break some poor boy's heart someday, a feeling he knew too well.

"Yeah."

"She'll be fine," she said, looking toward her sister. "She has to be."

"She has to be," he repeated.

Octavia reached up and gave her father a kiss on the cheek.

"Wow! Twice in one day," he said.

"Don't get used to it," she said. "After ballet, I'm going over to Susan's for a swim."

"Okay."

He watched Octavia walk over to the minivan that was waiting for her. He waved at Susan's mother. She had given birth to four girls, and now lived her life as the perpetual driver to her little heiresses.

"Will you be home for dinner?" he called after his daughter.

"Probably not," she said and climbed into the van.

☙ ❧

"Daddy?" Midnight joined her father on the front steps, her cheeks flushed, sweat dripping down her face. "I'm hungry."

"I'm getting a little hungry too," he said. "What are your taste buds craving tonight?"

Midnight pursed her lips and thought about it. "Kraft dinner?"

"Sounds like a plan," he said.

Midnight sat at the kitchen table and started drawing a picture on a blank piece of paper she'd pulled from her craft drawer, while Jim poured water into a pot and put it on one of the burners that he turned to MAX.

"Daddy?"

"Yes?"

Midnight looked at her dad. "I'm gonna marry Tyler."

"You are?"

Midnight nodded enthusiastically.

"But yesterday you said that he was never going to be your boyfriend ever again."

She gave him the look. "That was yesterday."

Jim waited for more but Midnight was busy colouring again. He shook his head, thinking that life should be so simple. He rather liked the five-year-old view of the world. Yesterday was yesterday. Old news. Move on.

"Did I scare you today, when I fainted?"

"Yes," he said while stirring the noodles. "It sure did."

"Do you think my cancer is back?"

"Why would you say that?"

"Tyler heard his mom talking to his dad." She put the crayon down. "She said she hoped it wasn't the cancer again."

Jim turned to face her. "Let's wait and see what the doctor says."

"She's not gonna poke me with needles, is she?"

"I don't know, honey," he said. "They might need to take some blood."

Midnight couldn't breathe as she fought back tears. "I h-hate n-needles."

Jim came over to her and crouched down. He stroked her hair. "I know you do, but these needles might be good needles."

She shook her head. "All needles hurt."

"I know," he said in his best soothing voice. "We'll just have to be brave."

"But you're not getting the needle, I am."

"I'll be there with you the whole time."

"Not the same."

"You're right, sweetie." He handed her a tissue. "We don't even know if needles will be needed so why don't we just wait until we see doctor Fournier, okay?"

She nodded and wiped the mess below her nose.

"Whose picture is that?" he said to draw her attention away. "Is that you?"

"No silly, it's Mommy," she said, brightening up. "See, she has long hair and hazel eyes, just like the photo on your dresser. She's beautiful."

"Just like you."

"I'll put it on the fridge, for when she comes back."

Jim quickly turned away and tried to breathe. Midnight's innocent optimism tightened his chest and he couldn't seem to draw enough air into his lungs. His daughter was always full of surprises, almost like she had clairvoyance. He knew she didn't, but moments like these made him wonder. Tiny arms wrapped around his leg.

"You okay, Daddy?"

He ruffled her hair. "I've got you, so I couldn't be more okay."

"I know you miss her."

"You're way too smart for your age," he said and pulled two bowls from the cupboard. "Let's eat."

☙ ❧

Once dinner was over, Midnight decided to make a card for Tyler. She spent nearly an hour working on it. On the front she drew a big heart and coloured it bright red, and then stuck a bunch of star stickers all around it. On the inside of the card, she drew a boy and a girl holding hands—her stick people were becoming much better lately. To the right, she drew a house and a car, a dog and a cat, and a stroller. She finished off with a rainbow above their heads.

"What have you got there?" Jim said, coming to see her latest masterpiece. "Wow! That's so great, honey."

"It's a card for Tyler."

First she'd drawn a picture of Karen, and now this very elaborate card for Tyler. Karen had been quite an artist, drawing charcoal portraits like a pro, without ever having taken any sort of training.

"I bet he's going to love it."

"It's me and Tyler, when we get married and have a house and a family."

"I see that," he said. "But it's not his birthday."

"I know. I just wanted to make him one."

"You're very thoughtful." He looked at the new picture on the fridge. "And very good."

"Will my kids have cancer too?" she said without stopping what she was doing. "I hope not."

He wasn't a doctor but hadn't he heard somewhere that we all carried cancerous cells, and if the conditions were just right—or wrong, depending on your point of view—then you got cancer? But were children of cancer survivors more likely to develop cancer themselves?

Was it hereditary?

"I don't think they'll be more likely to have cancer just because you had it. Mommy and I never had cancer."

"Good," she said. "Because I want to have lots of babies. Five."

Jim grinned. Poor Tyler had no idea that his life was already planned out. Jim knew the odds of the two kids dating later on when they were adults were next to nil, but his daughter's sweetness was rather precious. "That's a lot of babies."

Midnight arched an eyebrow, her right one, the one she

always raised when thinking hard about something. Her chin rested on her closed fists. "Tyler will have a good job, so we'll have lots of money to feed the babies."

Jim laughed. "You've got it all figured out, it looks like."

Midnight smiled. "Yep."

cs ɛ

The following day, Midnight, Tyler, and Jake were playing soccer at the park across the street, having a great time, when trouble from down the street showed up.

"Hey, I wanna play too. It's my turn, so gimme the ball," Bradley said.

Midnight hugged the ball and turned to Tyler, eyes wide and pleading. This couldn't be happening again.

"Why are you looking at him?" Bradley said. Then he began to cackle and walked toward Tyler. "Got something to say for your *girlfriend*?"

Tyler looked down at his feet. "No," he said so only Bradley could hear.

Bradley flashed a wicked grin at Midnight. "Maybe you should go. We don't need girls. Soccer is for boys only."

"No it's not!" she shouted. "We were fine playing without you."

"Is that right?" Bradley said to Tyler. "Your *girlfriend* making the rules now?"

Tyler just kept staring at his feet. Midnight glared at him but he didn't look her way. Was this the way the whole summer was going to be? This would be a horrible summer if it was. Tyler had to tell Bradley to go away, that they didn't want him to play with them. Tyler had to stand up for her.

"Tyler?" She felt her eyes well up.

"*Tyler*," Bradley mimicked.

Midnight started to leave but Jake took her hand.

"See?" she said. "Jake is braver than you."

At this, Tyler looked Midnight's way, and she could see the fear in his eyes. Bradley was probably three inches taller and ten pounds heavier.

"Bradley," Tyler said sheepishly. "If you want to play with—"

He didn't get to finish because Bradley pushed him hard in the chest with his two hands, sending Tyler backward. He lost his footing and fell to the ground.

"Ha, ha. What a wimp," Bradley said.

"Leave him alone," Midnight said as she rushed to help Tyler up. "You're so mean."

Tyler quickly got to his feet and ran off, his cheeks burning red.

"What a big baby," Bradley shouted. "Go get your *mommy*!"

Midnight turned. "I hate you," she said. "You're the meanest boy ever."

Midnight and Jake hurried away before Bradley could think of anything else to say.

☙ ❧

"Is Tyler okay?" Midnight asked Mrs. Murphy, who was waiting at the door.

"He said Bradley pushed him to the ground and that he hurt his bum falling on it," Mrs. Murphy said while trying to keep a straight face. "Thank you for bringing Jake."

"You're welcome," Midnight said. "Bradley is such a big meanie. He always brings trouble."

"He does at that," Mrs. Murphy said almost to herself. "Did you want to go see how Tyler is?"

"Yes," Midnight said. "But first I want to get something from home." She hurried and came back less than two minutes later.

"What's that?"

"I made him a card yesterday."

Mrs. Murphy smiled. "You have the heart of an angel. He's up in his room. You go ahead. I think his ego is more bruised than his bum."

Midnight stopped just before the first step to the second floor and looked at Mrs. Murphy with a furrowed brow. "What's that?"

"Ego?"

Midnight nodded.

"His pride," she said. "Being made fun of like that in front of you embarrassed him."

"Oh!" Midnight took a couple of steps and stopped. "At least he tried this time. So that makes me happy with him."

Midnight knocked on Tyler's door, and when he didn't say anything, she pushed the door open a bit and stuck her head in. Tyler was staring at the ceiling, his baseball glove in his left hand, a baseball in his right hand, which he threw up and caught in his glove.

"Can I come in?"

Tyler shrugged.

"You were good today," Midnight said. "I think Bradley won't be back now."

"Why not?"

"Because you stood up to him."

"No I didn't. He pushed me to the ground."

Midnight sat at the end of the bed and watched Tyler throw the ball a couple of times. She pursed her lips. "But you said something to him this time." She paused. "I think you were brave."

Tyler shrugged again. "He'll probably beat me up at school next year."

Midnight shook her head. "He'll forget by the time we go back to school. He's kinda dumb."

At that, Tyler smiled and sat up to look at Midnight. "He's really dumb," he said.

"Like a bag of nails," Midnight said. "Don't know what it means, but my dad says that all the time."

They stared at each other.

"Like a bag of doggy pooh," Tyler said, a grin spreading across his face, pleased at how clever he was to have come up with this all by himself.

"Ah, gross," Midnight said, laughing. "Maybe like a bag of dead worms."

Tyler nodded. "No. Like a bag of doggy pooh with dead worms mixed up in it," he said. "And big slimy boogers."

"With earwax."

They both laughed until their bellies were sore. In the safety of Tyler's bedroom, they were invincible; they could take on Bradley and destroy him, pummel him into a dog turd. He couldn't touch them now.

"I made this card for you," she said when the laughter had

died down.

Tyler took the card and admired it. "I didn't make one for you."

"It's okay," she said.

"It's really nice. I'll put it on my dresser and keep it forever." He placed it beside his t-ball trophy from last summer. His team had won the championship. "Want to play something?"

"Sure."

"Mom, we're going to play in the basement," Tyler shouted as they rushed by the kitchen where Jake was finishing a snack.

"Wait for me," Jake said.

"No. You can't come," Tyler said. "I just want to play with Midnight."

"Tyler," his mother said in that tone that meant business.

"Jake can play with us," Midnight said.

"But he's too little."

Midnight put her hand on Tyler's arm. "You're not Bradley, are you?"

Tyler sighed and shoved his hands in his pockets and stared down at his feet. "No."

"Good." Midnight leaned over and kissed Tyler on the cheek—her hero today, and the boy she was planning to marry one day.

☙ ❧

It was bedtime, and Octavia had just finished putting Midnight's hair into a French braid. They were sitting side by side on Midnight's bed, Octavia holding the book she was going to read in her lap.

"When did you kiss your first boy?" Midnight said.

"Gosh, I don't remember. Why?"

"I kissed Tyler today," Midnight said, a smile spreading across her face. "On the cheek," she added for clarity's sake.

"Of course," Octavia said and winked at her sister. "I only kiss boys on the cheek."

"No you don't," Midnight said. "I saw you kiss that boy the other day, on the mouth."

Near the end of school, Octavia and this boy, Carl Baumgartner, had hung out together for a few weeks. He'd been to the house a couple of times and he'd finally gathered the courage to kiss her before jumping on his bike and heading home one Saturday afternoon.

"He wasn't a very good kisser," Octavia said, sounding like she was trying to discourage her younger sister. "He almost bit my lip."

Midnight put her hand over her mouth and giggled. "Tyler's the only boy I'll ever kiss, so I don't care if he's not a good kisser. He'll get better."

"He will, huh?"

"Yep!"

Octavia took the *Hurry Up Franklin* book into her hands and flipped to the first page. "Well," she said. "Don't rush into it. And don't think that Tyler will be the only boy. When I was your age, I had a crush on Justin."

"Yuck," Midnight said. "He has things on his teeth, and stuff on his face."

"Pimples."

"Gross."

"Who's to say Tyler won't wear braces and have pimples when he's older?"

Midnight stared wide-eyed at her sister.

"That's a long ways away," Octavia said. "So don't worry about it. Let's read your story so you can get to sleep. It's getting late."

Midnight slipped under the covers and Octavia read a few pages, until Midnight's eyes were nearly shut. Then Octavia used a bookmark to keep the page they were at, and tucked Midnight in.

"Sweet dreams, my little princess." Octavia kissed her on the forehead. "I love you."

"Love you too, Tavia."

FIVE

~ September 2001 ~

Midnight had already hit the snooze button on her bedside clock twice, so the third time it went off she reached over and actually shut off the alarm. Reluctantly, she swung her legs over the edge of the bed, a deed that required way too much energy this early in the morning, and got up. Eyes half closed, she lumbered toward the bathroom for a shower. With any luck, the hot water would wake her up.

Her sleep had been broken by bouts of tossing and turning, staring at the clock, followed by more agitated sleep.

Every time she and her dad had a disagreement—okay, a fight—it left her feeling guilty. She was all he had now, with Octavia moved out, and Midnight didn't want to fight with him. And lately, their fights were always about her mother.

How could someone who'd been gone so long still cause so much turmoil in their lives?

Midnight waited for the water to be scalding hot before getting into the shower, and she stood there for ten minutes just letting the heat soothe the back of her neck and shoulders. She really didn't want to go to school today, mostly to avoid Samantha, who would badger her about the stupid party this weekend. Midnight didn't want to go, for no other reason than not wanting to be around a bunch of mindless teenagers doing stupid things simply because it was expected of them.

Again, the thought of volunteering came to mind and she knew that spending time at the Children's Hospital was the right thing to do—if they allowed volunteering, something she was going to need to look into. Let's face it, there was no one more in need of people to care about them than young children who didn't quite understand why they were sick in the first place and why they needed to have all these tests done on them.

Not that Midnight remembered much, because she'd been barely three when she was sick, but she knew her fear of needles dated back to that time, and at fifteen, she understood how scared these young kids going through these almost inhuman treatments must be.

The more she thought about it, the more the idea of helping out at the Children's Hospital appealed to her. She would seriously look into it.

Midnight shut off the water and felt a bit more alive. The day no longer seemed as dreadful as she'd expected and she picked up the pace to get ready.

She didn't want Samantha's mom to have to wait for her.

ଔ ଓ

Midnight looked passed Samantha and watched the van pull away. The ride to school had been very quiet, uncomfortably quiet, and she hoped she hadn't come across as rude to Mrs.

Carmichael. Other than her dad and Octavia, Samantha's mom was someone who Midnight really cared about, for all the obvious reasons.

"Didn't anyone tell the *sevies* that this is high school?" Samantha said.

The two friends started to walk toward the front door while grade seven students played tag or something like that, as if they were still in elementary school.

"They're not bothering me," Midnight said.

"You still mad at me?"

Midnight said nothing at first. "I'm not. I just don't want to go to that party and you trying to bully me into going made it worse."

"I just thought it would give us a chance to spend time together," Samantha said and put her hand on Midnight's left arm. She pulled it away once Midnight stopped walking. "You're becoming more distant every day. It feels like we're growing apart."

"I know," Midnight said. "I'm not like you anymore. And before you get defensive, I just mean that you're the normal teenager and I'm not. I need more. I need to make a difference, somehow."

"You make me sound vain and shallow."

Midnight could see that Samantha was hurt. "I don't think you are. You're beautiful and smart and I know you'll do great things."

"When I'm done being a stupid teenager."

This was more difficult than Midnight had expected. None of her words were coming out right. The ones she'd rehearsed in her head this morning in the shower seemed to have gone down the drain with the soapy water. It was obvious that she and Samantha wanted different things, that life was trying to pull them in opposite directions. It had been bound to happen someday. Midnight hadn't realized that day was now.

Samantha's face tightened. "We've been friends since grade one. How many people can say that? We're like sisters."

"You have a sister, who you fight with all the time."

"That's what sisters do. She's so much younger than me and we don't have anything in common except living in the same house."

"Octavia is seven years older and we never fought."

"That's different," Samantha said. "That's because . . ."

An awkward silence followed. Midnight knew that Samantha hadn't meant anything callous, but it still stung. It was a wound that kept reopening no matter how many defensive layers she wrapped around her heart.

"Sorry. I didn't—"

The bell rang. Students began to hurry past them but they remained outside, two statues frozen in place.

"I won't bug you about the party anymore. If you don't want to be my friend, I can't force you, but I know I still do. Maybe I'm a little selfish lately—okay, probably a lot—but like you said, I'm not you. I don't know who I am or what I want, so I pretend, like the other thousand students in this school. I wish I were more like you, but I'm me. It used to be enough."

Samantha walked away, leaving Midnight standing on the sidewalk, second-guessing herself.

☙ ❧

Midnight watched Samantha disappear into the school, wondering what exactly had just happened. She hadn't set out to have a fight, nor had she purposely wanted to sever their friendship, but it seemed like she'd done both.

Panic made everything around her spin and her legs almost gave out.

But then she recovered and ran after Samantha, hurrying down the hallway and hearing a teacher remind her that hallways were made for walking.

She ignored the teacher.

"Sam, wait up! Please."

Up ahead, Samantha stopped and turned, her features a barrier meant to protect her. "We're late for class."

"I know," Midnight said and stayed a couple of feet away. "I'm sorry. I don't know what came over me. I'm just . . . I don't know. Lately, I just see black and I'm trying to find a light."

Samantha's face went from hard to confused and she almost took a step back.

"I sound crazy," Midnight said. "I feel crazy, like nothing is in my control. I wish I was more like you, but I'm not. I'm cynical about everything teenagers represent. It all seems trivial, the things we deem important when the world is trying to . . ." She stopped when she realized a small crowd had gathered. She'd just given them more reason to think her weird. The urge to scream rose so quickly that she was surprised she caught it in time. "I'm sorry."

Midnight and Samantha didn't move, seemingly locked in some sort of telepathic conversation, which was enough for the crowd to get bored with and disperse.

"Truth is," Midnight said, "I know I embarrass you in front of your other friends, that you don't want to hurt my feelings so you put up with my idiosyncrasies, and involving me in your social circle is your way of trying to help me. Sometimes, I just think . . . maybe I'm as crazy as everyone thinks I am. When someone is different, well, they must be crazy, right? If you don't fit the mold society has so carefully created for us, well, there must be something wrong with me."

"Don't say that," Samantha said, taking a step forward. "I know why you're different, and I'm sorry if trying to include you in my life seems like I'm trying to fix you, but I'm not. Okay, maybe a little, because I care about you. I want to see you happy."

"I just don't know if it's something I'll ever be allowed," Midnight said and wiped her eyes with the back of her hand, smearing mascara. "I *don't* miss her. I don't remember her. But I hate what she did to us, to my dad."

Samantha reached out and hugged Midnight.

"You'll want to fix that," she said and led Midnight into the nearest girls' washroom. "The mirror never lies."

"Don't I look lovely," Midnight said with a hesitant laugh. "Guess I shouldn't buy such cheap mascara. It's the only makeup I wear, you'd think I'd splurge a bit."

"No biggie," Samantha said and helped her friend clean up. "Much better."

"Thanks," Midnight said. "For not abandoning me."

"I'm not going anywhere," she said. "You can depend on me."

"I know."

"You'd better."

The two friends hugged again, this time without the hidden tension.

"I've decided to volunteer at the Children's Hospital, if they'll allow that," Midnight said. "I think helping sick kids might be what I want to do with my life."

Samantha was washing her hands. "I can see you doing that."

"Me too." There was a hint of excitement in her voice. "Kids are so accepting. They don't judge."

"Too bad we lose that."

"I know."

"We better get late slips," Samantha said. "We'll tell Mrs. Lauzon that we had a female emergency, that time of the month. Works every time."

ᨀ ᨁ

Samantha and Midnight came out of history class forty-five minutes later, in a quiet stupor. In fact, the entire class was dead silent. Nothing like studying current events to sober up teenage angsts and put life in perspective.

"Well, that was depressing," Samantha said as the two girls made their way to their lockers. "Guess we could have skipped it."

"You know what happened in New York is real," Midnight said. "People died, people with families. Some kids lost parents. Some might even have lost both and are orphans now."

Samantha pressed her forehead against her locker. "I guess I don't want to think about that. It's so sad."

"It is," Midnight said. "Especially when your life is too perfect."

Samantha saw the smirk on her friend's face and relaxed. "It wasn't always that way and you know it. And I do feel sorry for those kids. I'm not totally self-centered."

"I see the possibilities in you."

"Real funny," Samantha said. "It's kind of scary though, right? I never think of war as being too real. It always happens far away."

"We've been lucky."

A couple of boys walked by and ogled Samantha. She gave them her too-hot-to-touch look and one of them stopped and the other ran into him.

Both girls laughed.

"Doesn't it bother you that boys look at you like you're some candy they'd like to eat," Midnight said. "It's a bit creepy."

"I guess," Samantha said. "But you know what?"

Midnight shook her head.

"I'm the one in control," Samantha said. "They can look all they want, but *I* decide what happens."

"I'm not sure about that."

"Explain."

"Well, once you decide to date them, don't you give up control? And by the count of the guys you've dated in the past year, seems like you've had little control."

Samantha smiled. "You need to date. Then you'll understand that we never give up control. We make them think they're in control, but really, boys never are. Look at your dad—" She practically choked on the words, her cheeks going red.

Midnight said nothing.

"I didn't mean that," Samantha said. "I'm sorry."

"No, you're right."

"I got carried away. I shouldn't have said that."

"You were just proving a point."

"I wasn't thinking."

"I'm fine."

"You sure?"

Midnight nodded. "You were just speaking the truth."

"Well, maybe I need to learn to filter my thoughts."

"I'm okay."

The bell rang again.

"Crap, class is starting. We can't be late again," Samantha said. "I'll talk to you at lunch. Come sit with us."

"I'll see," Midnight said and ran in the opposite direction.

Samantha watched her go, and then headed to math class. Something had bothered her as she'd watched Midnight run away, like her friend was leaving her, like she was never going to see her again. That feeling lingered for a while, unpleasant yet too real. Samantha couldn't help but think about what Midnight had said, about how some kids in New York might be orphans today, their parents killed in the collapse of the World Trade Center.

Life could turn unexpectedly, and Samantha didn't like that. She wanted to have control, like she'd told Midnight, but the truth was—and Samantha knew this—real life was full of moments where control was a thin rope of smoke that simply couldn't be grasped.

ꟹ ꟹ

Midnight tuned Mrs. Kerns out. English class was normally her favourite class, but right now she thought about what Samantha had said about her dad being controlled even after all these years, and that statement was truer than she cared to admit and it made Midnight ache deep inside her soul.

Oh Dad, what am I going to do with you?

If only she'd known her mother, maybe then she could understand why her dad was holding on to a memory that seemed to torment him more than make him happy. She understood how someone could love another person so deeply, and she knew that Samantha wondered about Midnight's own obsession with Tyler, but that was different. Or so she told herself. She couldn't be sure if what she felt for him was really love or simply a longing for a time that she regarded as perfect, when life was simple. How much of our early childhood do we truly remember as it was as opposed that what we believed it was?

What her dad needed was a date, a real, present-day date with a real woman, not a memory of a ghost fading into myth as each year passed.

"Midnight, you okay?"

Midnight looked at her teacher. "Yes, why?"

"Well, I was asking you a question and you weren't answering, and you look like you've seen a ghost. You look pale."

Midnight faked a smile. "I'm fine. I was just thinking about something. Can you repeat the question?"

"What conflict is being developed in *To Kill a Mockingbird*?"

"Oh, that's easy," Midnight said and spoke at length for the next ten minutes. Although the book was new to many of her classmates, she had read the story several times over the years, a favourite of hers and her dad.

When she finished talking, she felt her nose running and

wiped it with the back of her finger, only to reveal a smear of blood on her skin. She searched her backpack for a tissue and found a small package that had never been opened, something Octavia had told her a long time ago that she should always have handy.

In case of an emergency.

Midnight had never gotten a nosebleed before and there were no repeats that day—she knew people got nosebleeds all the time and it didn't mean anything; it was just another thing to add to her growing list of bodily defects—so that by the time she got home, she'd shoved it into the back of her mind.

☙ ❧

Jim was sitting at the kitchen table, his third beer of the day half done. Today wasn't a good day for writing. Nothing came to mind. The financial brochure he was supposed to write wasn't happening, so he'd tried to work on the novel he'd started ten years ago, but that hadn't fared any better.

So he'd thought that maybe a beer, even at eleven thirty in the morning, might be the oil that greased the wheel, but it hadn't. The second beer had done little to inspire, except to go for a third.

Jim stared at the bottle of Sleeman and disgust settled in the pit of his stomach. It was a wonder his liver hadn't given out yet. How many bottoms did he need to hit before he finally bounced back? He felt trapped in a hole he simply couldn't ever climb out of. He didn't like himself. He'd become a recluse, interacting with the outside world through his daughters, mostly Midnight. He'd retreated to the safety of his home so long ago that he really had no idea how to leave it, how to rejoin the world.

Live again.

He decided to make himself a sandwich, to sop up the alcohol and guilt in his gut. He looked in the fridge but found nothing of interest, so he raided the cupboard and found a can of tuna. Searching in the utensils drawer for a can opener, his finger brushed against a knife edge and his face crumpled in a wave of pain.

"Shit!" he said and looked at his finger as if surprised it was still intact. Then blood started to trickle out of the wound, so he grabbed a tissue and wrapped it around the cut. There were no Band-Aids in the powder room, so he went upstairs to the main bathroom. "You can't go on like this," he said to the stranger in the mirror.

Like all the other times he'd said that to the reflection in front of him, it provided no reply, no guidance, no hope. He picked up the towel that Midnight had left on the bathroom floor and hung it, gathered her dirty clothes and put them in the hamper in her closet. He stood in the middle of her room and noticed how dated everything had become—the dark pink paint on her wall, the worn cream-colored carpet, the collection of dolls on her shelves, the teddy on her pillow. A room locked in a time warp, like the rest of their lives.

He had neglected so many things.

Too many.

None of it was healthy. Not for him, and especially not for Midnight.

SIX

~ April 1989 ~

Over the course of winter, Jim noticed that Midnight wasn't eating much, and he suspected her weight had not increased in a while, maybe even a year. This concerned him and he made an appointment with Midnight's doctor.

When the paediatrician examined Midnight, she found a large lump on the left side of Midnight's abdomen, making her ribcage stick out a bit.

"I'd like to get an ultrasound done so we can get a better idea," she told Jim and Karen. "See Sylvie at the front and she'll make the appointment."

"What if she has cancer?" Karen whispered into his ear while they waited for Sylvie to book the appointment. "I don't think I could handle that."

"Let's not jump to conclusions," Jim said.

"Okay, I have the appointment for Friday morning, ten o'clock," Sylvie said and handed Jim a form with the address and instructions. "They like it if you can be there ten minutes early to fill out some paperwork."

"Sure," he said.

Midnight looked very sleepy, so he carried her to the car and put her in a booster seat. "We'll be home soon, honey, and you can have a nap."

"Okay Daddy."

Jim backed the car out and drove across the parking lot toward the exit. The light was red.

"Cancer," Karen said. "I just have this feeling."

"Can you keep it down?" Jim said, the annoyance in his tone obvious.

"She's already sleeping."

Jim glanced in the rear-view mirror and saw Midnight's chin against her upper chest. He smiled. He couldn't think of that sweet little girl having cancer. He wasn't going there until they found out more.

"We don't know anything right now," he said. "Let's wait for the ultrasound."

"I can't, Jim. I just can't. This is all too much. I'm sure she has cancer. She's just looked unwell lately. I knew something was wrong. What are we going to do?"

"My God, Karen," he said, slapping the steering wheel. "We don't even know anything yet so why do you have her in her grave already."

"I'm sorry. I'm sorry." She closed her eyes and took a couple of deep breaths. "I was never cut out for this, you know. If I hadn't gotten pregnant with Octavia by mistake, this wouldn't be happening."

Karen had often talked about going out to California, get a

band going, see how far they could go. "But you did, and this is our life, Karen. We have two kids that we love very much, and we'll get through this, whatever this is. Right?"

Karen was looking out the side window.

"Right?" Jim said again.

Karen didn't answer.

☙ ❧

Midnight was diagnosed with Wilms' Tumor a week later. The paediatrician tried to stay positive, telling them that if Midnight was to get cancer, that this one wasn't horrible, that the survival rate was close to 95%, and most kids lived a very long and happy life afterwards.

The doctor went over her recommendation, an aggressive course of action, but she felt good that the cancer was in the early stages and she liked Midnight's chances.

"Okay," Jim said several times while he listened to the paediatrician. "We'll do whatever needs to be done."

"Good, because it's going to be rough," the doctor said. "And she's going to need both of you to get through it. But she's a tough kid."

Jim and Karen left the doctor's office ten minutes later, both very quiet. They drove home in complete silence; not even the radio was turned on.

"You didn't say anything," Jim said once they were home.

"What was I supposed to say?" Karen said. "I told you last week that I had a feeling. I should be happy that I was right?"

"Of course not."

"Midnight has cancer." She plopped down on the edge of the

worn couch, her shoulders slumped. "She's got cancer."

"We'll get through this," he said as he sat beside his wife. "The doctor said it was detected early and her chances are good. Very good."

"Cancer," she said again. "Your mother died of cancer. How can you take this so casually? Our daughter has cancer, and you expect me to just take that? I can't, Jim. I don't think I can."

"What are you saying?"

She knotted her hands between her knees. "Just that I don't know if I can watch her die."

Jim stood too quickly, the rush to his head making him dizzy. He waited for the moment to pass and then walked to the front bay window. He stared outside. "She's not going to die," he said, his back to her. "Weren't you listening to what her doctor said?"

"She can't be one hundred percent certain."

"Of course, she can't, but Midnight is strong and she will beat this." Jim ran a hand through his hair, which seemed to be thinning rapidly lately. "That's our baby. She will need both of us when it gets really bad for her, because once she starts on the chemo, it will get really bad for her."

"I heard what the doctor said," Karen said, her eyes like a river. "Don't you think I know that? I'm scared. I'm really scared, and I wish we hadn't been dealt this hand. We had plans for our life together, remember?"

Jim turned to look at Karen, his eyes cold but determined. "That was a long time ago. Things change. People grow up."

☙ ❧

The weeks of treatment were pure hell for them all. Although the chemo was supposed to help Midnight get back on the road to recovery, it seemed to do the exact opposite. She looked worse after each treatment.

When her third birthday came just three weeks into her treatment, Midnight was too sick, so Jim suggested they postpone her party until she was better.

Spring came and went. Midnight couldn't have weighed more than twenty pounds by the end of June, at least twelve pounds underweight. And with a bald head, she looked so pitiful that Karen spent most of her time crying and smoking, a habit she'd given up when pregnant with Midnight.

"You reek of smoke," Jim said one night.

"It's keeping me calm," she said.

"I don't think it's working."

"Of course, it's not working," she said, sounding like a woman about to lose it. "When the fuck is she going to get better? I can't take this anymore. She's not going to get better. I just know she's not."

Jim tried to hold her but she pushed him away.

"Calm down," he said. "Octavia is old enough to see you losing it. She's ten, and she's not stupid. She needs her mother to show her how to handle this."

"I'm not cut out for this, Jim." She paced, stopped, glared at the walls as if the room was getting smaller and smaller. "I've been trying to tell you for weeks."

Jim took her into his arms and this time she didn't stop him. "It will be all right. I know it will. She's just about to turn the corner. Just trust me."

Karen cried into his shoulder.

"What's wrong with Mom?" Octavia said from the doorway of their bedroom. "Why is she crying?"

"Why don't you put Midnight to bed, honey? Please," Jim said.

"Yeah, sure."

Once Octavia left the room, Jim sat Karen on the bed and joined her. He pulled her back into the safety of his arms, and sat there without saying a word for a while.

Although he said nothing, plenty rushed through his mind. Karen had already given up. He knew that. Even if Midnight pulled through, even if she lived to be ninety years old, Karen had already given up on her . . . on all of them. This was her way out of this trapped life, and maybe she would leave tomorrow, or in six months, but Jim knew that she would leave. Whereas most couple would unite and grow stronger and closer in times of crisis, Jim knew this ordeal hadn't brought him and Karen closer. In fact, he felt utterly alone.

Jim looked at their wedding picture on the dresser. They had laughed and joked and been so in love. Karen had always had that free spirit in her, and being with her had been incredible. But, slowly, she had changed; he'd seen the fire in her slowly burn out. She hadn't been happy in a long time, not like him. He absolutely loved being a dad and husband.

She struggled with being a mother, with living the suburban life, with caring for a family.

Not unlike her father.

Jim's light blue eyes, normally radiating with life, were filled with sorrow. He knew he shouldn't do this, but his heart ached for the woman he had desperately yearned to be with. Sure,

Octavia had been unexpected, but so what? He had fallen in love with her the moment she was born, and the same when Midnight had joined them. But he had chosen to turn a blind eye to Karen, and how she had seemed less excited than him with each birth. He had told himself it was the entire process, nine months of feeling fat, being uncomfortable, and then the ordeal of giving birth . . . but he knew it wasn't just that. With each child, a part of Karen's spirit had vanished, a small part of her had died. He could see it in her eyes, the way they looked sometimes when things got crazy, full of regret and resentment. All the signs had been there for a very long time, but Jim had chosen to ignore them.

He should be angry with her.

He should yell at her.

He should tell her to suck it up and get her shit together, but it wouldn't do any good. In mind, she was already gone. It was just a matter of time before the rest of her followed.

Jim stood. "I'll go check on the girls."

Karen looked up at him and reached for his hand. "I'm sorry."

"So am I," he said and let go of her hand. "So am I."

ଔ ଓ

Jim peeked in on Midnight and she was fast asleep. Octavia had put her into pyjamas with bunny rabbits on them, and tucked her favourite stuffed bear in the nook of her arm. She looked so at peace when she slept, and just staring at his baby girl who was in a fight for her life, Jim couldn't understand how Karen had given up.

His little munchkin was going to survive.

Jim kneeled down beside her and kissed her forehead. He stayed that way for a while, just looking at Midnight, his love so overwhelming he felt paralyzed.

His thoughts turned to God.

Jim couldn't really say he was a religious man. Hadn't been to a church in years—neither girl was baptised, and he wondered if maybe they should be. He was Catholic, as his parents had been adamant churchgoers when he was a boy, but he'd pretty much stopped going when he reached adulthood. It wasn't that he didn't believe in God, or that his faith had disappeared, it just wasn't something that had stayed paramount in his life. He'd always been of the mindset that if he needed to talk to God, he could do it just as well from the comfort of his home as he could from the sanctum of a crowded church.

Tonight was a good time to have a one-on-one with God.

But he didn't make any empty promises that he'd attend church from now on, or that he'd be more generous with his donations from now on, or that the next time he saw a homeless person downtown, he'd give him or her a twenty so they could get something to eat. He didn't do any of these things because Jim didn't think God would be that foolish to believe him. Jim was pretty sure that He had heard it all, and Jim didn't want to be like everyone else, only needing Him when the good times were gone.

Jim simply said the Lord's Prayer.

After he was done, Jim kissed her again and stood. "Daddy is here, my angel. Daddy will always be here."

His emotions became too much and he wiped his eyes with his fingers. Midnight actually looked angelic with just her head sticking out of her blankets and her teddy against her face. He left her door slightly ajar and knocked on Octavia's door before letting himself in.

"Hey," he said and sat beside her on the bed. "Thanks for putting her to bed."

"Sure, Dad." She hesitated, pursed her lips. "Is Mom okay?"

That was a damn good question. Was Mom okay? How was he supposed to answer that? How was he supposed to tell his ten-year-old daughter that he didn't think her Mom was okay, that he was fairly certain that one day when she was at school and he was at work, he'd come home and Karen would be gone. Except that Midnight was with her during the day. So maybe, instead, she would simply go out to get milk one night, and never return. It could happen in a million different ways.

"She's a little overwhelmed," he finally said, feeling the bitter sting of the lie not in his mouth, but deep down in his soul. He was lying to his daughter to protect his wife. "We all are."

"I just never saw her like that. Mom never swears."

Jim grinned. Octavia had never met her mother when she was seventeen. She'd had a foul mouth on her. But it had been mostly around other people. When it was just the two of them, he couldn't really say that she swore much.

"It's a tough time. She loves you guys so much, and the thought of Midnight being sick . . ." His Adam's apple had grown to the size of a melon. "Well, you'd better get ready for bed too," he said and stood. "Do you have any homework?"

Octavia shook her head.

His voice was a whisper. "Goodnight, honey."

He turned to walk away.

"Dad?"

"Yes, Octavia?" he said and looked her way.

"Do you think Midnight is going to die?"

Jim saw worry in her eyes, but not hopelessness. He knew she loved her sister, but he also understood that her question was as much for herself as it was about Midnight, that if Midnight could get cancer and die, then what would prevent it from happening to her?

"Your sister is a survivor," he said. "She's not about to give up."

SEVEN

~ September 2001 ~

Midnight had butterflies in her stomach. She couldn't remember the last time she'd felt this nervous. She was also very excited. Tonight was the first time she was volunteering at the Children's Hospital and she couldn't wait to get there.

Normally the process could take quite some time, but Midnight had called on Thursday and managed to get hold of the Co-ordinator of Volunteer Resources, and after explaining why she wanted to volunteer, being a cancer survivor who not just wanted but *needed* to give back to the kids, the Co-ordinator, Valerie Beaucarie, had told her that there was a spot opening up on the first of October, but she would make an exception and let Midnight start this Saturday, as long as she committed to volunteering for twelve months and filled out all the necessary forms and met the requirements.

Midnight had agreed without hesitation and her dad had driven her out to the hospital to get all the paperwork done. She had gone back Friday after school for a one-hour orientation, where she learned about policies and procedures, and all safety measures meant to keep everyone safe.

And tonight, finally, she was going to start making a difference, and six o'clock couldn't have come sooner.

"Dad, ready?"

"Just waiting for you," he said from the family room. "Chauffeur Dad extraordinaire!"

"Do I look all right?" She was wearing blue jeans and a button-down white blouse. "I hope the kids like me. What if I don't know what to do or say? Is it warm here?"

"I have to tell you," Jim said, "I'm extremely proud of you. It takes a special person to give of herself."

"Thanks," she said. "We can go."

Twenty minutes later, Midnight was standing in front of the Children's Hospital, her dad driving away and giving her a couple of quick honks. Midnight took a deep breath and walked through the sliding doors, the cacophony of activity hitting her all at once and nearly overwhelming her.

She walked down the corridor, heading for the staff room where she checked in with Valerie.

"So, you ready?"

"Yes, absolutely." She wrung her fingers together "It's all I could think about today."

"Great. Let's go meet some kids."

☙ ❧

Samantha stashed a small bottle of whisky that was half empty into her purse. There were so many bottles of booze in the liquor cabinet that she doubted her parents would miss this small one, especially since there were three other bottles of whisky, two unopened and one nearly full.

She hadn't realized how much her parents drank, but then again, very few evenings went by that they—or at least her mom, since her dad was often not home until late—didn't have a drink or two. But tonight, she didn't care. She was going to have fun at the party and damned if she got caught.

Back in her room, she put on her makeup, going heavy on the black tonight. She wanted to look so hot that guys weren't going to be able to keep their eyes off of her. Her new tight blue jeans and tight black t-shirt accentuated all her curves, and she added a belt and a scarf around her neck. Small diamond earrings in all six holes, three per ear, and she combed her silky long blond hair straight.

She looked awesome.

The doorbell rang.

"Some guy is here for you," Emily said as she entered Samantha's room without knocking. "Whoa! Are you going out like that, looking like a tramp?"

"Shut up," Samantha said. "How would you know what a tramp looks like?"

"I'm not stupid and this is what a tramp looks like. I've seen some on TV."

"Maybe Mom shouldn't let you watch those shows."

"Maybe Mom shouldn't let you go out looking like this."

"Whatever," Samantha said. "And didn't I tell you not to come into my room without knocking?"

"Yeah, you did," Emily said with a defiant grin and walked out. "Hope you don't get pregnant. Or maybe I do so you'll stop thinking you're so much better than everybody else."

"Arrrgggg!" Samantha said. "You are such a *pain*."

"Blah, blah, blah."

Samantha checked herself in the mirror one last time and went down to the foyer. Her mom was talking with Derek, and Samantha wondered uneasily what they might be talking about.

"So," Tracy said, "Derek tells me he's planning to go to university after high school and pursue law or engineering. Both are very good fields to get into."

Samantha looked at Derek, her jaw dropping. Then she saw him wink and understood. "Sure does."

"It's good to have plans," her mother said. "So, you're going to the movies?"

"Huh, yeah," Samantha said. "A bunch of us are meeting there."

"What are you seeing?" Emily said in a skeptical tone.

"Uh . . ."

"We might catch *American Pie 2*," Derek said. "If everyone is up for it."

"Yeah, that sounds like fun," Samantha said. "I'm sure we'll find something if we have to."

"Well, you have a good time," Tracy said. "Don't be home too late."

"Sure, Mom."

Derek headed out the front door.

"Seems like a fine young man," Tracy managed to whisper into Samantha's ear.

An embarrassed look crossed Samantha's face before she stepped outside and closed the door behind her. Derek was waiting by the stairs.

"Oh my God!" she said, her hand over her mouth to stifle a laugh. "Seriously? *American Pie 2*?"

"Sure, why not? It's hilarious. I'd see it again."

"It's restricted."

"I'm eighteen, but I'm sure we could get you in. Nobody checks at the doors. You just buy a ticket for some other movie and then go see American Pie."

"Doesn't matter because we're not going to the movies to-night."

Derek flashed a smile that made his whole face, including his blue eyes, that much more electric. "No, we're not."

"Where's Kim?"

"Getting things set up at home."

"So let's go."

Just then, Derek surprised Sam by pulling her into him and kissing her, his tongue exploring her mouth. "Kim told me you had the hots for me," he said as he came up for air.

Samantha was speechless. Of course, she was hot for him, and she guessed Kim had figured it out because of all the times Sa-mantha talked about Derek, which was probably why Kim had stayed home.

"Well, I think you're dead gorgeous," he said and opened the car door for her. "We're gonna have fun tonight."

Samantha pulled the whisky out of her purse and took a swig before Derek rounded the car and got in the driver seat.

"Hey, you'd better share that," he said and grabbed the bottle from her. "Wow! That's good stuff."

"Don't get drunk yet. You gotta drive."

"I'm fine," he said and took another long pull before giving the bottle back. "Let's go."

He peeled out of the long driveway, Samantha looking back at the house to see if her mother was watching them. All she could see was Emily in the front window, waving at her in a sort of creepy way, that weird grin back on her face.

Samantha groaned and turned around.

"You okay?"

"Yeah. Just making sure my mom wasn't watching you drive like a maniac. Your outstanding status with her won't last long if she catches you."

"But I'm a *fine young man*," he said.

"You heard her?"

"I'm pretty sure she meant for me to hear."

"Probably." Samantha put the bottle in her purse. "She's so into impressions. I mean, you'd think she was someone important the way she parades herself."

"What about you?"

"I'm nowhere that conceited."

"You sure?"

"Why? What's Kim saying about me?"

A mischievous grin spread across his clean-shaven face. With his blond hair, Samantha could barely catch her breath. "Nothing I don't like," he said and gunned his father's Golf GTI to pass a couple of slow cars. "Nothing I don't like."

"Wow, your car goes."

"Yeah, it's the sporty Golf. My dad's been a Volkswagen diehard forever, even though he could probably get a BMW."

"Yeah, I have no idea what that is."

Derek grinned again and Samantha felt sudden warmth in her belly. He was so hot.

"Most Beamers are much more expensive and are typically held in higher status to the Golf. But this baby goes."

"Oh."

He laughed. She laughed. He looked at her. She stared back. Then he gunned the car again to pass a car and out of nowhere a cat crossed their path and Derek jerked the steering wheel and lost control. Front wheel drive cars have a lot of pull plus the GTI could really move, and Derek was unable to compensate as the car drifted into the gravel along the side of the road and he panicked and hit the brakes and jerked the steering wheel again and the car flipped onto its side and rolled several times before coming to a dead stop at the bottom of the ditch.

Samantha had blacked out after the first roll.

ʊ ɛ

Midnight met so many great kids in just half an hour and some were really sick that at first, she wasn't sure she was going to be able to handle this for one night, let alone twelve months. But then Valerie took her aside.

"It's a bit overwhelming, isn't it?"

"I guess I wasn't expecting that."

"I could tell. It was all over your face."

"I hope the kids couldn't tell."

"I'm sure some could, but don't worry."

"I feel like a fool now."

"You'll be just fine," Valerie said. "See little Jonathan over there? I think you'll be great with him."

"What do I do?"

"Just go over there and be a friend," she said. "That's really all these kids want."

Midnight rubbed her hands together.

"You'll be fine." Valerie checked her watch. "I have to be going."

"You're leaving me alone?"

"There are other volunteers," she said. "Barbara over there with little Gabriel has been here a long time. You can ask her anything. And Nicole's here somewhere. You'll get to know them. Just be yourself. The kids will tell you what they want most of the time. And if anything happens that you're not sure of, just get one of the nurses."

Midnight took a deep breath.

Valerie put a hand on her arm. "You'll be fine. I'm usually pretty good at judging people, and I get a feeling you'll be one of the good ones."

"I hope you're right," Midnight said and walked over to the little boy at the far end of the room. He was sitting on the floor and playing with a fire truck. He had the best-looking carrot-coloured hair she had ever seen. "Hi, my name is Midnight. Can I sit with you?"

The little boy looked up. "My name is Jonathan." He reached for her hand and Midnight sat down beside him. "You want to play with me?"

"I sure do."

His face, which had looked sad until now, lit up. "Is that your real name?"

"Midnight?"

He nodded.

"Yep!"

"It's sort of funny."

"Really?"

"I don't know anyone with that name."

"You know, I never met anyone with my name either. Do you know why my parents named me that?"

Jonathan shook his head, his beautiful orange hair swishing like a twirling mop.

"Because I was born at midnight."

Jonathan took a minute to absorb that. "Good thing you weren't born at nine o'clock."

Midnight laughed and many heads turned their way.

"I never thought of that, but I guess you're right," she said. "I think I would have hated to be called Nine."

Jonathan giggled, and then he began to cough, a deep, raw sort of cough. Midnight looked panicked and turned to find Barbara, but Jonathan stopped hacking just as suddenly as he'd started.

"You okay?" she said. "You scared me."

"I do that sometimes, when I get too excited."

"Guess we'll have to keep the fun down then."

"I'm fine. I'm used to it."

Midnight bit her lower lips. "How long have you been here?"

Jonathan shrugged. "A while. I think four weeks."

"Wow! Bet you can't wait to go home."

"I'm not going home," he said like it was no big deal. "I'm too sick."

Midnight wanted to wrap her arms around Jonathan and hold

him. His nonchalance about his condition was enough to make her fall in love with him for his strength and to mourn him for his fate.

"I have leukemia," he said. "My mom cries a lot."

Midnight pressed her lips together hard, very hard, and fought her own emotions. She had just met this little boy, barely knew anything about him, and already he'd stolen her heart. He was so sweet and innocent. If she could make him all better, she would.

"She must be a wonderful mom."

He nodded. "She's taking care of my older sister and baby brother tonight. My dad was here but went to get a coffee."

"Well, until he comes back, I'll stay with you. Is that all right?"

Jonathan nodded again. "I like you."

She gently caressed the back of his head. "I like you too."

"Why are you crying?"

Midnight felt a tear running down her left cheek and wiped it away with the back of her index finger. Why *was* she crying? It's not like she had anything invested into Jonathan's wellbeing, but she couldn't help but feel horrible about what he was going through, about what his parents and siblings were going through, and she wondered why this was happening to him. What had he done to deserve this?

Nothing.

It was that simple. She hadn't done anything bad either when she'd gotten sick, and Jonathan hadn't done anything bad to get leukemia, yet both of them had gotten sick. It made no sense. It was just something that happened. Randomly. Some people got sick and some didn't. It was like rolling the dice. Some got lucky and won, and others lost it all.

And that sucked.

"I guess I feel bad that you're here sick."

"My mom says that too."

"I think I'd like your mom," she said. "So, is this your fire truck?"

"It's the hospital's. I just play with it when no one else does."

Midnight reached for a yellow dump truck, one with enormous wheels, the sort of truck used for mining. She got on her knees and moved it around, making a loud motor sound in her throat. Jonathan joined her and for a few minutes they played, pushing their vehicles around the room, Midnight filling hers with other small toys she found along the way, and Jonathan putting out fires here and there. Then her knees began to ache and she sat.

"Sorry, but I need to take a break. My knees aren't as young as yours."

"How old are you?"

"I'm fifteen."

"Selena was fifteen."

"Who's Selena?"

"She's a girl that used to be here," he said, sounding like he missed her. "She was sick too. She lost all her hair before she died."

Jonathan said things so matter-of-factly that she was beginning to wonder if he'd sort of become desensitised to being sick and people dying because it was just a normal way of life for him. The thought saddened her.

"Was she your friend?"

He shrugged. "She played with me a few times before she got

too sick to play. She looked a lot like you. Are you sick too?"

"No, I'm not," she said. "But I was when I was three. I had cancer."

"You got better?"

Midnight noticed the surprise in his voice, like he didn't know people could get better when they had cancer. "I did get better."

She watched him process that. He had a dimple on his left cheek when he made a thinking face. "I'm not supposed to."

Again that matter-of-fact tone of voice.

"Maybe you will," she said and regretted it right away. She had no right to give him false hopes. She didn't know what he'd been told by his parents or doctor. She'd have to be careful in the future.

Jonathan shrugged. "Do you want to read me a story?" he said. "I can't read really good yet, just a few words."

She smiled. "I'd love to do that. Do you have a favourite book?"

Jonathan got up and went to the front of the room, by the door, and retrieved a book from a shelf. "Can I sit in your lap?"

"Sure." She waited for him to sit, then put the book on his lap and reached around him to hold it. "*Franklin Fibs.* Do you know what a fib is?"

"It's when you tell a lie," Jonathan said.

"That's right." She opened the book to the first page and started to read. Jonathan repeated each word. "Hey, you *can* read!"

He shook his head. "I just know the story."

"You actually remember the words?"

"I guess so."

"Wow, that's impressive."

He shrugged.

Midnight continued until she finished the book.

"I really like Franklin," Jonathan said. "I wish I had a best friend like Bear."

"Bear is a really good friend, that's for sure."

"Do you have a best friend?" he said while looking up at her.

"I'm lucky. I've had two," she said. "When I was your age my best friend was Tyler, but he moved away. That I met Samantha and we're still friends." It was a complicated relationship but she didn't think Jonathan needed to know that.

"I had a friend," he said. "His name was Johnny. But then I got sick and I've been here so I don't see him anymore."

"Does he live close to your house?"

He nodded. "Across the street."

Midnight felt bad that Johnny had not come to visit, but it wasn't her place to judge. Maybe Johnny's parents didn't want their son exposed to all the sick kids, or maybe it was Jonathan's parents that didn't want non-family to visit. In any case, Jonathan missed his friend.

"Well, I can be your friend."

Jonathan pulled himself up from sitting between Midnight's legs and hugged her, and she hugged him back. Then without a word, he took the book and returned it to the shelf before coming back. "Do you want to see my room?"

"I do," she said.

Jonathan took her hand and led her out of the playroom and down the corridor to his room.

"Wow! I wasn't expecting this," she said. There was a bed on wheels, of course, but also a walk-in shower, a built-in seat below the large window, a dresser, a flat-screen TV on the wall, a shelf with a flower vase, and a teddy lying back on a pillow. "Very homey."

Jonathan looked up at her. "I like having a TV in my room. I don't have one at home."

"I don't have one in my room either. I have to share it with my dad."

"What about your mom?"

Midnight took a minute. "My mom doesn't live with us anymore."

"Did she die?"

"No, she just left when I was a little younger than you."

"Do you have brothers and sisters?"

"I have an older sister. She lives with her boyfriend so it's just me and my dad."

Jonathan went to his bed and pulled himself up and grabbed his teddy bear. "Like Franklin, I have a bear for a friend."

"Cool. What does he think of your room?"

"He really likes it. Especially the chocolate pudding the nurses bring with dinner."

"I love chocolate."

"Me too," he said. "But I have to eat it first before Bear gets to it."

She smiled. "I'll bet."

Jonathan fell silent and his features seemed to darken.

"What's the matter?"

He shrugged. "I miss my mommy."

Midnight sat beside him and he put his head down into her

lap. She ran her hand across his head in a soothing manner. "I'm sure it's pretty hard for you. But I can stay with you as long as you want me to for tonight. I'm not your mom, but I'll do what I can to make this better for you."

"I'd like that."

"Great," she said, and they stayed like that for a while, Jonathan in her lap, her hand gently caressing his head, not a word spoken. None were needed.

She took in the room again, amazed at everything that was here, and then a disturbing thought crossed her mind. If he'd been here four weeks already, and had been undergoing chemotherapy, why hadn't he lost his hair? Why didn't he look like he'd been through hell? She didn't like the answer.

Were they not treating him because there was nothing they could do for him except to make the last of his time as pleasant as possible? And if that was the case, then why not have him spend it at home with his family?

She'd known this was going to be difficult, but to feel so deeply for a little boy she barely knew really took her by surprise. She really hoped she had the situation all wrong and that he was actually all cured and going home soon.

But she didn't think that was the case.

ঌ ৡ

Midnight heard footsteps and looked up to see a man in his mid-thirties standing in the doorway. He smiled appreciatively.

"I see you've met Jonathan."

"Is he your son?"

"Yes."

"I think he fell asleep."

"He has."

"I thought so," she said. "I didn't want to wake him so I tried not to move."

"I bet your back is screaming."

"A little."

He moved toward her. "I'm David."

"I'm Midnight."

"Really?"

"My parents were determined to give us different names."

"Us?"

"My sister's name is Octavia."

"Wow! That *is* different."

David moved Jonathan from her lap and put him down on the bed, covering him with a blanket.

"I don't mean to be intrusive, but what's going on with Jonathan?"

David took a long breath. "This is our third return in the past eighteen months. He's not doing well. Not much they can do really."

Midnight put a hand to her mouth. She hadn't cried so much in a very long time. "I'm sorry," she said as she took the tissue David handed her. "I barely know him but I'm already attached."

"Volunteering?"

"First time," she said." Doesn't it show? I was warned that I could find this difficult but felt pretty sure I could handle it."

"Why did you decide to volunteer?"

"Mostly to help. Hopefully to make someone happy for a few hours. I just wanted to do something."

"I'm going to guess you were sick once?"

"When I was Jonathan's age. I got better and now I want to give back."

"He's a special boy…"

Midnight heard the pain in his voice. This must be so hard, especially for a parent. Heck, she was finding it almost impossible to leave Jonathan, a boy she'd known for about two hours.

"What happens next?"

"We're going home tomorrow. For however long he has, we want to make it the best time we have with him."

"He told me he's been here four weeks."

"About ten days. He's been through just about every test they could think of."

"And they can't do anything?"

"Each time it comes back, it's harder to fight. He's still recovering from his last treatments. That was just last spring. It's into his bone marrow now. They have an experimental treatment they could try, but they only give it a 2% chance of success and it's going to make him feel worse than his last treatment, which was awful. We can't make him go through that. At some point, you have to stop being selfish and start thinking about what's best for him, not for you. It's hard to accept that he won't be with us for much longer, but we'd rather take him home and have him spend some quality time with his family than being here sick as a dog just because we don't want to let him go."

"I'm sorry."

"Thank you."

They stood in silence for a minute or two, kids' laughter floating through the air, coming from different rooms.

"I want to hear him laugh," David said. "We're thinking of taking the kids down to Disney World."

"Sounds like fun."

"Yeah, it does."

Jonathan stirred and peeled open his eyes. "Daddy!"

"Hey buddy, I met your new friend."

"Her name is Midnight," he said and sat up. "She read me a story."

"Franklin?"

"*Franklin Fibs*," Jonathan said.

"Your favourite."

He smiled a tired smile.

"Well," Midnight said. "Your dad told me you're going home tomorrow. Isn't that great?"

"We are?"

"Yes, we are."

"No more needles?"

"No more," David said.

The smile on Jonathan's face quickly faded. "I won't see Midnight again."

"But you'll see your mom, and your brother and sister. Bet they can't wait to see you."

"Will you come and visit?" the little boy asked her, looking hopeful.

Midnight looked at David, not sure how to respond to that.

"We live too far away."

Jonathan made a pouting face.

"You know," Midnight said. "It doesn't matter if we never see each other again. What really matters is that we did meet and spent a really nice time together. I had a lot of fun with you, and I will never forget the special time we've had. I'm so happy I got to meet you."

Jonathan got on his knees and crawled across the bed to hug her.

"I'll miss you," he said.

"I'll miss you too," she said. "You're a very special little boy."

☙ ❧

The ambulance arrived and wheeled Samantha straight through to the operating room. She had a fractured pelvis, a broken left arm just below the elbow, a sprained right ankle, a fractured right cheek, and several cuts on her face.

But she was lucky.

Derek was pronounced dead at the scene.

EIGHT

~ July 1989 ~

The bed felt much too big.

It had only been a few days since Karen had left, and Jim hadn't been able to track her down. Phone calls to her sister Maggie and her mother had led nowhere, neither having heard from Karen. She had a brother, Tom, who lived in Calgary, but he'd been much older and hadn't kept in touch much so Jim hadn't been surprised to hear that Tom hadn't heard from his sister in about five years. Tom promised that if for some godforsaken reason Karen did contact him or show up on his doorstep, he'd give her a piece of his mind and put her on the next plane home. Jim had thanked Tom for his good wishes for Midnight and promised to keep his brother-in-law up to date if anything developed, good or bad, with her illness.

Jim reached for the bedside lamp, and the sudden brightness was too painful for his sleepy eyes, so he shut them. Slowly, he opened them and squinted until they adjusted. He glanced at the empty space beside him and ran his hand over that side of the bed to confirm that Karen was actually gone. Falling hopes crashed in the pit of his stomach. Lethargically, he rolled himself over the edge of the bed and buried his face in his hands.

He was exhausted. Midnight's illness consumed all his time and energy, and he worried about Octavia, who suddenly had to fend for herself because he had no time for her. And as far as searching for Karen, he'd done as much as he could.

His daughters mattered more.

But at two in the morning, he missed his wife. He still hoped that she'd be back soon. She just needed a bit of time to figure out what was happening, come to terms with it, and then she'd be back.

He had to believe that.

Jim went to check on the girls, Octavia first, pulling the sheets over her that she had kicked back—lately, her sleep was troubled and she often cried out but never woke herself doing it—and then he went to sit with Midnight. The tranquil beauty of her innocence while she slept crashed over him like a wave so powerful that he felt like he was drowning. His eyes filled with tears that he welcomed. He could feel the wet streaks running down his cheeks and getting stuck in the three-day stubble he'd been too busy to attend to. If he thought of it, he'd shave in the morning.

He touched Midnight's face with the back of his fingers.

"You are my sweet little angel," he whispered. "God has plenty already. I won't let you go without a fight. Daddy will not give up on you like Mommy."

As soon as he'd said it, he wished the words back. That wasn't him talking, it was his exhaustion. But wasn't there a bit of truth to it? He didn't really want to believe it, but sadly, there was. She had grown up in a tough household, her father leaving when she was just ten. Her mother had been an alcoholic and her sister Maggie, who was five years older, had moved out at seventeen. Tom was ten years older and had moved out the year before his father had left, tired of his parents' constant fighting.

The Karen he had fallen in love with in high school had never been a quitter. Even with the crappy life she'd had at home, even with the way people looked at her and whispered bad things behind her back, even when everyone had given up on her, he hadn't. There'd been something beautiful and vulnerable about her, and when an unexpected relation flowered, he had discovered a strong and fun and vibrant young woman who quickly stole his heart.

Had he seen in Karen what he'd wanted to see? She had been so different from him, a little dangerous, a spark that he'd lacked. Had he been fascinated by her fire?

Fires will burn out when they're suffocated.

Had Karen felt suffocated?

Jim leaned over and kissed Midnight's forehead and watched her stir. She looked more like Karen than Octavia did. He remembered seeing pictures of Karen at this age and they could have been twins. His eyes were drawn to the family photo on Midnight's bedside table, taken last Christmas, and looking at it now, he noticed that while all three of them had genuine happy grins on their faces, Karen didn't.

She looked very unhappy.

Jim rubbed his face.

He really hadn't noticed. He'd been content—no, not just content, but truly happy—and had assumed that Karen felt just the same. He had seen what he'd wanted to see.

Just like in high school.

He sat by Midnight's side for some time, maybe an hour, until finally, drained, he returned to bed only to stare at the darkness of his empty room. Sleep didn't come quick, and when his alarm pulled him from deep sleep at seven, he felt as if a truck had run over him a few too many times.

He wanted the day to be over already.

☙ ❧

"Octavia, your bus will be here any second now," Jim shouted from the bottom of the stairs. "Hurry up."

"I can't find my earphones for my Walkman," she shouted back from her room.

"You need to catch your bus because I need to take Midnight to the hospital this morning for her treatment. Forget the earphones for today."

Octavia came sauntering down the stairs, her Walkman in hand. "Why do I have to go to a stupid summer camp? It's boring and I don't know anyone."

"You've always liked summer camp."

"That's when I was a kid."

"Huh . . . you are still a kid."

"I'm—"

"Daddy . . ." Midnight said. She was standing at the top of the stairs. "I don't feel good. I'm gonna throw up."

"Quick. To the bathroom, honey. I'll be right up."

He turned to Octavia.

"Your bus will be—"

Too late. It was right in front of their house. The bus driver honked a couple of times.

"Shit!" Jim said. "Octavia, get going. Now!"

Octavia brushed passed her father, an angry frown on her face, grabbed her lunch bag and stuffed it in her backpack, and left without saying goodbye.

Jim rushed up the stairs, taking them by twos, to find Midnight on her knees with her head in the toilet, the loud retching noises sounding like she was going to puke out her guts and more. Jim stood in the doorway for only a second, wishing he could trade places with her, and then went down on his knees beside her and gently rubbed her back while she threw up.

☙ ❧

Midnight's chemotherapy treatment was spread out over eighteen weeks. This was week 9, halfway through, and Jim couldn't wait for these gut-wrenching trips every three weeks to be over. After this week, there would only be three treatments left.

Three left.

Midnight's treatment was half over, so why couldn't Karen have just hung on a little longer? Just a little longer. Sure, there were no guarantees that Midnight would be cured one hundred percent, that she wouldn't suffer a relapse at some point in the future. No one had any guarantee. People died every single day in car accidents, work accidents, all sorts of accidents. And of all sorts if illnesses. In life, there were no guarantees.

None.

After her treatment, Jim carried his daughter to the car and took her home. Midnight looked completely drained. He drove in silence, his mood darkening as he passed by a herd of healthy kids playing in a park, worried mothers telling them to be careful, not to do this or do that. If those mothers only knew that broken bones were the easiest thing to mend. He would give anything to trade places.

Jim pushed back his anger and looked into the rear-view mirror at Midnight, who was sleeping, the hat on her head hiding the little hair she had left. But even without hair and with dark sunken eyes and a sad, tired expression on her face, Jim couldn't be more proud of his little warrior. Midnight was the strength that he sometimes lacked, the reason that helped him push on and fight.

Midnight made strained noises as she slept, and Jim wondered if she was having a nightmare, if the brutality of the treatment haunted her.

This is killing her as much as it is me.

He'd added years of grey hair and wrinkles in just a few months. It was a small price to pay. Very small.

Jim slowed the car and turned into the driveway, shutting off the engine. He sat for a moment looking at his home. Homes were supposed to be filled with fond and happy memories. He knew they were there, somewhere in the attic of their lives, but in the shadows of this tragedy, he couldn't find them.

Jim took Midnight up to bed, and then went down to the kitchen looking for something to help him make it through the rest of the day—hell, make it through the rest of this dreadfulness.

☙ ❧

She wasn't coming back. Two weeks gone, Jim knew that the

mother of his children wasn't going to walk through that front door ever again. He wanted to hate her, but lying in bed, his hand on her pillow, he couldn't find the energy to do so.

Midnight had just gone back to bed after being sick. Jim had had to change her bedding and pyjamas, and wipe up the trail of vomit from her bed to the bathroom. He'd washed her face and hands, and tucked her back into bed, sitting by her side until she had fallen back to sleep.

On top of that, he had to deal with Octavia. She'd been kicked out of day camp for fighting with another girl. The camp counsellor had told him that Octavia couldn't come back, that she'd initiated the fight, and they simply couldn't allow that sort of behaviour.

Not much he could say to that.

Jim couldn't really be angry with Octavia or reprimand her. He needed to find time for her, yet there was so little. Not much of an excuse, he knew.

They just needed a few more weeks and hopefully their lives would find some sort of normalcy.

☙ ❧

By the summer of 1990, Midnight's hair had grown back a few inches, her weight had increased a little, and her skin no longer looked washed out. And best of all, she had found her smile again, that smile kids have, so sweet and genuine, that smile that Jim had missed terribly.

And that gave him hope.

Hope that Midnight's future wasn't as bleak as it had been just one year ago, hope that she'd go to school come September—

junior kindergarten already—and make lots of friends, hope that she'd beaten the odds and could just be a normal kid.

That's all a parent could want.

He watched Midnight and Tyler playing on the front lawn, and for the first time since Midnight's diagnosis, he felt he could breathe, the burden of the past fifteen months finally gone.

He'd taken an extended leave of absence from work and didn't see much point in returning. Being a copywriter, and a very good one, made the transition to working from home easy. When his former employer became his first client, it didn't take long for others to seek his talent. It wasn't always easy, and he had to be careful with the money that did come in, but for Jim, being available for his daughters, at all times, took priority.

It was the only thing that mattered.

The only thing.

NINE

~ December 2001 ~

Samantha was going home for Christmas. It had been three months since the accident and luckily her pelvis had had just a small fracture and bedrest had been the best remedy. Her left arm had been worst, broken in two places, below and above her elbow. She'd had a cast for ten weeks, starting at the shoulder all the way to her wrist. Also, her ankle had not been sprained but broken—the fibula and tibia—and there had been some ligament damage too, so she'd had a cast to stabilise the area and allow proper healing.

Her cheek was just bruised, so that was good, but she did have a horrible scar that started below her right eye and went all the way to her right ear. She'd been told it would fade but not go away entirely. The small cut on the bottom of the left side of her jaw had healed and was fading, as was the cut above her right eye.

It had been a gruelling three months and she'd missed Derek's funeral. She couldn't believe how quickly the accident had happened—one minute she and Derek were having fun and the next minute she was in a hospital bed and he was dead. It just seemed surreal.

He was the first person her age that she knew who had died, a fact that didn't seem possible. And all because he'd come to pick her up to go back to his house for a party. She didn't think she'd ever shake the guilt she felt, no matter what. Derek was dead because of her.

It wasn't something she could forget.

"Ready to go home?" the nurse said, a woman in her late fifties that was full of positive vibes. Her name was Georgette and Samantha had gotten to know her over time. She was divorced, had three kids and five grandkids, and a seventeen-year-old light-grey-haired Siberian cat named, appropriately, Greyon. "I know I'd be glad to get out of here."

"It hasn't been so bad," Samantha said, knowing that being at the hospital this long, she'd been able to put her life on hold, not have to face what had really happened. "I'm actually going to miss a lot of the nurses I've met, including you. You've all been so wonderful. My mom won't be able to look after me like you all have."

"You're going to be fine," Georgette said. "The worst is behind you. You healed up quite nicely. A few weeks of physio and you'll be back on your feet."

Samantha smiled but it felt empty.

"I know it seems like your whole life has been disrupted, but you're young and when you're my age and look back, this will seem so far into the past that you'll hardly believe it happened at all."

"Except a boy I liked died because of me."

Georgette was quiet. "I'm truly sorry. It was an unfortunate accident, that's for sure. It will take time."

Samantha sighed. Maybe someday she won't hurt so much—emotionally, that is. And when it does happen, she'll have the ugly scar on her face to remind her, to make sure she doesn't forget. She was glad to be alive, but it was riddled with guilt.

"Eh, honey," her mom said as she came in with a bouquet of balloons. "You're coming home!"

"Lucky me."

"Hi Georgette," Tracy said as she tied the balloons to the bed railing. "Our little girl is still in the dumps?"

"She'll be fine once she gets out of here," the nurse said. "You all take care."

"Thanks, Georgette," Tracy said. "For taking good care of my baby girl."

"Mom, really?" Samantha said. "Emily is the baby."

"All our kids are our babies," Georgette said. "Mine are all grown up but they are still my babies. A mother never stops worrying."

"See?" Tracy said to her daughter.

Samantha rolled her eyes. "Georgette, I'm really going to miss you."

The older woman came over and hugged Samantha. "You'll be fine."

Samantha nodded and swallowed a lump. "I know. It's just that I feel . . ."

"Go live your life," Georgette said. "Beating yourself over what happened won't change it."

"I know."

Mom and daughter waited for the nurse to leave, and then

Tracy got busy gathering Samantha's belongings.

"Where's Emily anyway?"

"At school, honey. Today's the last day before Christmas break and she didn't want to miss it. Everyone brought something to eat and they were all going to share and watch a movie and play games."

"A lot more fun than coming here, that's for sure."

"I know this is hard, honey," Tracy said. "But you heard what Georgette said. Time to go home and get back to your life. You're healed up, I've got a fabulous physiotherapist who's going to come to our house and work with you for the next four weeks to help you get back on your feet, and soon everything will be back to normal."

Samantha shook her head. "Maybe for you, but not for me. I almost died. I lost a friend. Nothing will be back to normal for me."

"Honey."

"Mom, are you not listening to me?"

Tracy tried to touch her but Samantha pushed her hand away and pulled the bed sheet up to her neck.

"Samantha, what's going on?"

"I'm scared, Mom," she finally said, unable to look at her mother. "I don't think I can get into a car ever again. Just the thought of it turns my stomach. What if we get into another accident? What if I die next time? I can't. I just can't."

"Oh, honey," Tracy said and sat down on the edge of the bed. "What happened was horrible, and I can't express how profoundly sorry I am for your friend and his family. But you are alive and you can't stay in the hospital. You'll come home and finish with your rehab, and you'll be back at school with your friends before you know it, and someday, hopefully, all of this will be forgotten."

"Friends? Really? You think I'll be back at school with my friends? Do you know how many of my friends came to visit me more than once?"

"I'm sure all your close friends came."

Samantha shook her head. "Well, turns out I only really have one close friend. Midnight is the only one that came here regularly. Isn't that funny? I thought we were growing apart before all of this happened, and turns out she was the one friend I should have spent more time with."

"Well, Midnight has always been a special person. I've told you this more than once."

Samantha ran a finger along the scar on her face. That's all her so-called friends saw—the new hideous Samantha. Except for Midnight.

"I know. It just wasn't the sort of special that I wanted to see, or wanted to be around with. I thought being popular was what I wanted, what was important. It's what all kids my age want."

"Not all kids, honey." Tracy took her daughter's hand. "Being popular is one thing. But it doesn't last. I was popular in high school and trust me, it really didn't help me in the long run."

"What do you mean?"

"It doesn't matter."

"Mo-o-om," she said, stretching the word into three syllables. "What are you talking about?"

Tracy took a long breath. "A girl like me was expected to go out with a certain type of guy, sweetie."

"A guy like Dad?"

"A guy like Dad."

"What is going on with you two anyway?"

Tracy pulled her hand away, stood, and paced. She kept her back to Samantha. "We're not in high school anymore."

"Mom?"

"Your dad and I aren't as made for each other as we once thought," she said while going over Samantha's things, making sure she hadn't forgotten any. "Maybe we never were, and yet people convinced us that we were. But those people aren't in our lives anymore."

"Mom, what are you saying?"

Tracy Carmichael turned and looked her daughter in the eye. "We didn't want to tell you earlier, but your father and I separated four weeks ago."

☙ ❧

Midnight was sitting on Samantha's bed, sucking on a candy cane. Outside, she could see big snowflakes cascading down lazily, swinging back and forth. Instead of being dropped off at home after school, Mrs. Carmichael had suggested she come visit with Samantha and try to cheer her up.

"That's a pretty cool wheelchair," Midnight said. "But you're going to have to ditch it."

"Easy for you to say," Samantha said, crunching on a candy cane of her own. "I've been on my back for months and my leg muscles have become so useless they can't even hold my skinny ass up."

They looked at each other, and burst out laughing.

"News flash, your ass has never been that skinny."

"It might not be as skinny as yours, but it ain't fat."

Midnight nodded. "I'll give you that."

"Besides, no one is as skinny as you are," Samantha said. "I swear you get thinner every time I see you. Eat up, will you?"

"Got my fix of sugar right here," she said. "I'll have to do a blood test in a bit."

"Do you ever get tired of that?"

"Not like I have a choice."

"Yeah, that kind of sucks."

They finished their candy canes.

"I bet you're happy to be home for Christmas," Midnight said. "Sleep in your own bed."

"I'm stuck in the main floor guest room for a while. My mom can't carry me up the stairs." She was quiet for a moment. "Did you know my parents split up?"

"What?"

"Yeah, my mom dropped that bomb on me when she came to get me," Samantha said. "Can you believe it? Like, I knew they fought a lot, but you kind of get used to it and it becomes normal. I guess I didn't realize they actually didn't love each other."

"Wow!" Midnight said. "Your mom and Emily never said anything to me. I guess they didn't want me to tell you."

"Guess not."

Midnight hesitated. "You okay?"

Samantha looked at her and then began to laugh hysterically. "I haven't been okay in months. I'm living in hell."

"My dad told me once, and I've never forgotten. He said 'There's always someone worst off than you.' I think it was after my cancer went away."

Samantha looked at her. "You always have to one-up me?"

"That's not what I was doing."

"But it's how it feels."

"I'm sorry," Midnight said. "I was just trying to tell you that your life probably isn't as bad as many others have it. I see a lot of pretty sick kids at the hospital."

Samantha sighed. "See, you're doing it again."

"Maybe once you're walking again, you can apply to volunteer with me."

"If I never see another hospital as long as I live, I'll be fine with that."

"Didn't you say you liked it there?"

Samantha touched her scar. "It was nice to have all those nurses looking after me, but . . ."

"Home is home."

"Except that now it's not, anymore. After everything that's happened, it sucks." She took a moment. "I'm . . . I'm scared."

"I'm here for you," Midnight said. "Anything you want to talk about. If it helps, I'll listen. A lot of the kids I see, that's all they want: a friendly face that will listen to them."

"Well, you're the only real friend I have and I was too dumb to see that," Samantha said with a slightly shamed expression on her face. "Will you spend Christmas with me?"

"I'd like that."

"Bring your dad," Samantha said. "I'm sure my mom won't mind, now that she's single."

Midnight gave her a questioning look.

"We were talking one day," Samantha said. "That was before

the accident, and you and your dad came up. The way she talked about him, it sounded like she might have liked him, you know?"

"Not sure what to think of that," Midnight said. "A little weird."

"That's what I thought and when I asked her what she meant, she just blew it off."

"I guess we forget they were young once, before we came along."

They sat in silence.

"Hey, that would make us step-sisters," Samantha said.

"Now *that* would be weird."

They laughed.

"I'm glad you came over," Samantha said. "I'll think about it, what you said about volunteering."

"Good. I think you'll be surprised what great people you'll meet. And the difference you'll make for someone."

"But isn't it hard if, you know?"

"Yes, it is," she said. "I only had a few hours with this little boy, Jonathan, but he was so special. And I feel that he's made me a better person."

☙ ❧

Jim and Midnight walked up the steps and rang the bell. Jim had bought a bottle of Chateau Pineraie, not knowing much about wine but going with the recommendation of one of the staff at the LCBO. Plus, at $39.95, it was way out of his budget, but he figured it had to be pretty good. And to make up for all the times Tracy Carmichael drove Midnight to school, a really good bottle of wine seemed appropriate.

He also figured it would keep his drinking to a minimum.

At first, he hadn't wanted to come, feeling a bit strange about the invitation, especially after Midnight had told him that Samantha's parents had separated. But since Octavia and Mark were going to spend Christmas with Mark's family this year, Jim realized the house would be very quiet with just him and Midnight, and he'd finally agreed to come.

"I think our house can fit into this one five times," he said.

"I know," Midnight said. "If our house was this big, we'd never find each other."

"Which probably would be fine on days we're mad at each other," he said as a tease, "but not the rest of the time."

"I like our little house. It's home."

"That it is."

Jim pressed the doorbell button. "Crap, that's loud," he said when some sonic atrocity erupted inside.

Before Midnight could say anything, the door opened and Emily let them in. Jim was speechless. The foyer was spacious with two-by-two marble tiles. To the right, there was a small black leather bench against the wall with an expensive-looking framed mirror above it, and a three-door closet to the left where they hung their jackets and placed their winter boots. Straight ahead was a curving staircase leading up to the second floor and a wide hallway that led to the back of the house. Once past the foyer, to the right, there was a den that filled Jim with envy, and to the left, a sitting room that was so ridiculously large, he could only shake his head.

"I'm so glad you could make it," Tracy said, coming down the stairs.

"Thanks for the invite." Jim handed her the bottle of wine. "Not sure if you're a wine connoisseur, but—"

"I've actually had this one and it's very good," she said. "You didn't have to, but thank you. Please come on in. Samantha is in the kitchen."

They followed Tracy and Emily into the back. Again, the kitchen was so big it was insane, and the dining room boasted a table that could accommodate sixteen people.

Jim had no idea that Samantha's family was that well off. He remembered when they lived just a few streets over from them, their old house no bigger than theirs. It would have been nice to have been able to give his girls a bit more while they were growing up, maybe not *this* much more, but a little more nonetheless.

"Mom, we're going to the theatre room to watch something," Samantha said.

"Sure, honey."

Jim and Tracy watched the three kids head toward the east side of the house. Midnight was pushing Samantha in her wheelchair.

"How long will she be in the chair?"

"Not too long, I hope," Tracy said. "I hired a physiotherapist. He starts right after New Year. She should be back at school by the end of January."

"That's good."

"I think the sooner she can get back to a normal life, the better," she said. "Right now, she can be a bit dramatic, and so moody."

"She went through a lot."

"She did. But she's alive, so I'm not complaining."

"Yes, that's certainly something to be grateful for."

"We should open that bottle." Tracy handed Jim the bottle and a corkscrew. "How about you pour us a couple of glasses? You'll find those in the hutch in the dining room."

Jim returned with a couple of wine glasses, pulled the cork, and poured a generous amount for each glass. "This is a *mansion*," he said.

Tracy blushed. "It is a bit extravagant. David insisted we buy it. I would have been fine with a slightly bigger house than what we had on Avery Crescent."

"It's lovely."

"Thanks," she said and raised her glass. "Merry Christmas."

"Merry Christmas," he said.

They clinked their glasses lightly and drank.

"Wow! That's really good," he said, reminding himself to not overdo it tonight. "I'm mostly a beer-and-scotch kind of guy."

"That's not a bad sort of guy," Tracy said.

Jim swallowed. "Is David joining us?"

"Didn't Midnight tell you? Dave and I have separated."

"She did mention that," he said. "I just wasn't sure if it was for real."

Tracy took a sip of wine. "It's been happening for a while, I'm afraid. It got worse once we moved here. He worked more and more and spent less time here with us. I sometimes smelled perfume on him. It wasn't mine."

"I'm sorry."

"Funny thing," Tracy said, running her index finger along the rim of her glass. "I wasn't even angry when he told me. I was sort of relieved. I finally knew the truth."

"Still, after all these years. I mean, you've been together since high school."

"That's an awful long time not to be happy," she said and took another sip of wine.

"Really?"

She tucked a loose strand of hair behind her right ear. "I'm sure we had some good times at first. We waited long enough to have kids. After a while, partying like you're still in high school got old. And then, he just became obsessed with work. I became lonely and stopped taking my pill. I wanted to have a baby. When I told him I was pregnant, he didn't exactly jump for joy. In fact, he was worried that I might have derailed his plans."

"Plans for?"

"I asked him the exact same question. He said his plans to make something of himself. It was hard enough to make ends meet with just the two of us, he'd say, and now with a baby on the way, well . . ."

"Guess we never know what goes on behind closed doors," he said. "You guys were the talk of the school."

"From my point of view, you and Karen were the talk of the school. So many of us never understood why you . . ." She trailed off, realizing her faux pas. "I'm sorry."

He gave her a reassuring smile. "There was something about her. She was like a drug I couldn't get enough of."

"But you had so much to offer," she said and leaned forward on the counter. "I mean, any other girl would have been thrilled to go out with you."

He felt a little red in the face. They stared at each other, Jim sitting on a stool and Tracy standing on the other side of the peninsula. After a minute, she went over to the oven to check on the turkey.

"I surprised the girls and did everything myself today," she said with a small laugh. "They were dumbfounded that I actually knew how to cook. I had to remind them that until a year ago, before we moved here, I cooked all our meals. Again, it was Dave's idea to hire a cook, a gardener, and a maid. I actually have no idea how much money he makes, but he seems to have no problem spending it."

"By the looks of this place, I'd say quite a few millions."

"I think so too," she said and bit her lower lip. "I have no idea what's going to happen. I don't care about me, but he'd better make sure the girls are taken care of."

"What will you do?"

"Dust off the old resume and university degree."

"Right, you did go to Ottawa U?"

"Psychology major. Not sure what that will do for me now. Last job I had was as a secretary before Emily was born. I'm probably unemployable."

"I'm sure you're not."

"You need an assistant," she said and laughed nervously.

"You wouldn't want to work for what I could pay you."

She stared at him while taking a sip of wine. "How have you done it, all these years?"

"Not living like this," he said. "The girls never asked for much. I gave them my time, my love, my devotion. I think it made up for all the things I couldn't buy them. I like to think it made us close."

"I used to think Sam and I were close," she said, looking

toward the back of the house where the girls had gone off to. "And now that she's home since the accident happened, I'm sort of lost and a bit afraid. You should have seen her face when I told her Dave and I had split up. It was like she was accusing me of fucking it up."

Jim's eyes bulged.

"Oh, don't look at me that way. I can drop the F-bomb like anyone. I just try a little harder than most not to do it too often, and never in front of the girls."

"Unfortunately," he said, looking embarrassed, "when I've had a few too many beers, my tongue gets a little too loose. I'm sure Midnight will attest to that."

Tracy snorted. "We seem to make a great pair. Here's to failed marriages and two decades of wasted time."

She lifted her glass, but Jim didn't.

"When you put it that way, maybe Midnight is right. Maybe it's time to close the door on misery and start looking for a spot of happiness."

"Hear, hear," she said and downed the last of her wine. "Maybe we could go out to dinner sometime."

Jim studied Tracy for a moment. She was actually a very attractive woman, and he felt comfortable just talking to her. Part of him didn't hate the idea, but a bigger part felt that he wasn't good enough for her.

"I wonder how the girls would feel about that," he said.

଒ ଓ

Midnight, Samantha, and Emily were watching The Matrix on DVD. If there was one room she loved about this house,

Midnight loved this one. There was one of those really new 50" flat-screen plasma TVs on the wall and so many speakers all around that sound came from everywhere. It was rather awesome.

She knew her dad could never afford one of those TVs. He didn't have the kind of money Samantha's dad had. Still, she wondered if they could get something a little bigger than the 20" TV they had, and do something in their basement that would be decent enough to feel like you're watching a movie at the theatre.

A small theatre.

"Did you see that?" Emily said. "Neo is so cool. He's dodging bullets in slow motion."

"Not like you haven't seen the movie before," Samantha said. "You've probably watched it fifty times. You're so in love with Keanu Reeves."

"Shut up," Emily said and made a face. "I just like this movie."

"Uh-huh, sure. You have a crush on Keanu."

"Just shut up."

"*You* shut up."

"Girls," Midnight said. "It's Christmas, after all. Let's be nice to each other."

Emily and Samantha stared at Midnight as if to say, *really?*

"So, what do you think they're doing out there?" Samantha said, a mischievous look in her eyes. "Think they like each other?"

"You're not trying to set them up, are you?" Midnight said. "Didn't we sort of agree that that was kind of weird?"

"Yeah, yeah. Don't worry about it. I just want to see what

happens."

"You're a weirdo," Emily said. "Dad could still come back."

"Uh, did you see the slut he's banging?"

"Really, Sam," Midnight said. "Your sister is just twelve."

"Ah, she knows all about sex anyway. They learn it in grade three nowadays."

"That's not the point," Midnight said.

"You know we're going to be with them on Boxing Day?" Emily said. "And I want presents, so I'm going."

"Have fun," Samantha said. "Because I'm staying here. I have no intentions of making friends with her."

"Her name's Carol," Emily said.

"Kind of an old name for a twenty-something whore."

"Sam," Midnight said. "Come on, you don't know her."

"She might be nice," Emily said.

"I don't care. She broke up our parents. Why would I want to be nice to her? I'm sure as hell not calling her *Mom*."

"It's not like you like Mom all that much," Emily said.

"Yeah, but . . ." Samantha said. "She's our mom and it's our right to not always like her and give her a hard time."

"You are so weird," Emily said.

"Whatever," Samantha said with a snarly face. "Just watch your boyfriend on the screen."

Emily screamed. "Just because you're all crippled and all doesn't mean you have to be such a bitch!"

"Emily!" Midnight said.

"Well, she is!" Emily said. "Mom told me I had to be nice to her but she needs to be nice to me too."

Samantha sat in her chair, her face turning to granite, her eyes like daggers. And then she broke down and started to cry.

"She didn't mean that," Midnight said.

"She did," Samantha said, quietly, as if acquiescing to her new reality. "And she's right. I am a cripple now."

"No you're not," Midnight said. "You'll begin your physio and you'll be walking in no time. Didn't the doctor say a few weeks and you can ditch the wheelchair?"

Samantha didn't answer.

"Yes, that's what Mom said," Emily said. "Except that Samantha doesn't want to try. Mom had to send the physiotherapist away yesterday when he came. He'd made a special appointment just for you on Christmas Eve Day, so he could meet you and go over things."

"I wasn't in the mood," Samantha said. "I'd just gotten home Friday. I wanted a break. We're not supposed to start until next week anyway, so he can tell me his plan then."

"The sooner you start, the sooner you'll be walking," Midnight said.

"Now you sound like my mother."

"Well, she's right."

"Yeah, Mom is right."

"Why don't you just be quiet and watch your loverboy?"

Emily stuck out her tongue.

"Real grown up, Em."

"Real grown up, *Sam*."

Midnight shook her head. She and Octavia had never bickered liked this. Sisters shouldn't fight as if they hated each other.

"Maybe we should go see what the real grownups are doing?" Midnight said.

"Yeah, I'm hungry," Emily said and left the room.

"Please don't say it," Samantha said. "She can really get on my nerves."

"And you probably get on hers," Midnight said as she started pushing the wheelchair. "And if your mom and my dad hook up, *I'll* be getting on your nerves, *sis*."

A burst of laughter erupted from the room.

☙ ❧

When she got home, Midnight pulled out her journal and read the last few things she'd written. She put the end of her pen in her mouth and thought of the evening she and her dad had just spent. She had seen something in her dad that she hadn't seen in forever.

He had seemed relaxed and happy, chatting it up and laughing. When last had he laughed so hard? Midnight couldn't remember. He usually laughed at comedies on the television, whether a show or a movie, but it had always seemed somewhat held back, like he was afraid to let it all out.

Tonight, he had held nothing back.

And she'd noticed a bit of a twinkle in his eyes, and in Samantha's mom's too. It was sort of weird, granted, but only because she was friends with Samantha. If she weren't, the situation wouldn't feel awkward at all. In fact, she'd be thrilled her dad was finally, *finally*, looking at another woman.

Just then Midnight felt her nose running and snatched a tissue from the box on her night table. She tried to recall how many nosebleeds that was, and she thought it was just the third time since that first one back in September. The first couple she'd dismissed, but now she wondered if maybe she should mention it to her dad.

And worry him after seeing him so happy tonight?

She decided to wait and see if it happened again. Maybe it was just the dry, cold winter air. Everything was so much dryer in the winter.

Getting back to her journal, Midnight wrote: *If it makes my dad happy, I'll be fine with him dating Mrs. Carmichael.*

TEN

~ May 1991 ~

Midnight's fifth birthday was a celebration, but also a time to be grateful and thankful. It marked a full year free of hospital visits, a full year where life was slowly returning to normal, a full year that made Jim believe that miracles could actually happen.

He watched Midnight sitting at the table and heard her giggle. It was nice to hear again, like a favourite song from a time long gone that you'd almost forgotten. His chest felt tight for a moment and his throat started to close.

Kids did that to you.

But she wasn't like other kids. So much had happened already in her short life and he just wanted her to be left alone so she could live normally. She still had nightmares, and every time she sneezed, he practically jumped out of his skin, ready to pack her in the car and rush out to the hospital. Maybe he'd never get back to living normally, but he hoped that she would.

He didn't think that was too much to want.

"Dad? You okay?" Octavia said.

An overwhelmed look spread across his face. "Been a long year."

"She'll be here a long time," she said. "Midnight will live to be an old woman."

He nodded and lit the five candles spread across the chocolate cake he'd bought at the grocery store. Baking wasn't one of his talents, a fact that was painfully clear after several attempts to make chocolate chip cookies and burning them each time. Ruining a birthday cake would be unforgiveable.

"Happy birthday to you," he began and Octavia and all five of Midnight's friends—Emma, Jill, Becca, and of course Tyler and his little brother Jake—joined in.

Midnight blew out the candles and they cheered and clapped. Jim cut generous pieces of chocolate cake and enjoyed watching them eat. Seemed there was as much chocolate smeared on lips and cheeks as was eaten.

It was such a wonderful sight.

"Slobs," Octavia whispered.

"You were no better," he said, the joy in his voice unmistakeable. "And it wasn't that long ago."

"It's nice to see her having fun."

"Yes, it is."

"Tyler can't keep his eyes off of her," Octavia said. "Won't it be something if someday they actually do date?"

He put a fork full of cake in his mouth. "The odds are probably pretty low. Right now, at their age, boys and girls aren't that different so playing together like they do is normal. But come your age, things get awkward, and they'll likely grow apart."

"And maybe they won't."

"Maybe they won't," he repeated. "I probably don't tell you enough, but I appreciate all you do for her . . . and for me. You've become the lady of the house."

He put an arm around her shoulder.

"No worries, Dad."

꧁ ꧂

In early July, Jim took the girls camping for a week over at Fitzroy campground, less than an hour away from Ottawa. He'd bought a four-men tent, sleeping bags, a portable BBQ, a Coleman, and a cooler that he'd stuffed with plenty of food for a couple of days. They arrived Friday afternoon and set up camp before heading out to the beach. The water was nice, even if a bit cool, which felt good on this hotter-than-average day.

Later that night, they sat around the campfire and enjoyed the constellations. In the city, only the brightest stars were visible, but out in the countryside, the night sky lit up like an over-crowded heaven.

"Pretty cool," Jim said.

"Daddy?" Midnight said. "Is it true that stars are all the people who died before us and went to heaven?"

Jim looked at her. "I'm not sure, honey. Where did you hear this?"

"I think it was Becca. Her Nana died and her mom told her that her Nana was up in heaven, shining down on her. So I guess she's a star now."

Jim glanced at Octavia, who shrugged. "If it's true, it wouldn't be a bad way to live forever," he said.

Octavia got something from the tent and held it up. "We need to check your blood sugar."

"Can't we skip it tonight?" Midnight said with a whine. "We're camping."

"No, honey," Jim said. "You know what the doctor told us last week about your fainting spell. You have diabetes. We need to keep an eye on it all the time."

"Why am I always sick?" she said glumly. "Mommy will never come back now."

"That's not—" Jim started to say.

"Don't," Octavia said, looking at her dad for a brief moment before giving her sister the test. "You're good."

"Can I have a snack?" Midnight said.

"We'll have to do the test again after," Octavia said.

"Never mind," Midnight said with a yawn. "I'm tired anyway."

"I'll take her to the washroom," Octavia said.

"Take one of the flashlights on the table."

While they were gone, he poked the fire, moving logs around until the flames caught again. He pulled a beer from the cooler and downed half of it. He'd seen the way Octavia had looked at him when he'd tried to defend Karen. He hadn't meant to. He just did it instinctively, like he'd defend them. Still, he understood her irritation.

He heard the girls coming and finished his beer.

"All done?" he said. Midnight fell into his arms. "Tired, baby-girl?"

"I'm not a baby anymore," she said.

"You'll always be my baby-girl," he said and kissed her forehead. "Both of you," he added, looking at Octavia.

"Can you tuck me in, Daddy?"

"You bet."

"Night Tavia," Midnight said and hugged her sister. "Love you."

"Love you too."

Jim helped Midnight into her sleeping bag and zipped it up.

"Did you have a good day?"

"Yes. I like camping. Can we do it again?"

"I think we should plan on it. Make it a yearly thing."

She smiled. "Daddy, do you think Mommy is a star?"

The question took him by surprise. "That would mean Mommy has died. I'm not sure that she has."

"Then why hasn't she come back home? It's because I'm dia . . . dia . . ."

"No, honey, that's not why." He took a deep breath. "I don't know why, really. But she has no idea you're diabetic, so that's not why."

"I miss her. I think." She began to cry. "I don't really remember her. I look at the Christmas picture in my room but I don't really remember what her voice sounded like."

"She had a beautiful voice," he said. "She could sing. When she thought I wasn't around, she'd sing to you while feeding you."

"Is that why she went away? To sing?"

Karen had had the voice of an angel when she sang, the exact opposite of when she spoke, which could be rough and raw at times.

"It's possible," he said. "It's quite possible that's what she's doing."

"Maybe she'll come back when she gets tired of doing that."

"Maybe," he said and kissed her cheek. "You sleep tight, sweetie. I'll see you in the morning."

"When are you and Tavia coming to bed?"

"Soon," he said. "I just need to put things away so the racoons don't get into our stuff, and then put the fire out."

"Night Daddy."

"Goodnight, honey."

He walked out of the tent and joined Octavia by the fire pit. It still surprised him how quiet it was even though they were surrounded by other campers.

"Is she good?" Octavia said.

"I wouldn't be surprised if she was asleep already." He went to the cooler and was about to pull out another beer when he felt Octavia's eyes on him. "I didn't mean . . ."

"But you did," she said. "You always bring her up when you don't need to. We don't need her, Dad. I don't need her. Midnight doesn't need her. You don't need her any more than you do that beer. I'm old enough to see you drowning your pain in alcohol."

Jim closed the cooler, empty-handed.

"She's gone," Octavia said. "We need you. *You.*"

Jim sat in his chair and felt the weight of his daughter's words pushing him down. They'd had their ups and downs lately, and for a twelve-year-old, she could be so damn right.

"I'm tired," she said. "I think I'll turn in."

Jim watched Octavia disappear into the tent, and then sat staring at the fire for a while. He felt like he was failing her, maybe both of them. And he did drink too much.

ଓ ୧

On Sunday morning Jim made scrambled eggs and toast, and while they ate, Midnight wouldn't stop talking about Tyler. It was Tyler this, and Tyler that. She couldn't wait to get home and see her Tyler.

"Someone is missing someone," Jim said.

"I can't wait to tell Tyler about our camping trip," she said through a mouthful of food. "Specially the sand castle we built yesterday at the beach, and the seagulls we chased, and the friend I made—what was her name?"

"Samantha," Octavia said. "And she lives just two streets from us, on Avery. What a small world."

"And we're going to play together when I get home," Midnight said. "I got her phone number and address. Right Dad?"

Jim nodded. "I wrote it all down so we wouldn't forget."

"Too bad she couldn't stay for today," Midnight said. "We could have played."

"Well I'm sure you'll see her plenty this summer, Jim said. "They just moved into the neighbourhood last week."

"She has a little sister," Midnight said. "But she wasn't feeling good. That's why they have to go home."

After breakfast, they headed for the beach, enjoyed the hot sun and cool water, and came back around noon to start packing. Checkout time was at two.

ଓ ୧

Midnight was giddy the entire drive home. No one could get a word in, and it was mostly about Tyler, with Samantha thrown in as an afterthought, it seemed. When the car started to go down their street, Midnight started to screech, but then when they pulled into their driveway, silence filled the car. There was a sign on the Murphys' lawn.

"What does the sign on the lawn say, Daddy?" Midnight asked.

"Uh," Jim said and glanced over at Octavia. "It says for sale."

"What's for sale?" Midnight said.

"Their house?" It came out like a question.

"Why is their house for sale?" Midnight said. "Daddy, why is Tyler's house for sale?"

"I don't know," he said. "I'm as surprised as you are. Tyler didn't mention they were moving?"

Midnight shook her head and got whipped by her pigtails. She saw Tyler running out his front door and she got out of the car. "Why is your house for sale?"

Tyler's face went from I'm-so-happy-to-see-you to a frown that was full of disappointment. He crossed his arms. "*I* wanted to tell you."

"There's a big sign on the lawn," she said in a tone that could have slapped Tyler across the face. "Why are you moving? I thought you were gonna live beside me always."

Tyler shoved his hands in his pockets, stared at the ground, and spoke in a sad monotone. "My dad got a new job and we have to move to a place called Washton."

"Washington?" Jim said.

Tyler looked up and nodded. "Yeah, that's it.

Midnight looked at her dad.

"It's the capital of the United States," he said. "Just like we live in Ottawa, which is the capital of Canada."

Midnight continued to stare at her dad, a stare that was as empty of understanding as her mood was of happiness.

"It's far away," Jim finally said.

Midnight turned to Tyler. "Can't you and your mom and Jake stay here, and only your dad move away?"

"No," Tyler said. "We all have to go."

Midnight felt her chest heave. "But I'll miss you. I don't want you to move away. I won't let you." She crossed her arms, resolved that this would keep Tyler from moving to a far and strange city.

"Honey . . ." Jim said, crouching down beside Midnight. "This isn't Tyler's fault. He can't stay here. He has to go with his family."

"But—"

"Sweetie . . ."

"My dad said it's only for ten years," Tyler said. "And we can move back."

"That's like forever," she said, the tears breaking through her armour. "I'm only five. It's like I'll be . . ."

"Fifteen," Octavia said.

"Fifteen!" Midnight felt like her heart would explode. "That's older than Tavia!" Midnight buried her face in her hands.

"Honey," Jim said and swooped her into his arms. "I know this is hard, but Tyler's probably going to be here all summer and you can play with him until he moves."

She tried to talk but the words wouldn't come, her sadness so big in her throat that it nearly choked her.

"I'm sorry," Tyler said in a voice full of sorrow. "My mom

said it's a great op-opp . . ."

"Opportunity," Jim said and stood, his left knee popping.

"Yeah, that's what she said. For my dad. So we have to move." He looked devastated. "I'm sorry, Midnight, I really am."

"You said that already," Midnight said with a touch of vinegar in her tone. She wiped her eyes and her nose. She smiled but it was flat. "I made a friend when we went camping."

"You did?" Tyler said, cautiously curious.

"Her name is Samantha," Midnight said. "Samantha Carmichael and she lives over on Avery. Right Daddy?"

"That's right. She lives over on Avery Crescent."

"So she can come over and play anytime," Midnight said, sounding like she hoped it hurt Tyler's feelings that she'd made a new friend. "Because it's not *far*."

Tyler pressed his lips together and his eyes seemed a little sad. "I'm glad you have a new friend to play with. I hope I can make new friends when I move."

Midnight grabbed a pigtail and picked at it while she talked. "Are you scared?"

"No," he said, unable to look at her. He sucked at his lips. "Maybe a little. What if I don't make friends?"

"I'm sure you will," Jim said. "Once you start school, you'll meet lots of other kids."

"That's what my mom said," Tyler said, scratching the bridge of his nose, then his arm. "It won't be like playing with Midnight. She's my best friend."

Just then, Midnight did something that surprised them all. She walked up to Tyler and wrapped her arms around him and put her cheek against his.

It took a moment, but Tyler eventually wrapped his scrawny little arms around her, and they stood like that for what seemed a lifetime, two friends understanding that what they'd shared, this friendship that had come together as easily as a breath, was soon to breathe no more.

When she was done, Midnight pulled away and ran toward the house, desperately trying to outrun a pain that she would never completely leave behind.

ELEVEN

~ January 2002 ~

When Christmas vacation ended and the first day of school of 2002 arrived, the atmosphere in the hallways resembled that of a funeral home, as weary students still in Christmas holidays mode, dragged themselves back to class. Everyone complained the break had been too short, or had been wasted travelling to see relatives they barely knew, and that exams were coming way too soon and no one was ready. For the grade twelve students, this was the beginning of the home stretch, the last year of high school, and if you were heading off to post-secondary education, it was time to get it in gear and work those grades up if you expected to be accepted at one of the better universities.

Others couldn't wait to just get out of school and get on with life. Those were the kids that always had the attitude they were better than everyone else and didn't need more education, or just hated school so much and viewed it as a waste of time, so why go off to college or university? Some of them were about to find out what life was really about.

A punch of reality was often the best teaching tool.

Midnight sat in the second row from the front. She scanned the room and pictured those kids who, in five years' time, would be working dead-end jobs with wives who didn't look as good as they had back in high school, and would wonder where their dream life had gone. Of course, her own sophomore classmates had another couple of years to change the course of their lives, but Midnight had known most of these kids a long time and knew that very few had changed.

She just had to look at Bradley Eriksson, a year older and a grade behind. If only Bradley, who had been a thorn in her side forever, had moved away instead of Tyler.

Bang!

She hadn't thought about Tyler in quite some time, which in itself surprised her. Then again, she'd been busy volunteering at the hospital and helping Samantha. Not much time to wallow in the past.

Still . . .

Her thoughts drifted to the summer he'd moved away. They had spent every day together, playing in each other's back yards or at the park, sharing lunches, often as a picnic out in the yard sitting on a blanket. Her dad made peanut butter sandwiches most times while Tyler's mom made ham and cheese sandwiches with carrot sticks and cherry tomatoes on the side. And sometimes chips.

A slow smile spread across her face, a smile that warmed her like a thick wool blanket on a cold winter's night, a smile that gradually turned into an ache she couldn't quite soothe.

Ten years.

It had been more than ten years now since he'd moved. She recalled Tyler saying they'd move back after ten years and she wondered whether they had, and where in Ottawa they had moved back to. Was he still as cute as back then with his red hair and blue eyes and those freckles across the bridge of his nose? And that dimple on his left cheek that always seemed to be there no matter what, even when he couldn't look her in the eyes because he was embarrassed or ashamed for not standing up to Bradley Eriksson.

Funny how she kept telling her dad to move on, to let go of her mom, yet in a sad sort of way, she hadn't either.

She still hoped that Tyler would come back.

Bradley Eriksson's sharp and grinding voice, like a diamond blade cutting through concrete, pulled her back to the present and she closed her eyes. She loathed Bradley so much her stomach churned, like he'd punched her in the gut. Why couldn't he have been in a different English class?

Thankfully, the semester was almost over, with exams at the end of January and then hopefully she wouldn't have any more classes with him next semester.

It wasn't easy, but she cleared her mind and pushed away her disgust for Bradley, and then she heard words coming out of his mouth that didn't make sense, even less so than all the usual nonsense and gibberish he spewed out.

"Well, well," Bradley Eriksson said. "If it ain't Carrot-Top himself. Hey Midnight, your *boyfriend* is back in town."

Midnight opened her eyes and she felt the skin on her face become cold.

She blinked.

Her mouth went dry.

Everything and everyone around her faded out, like the last scene in a movie that zoomed in on the main character. There he was, standing in the doorway, the intensity of his gaze feeling like a warm caress sweeping her face, bringing the blood that had drained away seconds ago back to it.

He couldn't be real. He simply couldn't be standing there.

Could he?

Midnight felt her hand start to reach out and she pulled it back before she embarrassed herself.

She blinked again.

He didn't vanish like the mirage she'd expected him to be. He was still standing in the doorway. After ten long years, he had returned. Just like he'd promised.

The boy next door.

Tyler Murphy.

☙ ❧

Jim sat on the floor of the walk-in closet, the box he'd tucked away at the back years ago now pulled out and open, pictures of him and Karen spread all around him. She had loved to take pictures with her camera. He remembered giving it to her as a gift for her eighteenth birthday, neither one aware that in fourteen months they would become parents to a beautiful baby girl.

During that year and two months, Karen had taken hundreds if not thousands of pictures, but had suddenly stopped once Octavia was born. Luckily she'd left the camera behind, so he'd taken plenty of photos of the kids.

He pulled a picture of them from the mess on the floor and

studied it. They were in the basement in her house, he was sitting on the couch and she had her head in his lap, looking so coy. At first he wondered who had taken the picture, but then, even in his inebriated stated, he remembered that he'd also given her a tripod so she could set the timer on the camera and join him.

"You broke my heart," he slurred. "Why?"

Jim raised a glass to his lips and downed half of his Crown Royal. The fiery liquid left a burning trail down his throat. As soon as Midnight had left for school, he'd grabbed the bottle and a glass and had made his way up the stairs to his bedroom, intent on getting rid of this box of memories, the last remains of a life long gone, but as always when it came to Karen, he'd fallen under her spell and instead of carrying the box down to the garage to empty into the trashcan, he'd started pulling out pictures and looking at them, remembering the good times.

Maybe he'd known he wouldn't be able to simply throw it all out and that's why he'd brought the bottle of whisky with him.

Here was a picture of them at Britannia Beach.

Another at the Ottawa Exhibition. He pulled the photo closer. Karen had been two months pregnant then. He thought he could see a small bump, but it was most likely the way she was standing. Two months was too soon to show.

Still, Jim couldn't help but feel both joy and despair looking at the photo. Octavia was becoming a person inside of Karen, but Karen's eyes were filled with dull unhappiness.

He couldn't remember seeing her this way. He'd been on cloud nine back then, knowing that he was going to be a dad soon. Sure, they'd still been teenagers when the baby came, but that hadn't bothered him.

He now realized it had been the beginning of their troubles. Karen's moods would swing unexpectedly, and like the naive boy he'd been, he had convinced himself that it was just the changes her body was going through. And some of it had been exactly that.

But after Octavia was born, Karen was never the same. A part of her had died with the birth of his daughter.

And the other part had died when Midnight was born.

How could he not have seen this?

Jim finished the last of his drink. It was barely nine o'clock in the morning and he was so drunk he couldn't even get up. He'd been drunk back then too, but not with alcohol. No, he'd been intoxicated by the love he'd felt for the three beautiful women in his life.

One had run away.

The other was all grown up and moved out.

And soon Midnight would be all grown up too and he'd have no one.

Suddenly, he felt old.

Suddenly, he felt lonely.

Suddenly, he tore the picture of him and Karen at Britannia Beach—first into two, then into four, then into eight pieces.

Once he'd started, he couldn't stop. Souvenirs he'd held dear to his heart had become meaningless pieces of paper scattered all around him. Midnight had told him not so long ago that he was broken, that he had to let go of Karen to get fixed.

Jim brought the bottle of whiskey to his lips and drank the rest of it.

He wasn't broken.

He was shattered.

☙ ❧

Midnight put a hand to her face, certain her skin was on fire. She felt warm, but no flames. Still, her heart beat so loudly she was sure everyone could hear. When last had she felt this way, so out of control?

Probably the day Tyler had left.

And now he was back.

Midnight dug her short nails into the skin of her right forearm to wake herself from this dream. This couldn't be real. Tyler couldn't possibly be standing in the doorway of her English class, tall and lithe and so handsome. He looked exactly as she had pictured he would look. There was still a hint of the little boy she had known, but she could also see the man he was becoming.

Suddenly, ten years of waiting evaporated.

Ten years of yearning were a distant memory.

Ten years of wondering if he would ever come back had been answered.

And then something changed—the look in Tyler's eyes went from fiery and inquisitive to hazy and confused. It was the look someone gets when they realize they don't recognize whoever they thought they knew, a look that left Midnight a little saddened and bruised.

Although he still looked like an older version of the Tyler she had known, she didn't look anything like the Midnight he had known. That girl had had dark hair almost touching her shoulders—after losing it to chemo she had wanted to let it grow forever—and no earrings, while the fifteen-year-old version had short hair cropped around the ears that she'd dyed purple during the Christmas break because she'd felt like a change, and she'd gotten two more piercing in each ear for a total of eight piercings, four per ear. She wore no makeup today, not even her customary mascara.

Fact of the matter was, she'd had no reason to put on makeup today. There simply hadn't been anyone in particular she'd wanted to impress, most boys her age being too immature to bother with. Honestly, no other boy had ever been able to measure up to Tyler. As she pulled her eyes away from the boy who had stolen her heart so long ago, she realized that like her dad, she'd been holding on to a ghost, trapped by memories that may have seemed better than they'd actually been, unable and unwilling to move on.

Midnight wanted to shrink back into her seat, to let it swallow her whole. All the times she'd told her dad to forget about her mom, that she wasn't coming back and that he should start living again, she had been doing the same.

She felt like a hypocrite.

Mrs. Dunlap, the English teacher, came in and everyone scurried to take a seat. Tyler grabbed one in the third row—away from Bradley, but also away from her.

Sadly, the two seats on either side of her had been available.

೧೫ ೫೧

Samantha hated her physiotherapist. His name was Michel Lapointe and he didn't speak English all that well so she didn't have a clue why her mom had gotten this guy. Except that he was a wall of muscle, had blond short hair and blue eyes, and filled the room with more testosterone than she'd ever smelled in the boys' gym class, but other than that she simply hated him.

He was torturing her and seemed to be enjoying every second of it, with his all-white-teeth smile plastered on his incredibly gorgeous face. At least, he wasn't as old as her mom, which was a bonus, but he was too old for her, probably late twenties.

"Can I take a break?" she said in a voice that was whinier than she'd wanted. "I need a break."

"We take a break soon," Michel said in thick French accent. "Walk like your life is in danger."

Samantha glared at Michel.

"Oh, please," he said. "I see worse looks from much tougher than you. Do you want to be in wheelchair forever?"

"I'm tired," she said. "Every bone in my body hurts. Just a short break. Please Michel."

"Your mother pay me to get you back on feet, not take breaks every ten minutes."

"We've been at it for over an hour—"

"And we take break when done. Now, you walk across the room without walker."

"Are you crazy?" she said. "I'll fall flat on my face."

"Maybe you do, maybe you don't. Go!"

"Has anyone ever told you you suck at people skills?"

Michel smiled a smile so wide that she guessed he'd been told more than once and that smile told her that he really didn't care. The bastard was so full of himself it irked her.

"You can do it," he said. "You dance all night at your prom."

"I'm only in grade ten," she said. "I have two years before prom."

"Really?" he said, pretending to be surprised. "I thought for sure you were a senior. Maybe a nice senior boy will ask you so we need to make sure you are ready."

Fat chance. They'll take one look at the ugly scar on my face and run away.

Michel walked up to Samantha and pulled the walker away. He took her hand and started walking. After a few steps he let go and moved away so that she stood on her own.

Samantha pinched her face, concentrating. The tip of her tongue parted her lips slightly. She took one unsteady step forward, feeling the effort through her entire body. She took another step. She felt like an infant learning to walk. It's a wonder babies didn't just give up every time they fell on their bottoms.

She took three more steps, then stopped.

"I can't do any more," she said, breathless. "My legs are so shaky right now. I need to sit."

To her surprise, Michel brought her wheelchair and helped her sit.

"You did really good for your first day," he said. "More than most people with injury like that."

Samantha was too tired to bother with a snide remark.

"We take a break and then work on upper body strength and ROM."

"What's that?"

"Range of motion exercises. We want all your joints to move freely. Then some light weights, to help make your arms and shoulders stronger."

"Why? It's my legs that need to get better."

"Yes, but your body is one unit and all parts must work."

Samantha looked him up and down. "Yeah, well I don't want to look like you."

An explosion of laughter filled the room. "It took years to build body like this, not a few weeks of physio."

"Great," she said with little enthusiasm.

Ten minutes later, they were back at it, starting with neck rolls and shoulder stretches and eventually arm work with two-pound dumbbells.

At one, Michel left, leaving Samantha completely spent. She had her mom wheel her down to the guest room next to the kitchen.

"You want lunch?" her mom said.

"I'm too tired to eat," she said and climbed into bed with some help from her mother. "That was brutal."

She fell asleep within seconds, haunted by the fact that she would have to endure this torture again tomorrow, and the day after that, and the day after that.

God! She had weeks to go.

☙ ❧

Midnight heard Mrs. Dunlap but she had no idea what her teacher was saying. Her mind was still clinging to when Tyler's eyes had pulled away, not recognizing her. She couldn't really blame him. If only he had come by her house when he'd moved back, to say hi. They could have gotten reacquainted. That would have been nice.

She wondered why he hadn't.

Because you're some girl he once knew, she thought. He didn't know her now. They hadn't stayed in touch. They were strangers.

But were they?

She remembered the day they had shared their first real kiss on the lips, out behind the spruce trees at the park, a few days before he had moved. His lips had been soft and pleasant. A girl never forgot her first real kiss. But what about boys? Had Tyler forgotten? How many girls had he kissed since then? My God! Why was she thinking this? How pathetic. Why would something that had happened so long ago still matter? Of course, he had kissed other girls. Just look at him. He was gorgeous.

She couldn't wait to tell Samantha. Or maybe she shouldn't. That would only give Samantha something else to tease her with. She definitely didn't need to give that girl more ammunition.

Suddenly, she felt light-headed and noticed her hands were trembling. She put them underneath her thighs, but then suspected her blood sugar level might be too low. Her diabetes had not been a problem in years, but at the moment, she was worried. Midnight pulled her kit from her bag, inserted a test strip into the meter, used the lancing device on the side of her fingertip to get a drop of blood, and touched the edge of the test strip.

While she waited for the result, she clued in that people were looking at her. Okay, she didn't normally do this in class, but she'd had no choice. She ignored them, her eyes glued to the meter until her result appeared on the display. She was fine. It was just the excitement of the moment. Nothing more.

"My brother is diabetic too," Tyler said. "Not a lot of fun when you pass out."

When she looked at him, she thought that there was recognition in his eyes this time. That made her relax. "How is Jake?"

ꕥ

Tyler took his seat after Mrs. Dunlap told them all that the show was over, that it was time to get back to the lesson. He frowned as he wondered how the strange looking girl knew the name of his younger brother. In a class of sameness, she definitely stood out, not just because of her short, purple hair, but also the way she was dressed wearing a long black sweater over black leggings tucked into black combat boots.

She looked like those punk girls of the late seventies. He glanced back at her but she was busy putting her kit into her backpack. There was something about her that intrigued him, something almost familiar. Maybe she just reminded him of a girl back in Washington. That must be it. He rolled through the names of girls he had known, and others he had wanted to know, but that wasn't helping.

He glanced at her again.

Something deep in his memory slowly came to surface.

Another look.

Couldn't be.

Could it?

If that was who he thought it was, she had not grown up the way he would have expected. This was not the Midnight that had lived next door.

Not without guilt, he had to admit that he'd not thought of her in a long time; his life here before he'd moved to Washington was a very distant memory.

Still, when he'd learned he was moving back, his mom had suggested that he should get in touch with Midnight, but he'd figured that she'd probably forgotten about him and had friends of her own. His mom had said it may be so, but there was nothing wrong with ringing up an old friend.

It had felt a little too strange to him to just drop by her house and say what? Hi I'm Tyler Murphy, I used to live beside you.

That was just not cool.

Tyler looked at the girl again, and she was staring at him this time. He saw it then, in her eyes, those light green eyes that had so often glared at him whenever he'd done something stupid, filled with regret and disappointment, eyes that had seemed to reach down into his soul and demand that he be better.

Now he remembered all the times he had spent playing with her and how she had cried as she watched his car drive away on the day they had moved.

And yes, he had cried too.

Suddenly, he missed her. He'd never had a friend like her in Washington. Even his girlfriends hadn't connected with him the way she had.

How could he have forgotten her?

That little boy in him suddenly looked down.

He'd forgotten.

He looked at her again.

Yes, he remembered her, now.

It was definitely her.

The girl next door.

Midnight Madison.

☙ ❧

Midnight was sitting somewhat askew so that from the corner of her eye she could see Tyler. It was all she could do to keep a straight face, knowing that he was looking her way every few seconds, trying to figure out who she was. When she'd first seen him, all she'd wanted was for him to recognize her and come sit beside her, but since he hadn't, it had sort of become a game.

When would he put it together?

She covered a grin with a hand. Seeing him agonizing, trying to figure out who she was, knowing but not quite able to put a name to the face, was rather amusing. She kind of liked the idea of driving him crazy, so she wasn't about to make it easy on him.

Maybe she'd bolt once class was over, keep the mystery burning a while longer.

A little torture never killed anyone.

She glanced at him.

He looked back.

She thought she saw a flicker in his eyes, like he'd finally figured out who she was. She turned away and concentrated on what the teacher was telling them.

Tried to, anyway.

When class finished, she grabbed her things and escaped, seeing that Bradley had cornered Tyler, who didn't seem pleased. She felt his eyes following her across the room.

Once out in the hallway, she hurried to the women's washroom.

⁂

Tyler grabbed his things and bolted, wanting to catch up with Midnight, to tell her he remembered her, but a big fat dude stopped him.

"Hey, get out of the way."

"Don't you know who I am?" the boy said.

Tyler watched Midnight step into the crowd, and then she was gone.

"No, and I don't care," he said.

"Whoa, big tough guy, are you?" the boy said. "Guess moving away turned you into some kind of American stud."

A couple of his friends laughed and slapped each other on the arm. Tyler looked at all three, his head not moving but his eyes shifting quickly, assessing the situation, getting ready. The fat one looked soft, so one punch to the gut would double him over, and the other two were much shorter than him, maybe five inches, so he figured he could take them easily. He'd been training in martial arts for years, something that had come handy a few times in Washington. Unfortunately, a lot of girls seemed to have boy-friends or ex-boyfriends that were jealous. He didn't care to fight but did when it was needed.

"What's your problem?" he said to the fat boy.

"Bradley Eriksson. Ring a bell?"

At first Tyler didn't clue in, but then it all came back. That fat little boy had grown into a fat teenage boy.

"Bradley Eriksson," Tyler said, stretching the last syllable into a sneer. "Well, looks like you haven't changed a bit."

"You being a smartass?"

"Yeah, I am," Tyler said and jutted his chin up ever so slightly. He looked down at Bradley with ice in his eyes. "We weren't friends then and we're not going to be now."

The two boys didn't move.

"Let's get going," Mrs. Dunlap said. "Next class is about to begin. You two can get reacquainted later."

"Yeah, later," Bradley said and walked away, followed by his two minions.

"Tyler?" Mrs. Dunlap said. "Everything okay?"

"Yeah, fine," he said and hurried out into the hallway. He scanned above the heads of his fellow students, but couldn't spot anyone with short, purple hair. "Damn it."

The bell rang, so he headed to his next class.

Maybe he'd been mistaken. If it had been Midnight, she would have stayed behind to say hi.

Wouldn't she?

He started to feel foolish for feeling . . . what? Excited about seeing her again? He'd had to break up with Monica back in Washington, and sure they had been seeing each other for almost a year and he'd really liked her, but it hadn't exactly torn him apart to leave. He missed her a bit, probably a lot, but now—

Was that really Midnight? She was just an old friend. Right? And there was nothing wrong with wanting to catch up with an old friend. His mom had even told him so. Besides, he would never see Monica again, unless he moved to Washington after high school. But that was two years away and lots could happen between now and then.

And Monica wasn't the sort of girl who waited.

And he wasn't moving back to the States. He was from Ottawa and this is where he was going to stay. Maybe things would be better here, with fewer opportunities to get him into trouble.

Probably fewer shootings, for sure.

One of his buds, Jackson, had been shot last summer. There was a lot of violence in Washington and his mom had had a lot to do with them coming back. Besides, she'd missed her family, and Grandma wasn't doing well.

Tyler had to admit, he didn't remember much of Bridgehaven, and they'd only been back three weeks. Maybe, if that was Midnight, she could show him around.

He sort of liked the idea.

Midnight?

With short purple hair?

What was that all about? What was she like now? Maybe she was one of those girls with attitude? Might explain why she hadn't waited for him. Ten years. It had been ten years since they'd last seen each other. People changed in that span of time.

He had changed.

Still, he remembered that Midnight had been the first girl he'd kissed. He'd pretended it was no big deal . . . but thinking back, he realized he'd never forgotten it.

They'd been best friends.

Tyler reached his next class, scanned the hallway one last time as students seemed to vanish into open doorways, and not seeing Midnight, he shrugged and entered the classroom.

☙ ❧

Even though Samantha wasn't at school, Mrs. Carmichael still had to drive Emily and insisted she come by and drive Midnight to and from school.

"Is it okay if I come over and see Samantha?" Midnight said as soon as she was in the van. "I have to see how she is and tell her about my day."

"She was sleeping when I left, but it's probably fine."

"Sleeping?" Midnight and Emily said together.

"Her physiotherapy was rather gruelling," Mrs. Carmichael said. "She was exhausted."

"Oh," Midnight said. "Well, maybe I should just go home and call her later."

"No, no. I'm sure she'll be happy to see you."

Ten minutes later, Mrs. Carmichael pulled into the long winding driveway and stopped right in front of the house. Midnight was bursting to tell Samantha about Tyler.

"You know the way to the guest room?" Mrs. Carmichael said once inside the house.

Midnight had already stepped out of her boots and was walking toward the back of the house, her jacket still on. "I do."

She got to Samantha's temporary room and knocked lightly on the door but didn't wait for a response. She stuck her head in and saw Samantha lying in bed, reading a book.

"He's here," Midnight said and sat on the edge of the bed.

Samantha set a bookmark and closed her book. "Who's here?"

"Tyler."

Samantha looked puzzled. "Tyler?"

"Yes. Tyler," Midnight said, relieved to finally tell someone. "My old neighbour. Tyler. You know?"

"Oooooohhhhhh . . ." Samantha said and sat up, propping a pillow against the headboard. "*That* Tyler."

"I can't believe it," Midnight said, her face flushed. "I had no clue. But there he was, in English class. Funny how we were talking about him just before Christmas, and here he is. I mean . . . I don't know what it means. Isn't this, like, weird? It has to be.

Because it makes no sense that he's suddenly here. What are the chances of that happening? I've been hoping for this for ten years and now that he's here—"

Samantha was laughing.

"What?" Midnight said.

"Listen to yourself."

"What?"

"You sound like a freaking psycho," Samantha said. "All the years I've known you, you've never talked so much and said so little."

Midnight was too excited to be bothered by Samantha's comment. She just went on, telling Sam all the minute details of how Tyler hadn't seemed to recognize her, and then how she'd pretty much played a game of cat and mouse the rest of the day.

"Playing hard to get," Samantha said. "Are you sure that's the right strategy?"

Midnight shook her head. "To be honest, I sort of freaked and panicked. I mean, I think he recognized me by the end of class and then I was just too scared to talk to him."

"You? Scared?"

"I know, right?" Midnight said. "But if you'd seen him, you'd get it. He's like, so grown up, probably over six feet and lean but solid. You know? He was gorgeous. I just didn't know what to do."

"Wow," Samantha said. "I've never seen you like this. Ever. He's really got you bothered."

Midnight was quiet for a moment, struggling with her feelings, not knowing what she should do, afraid that what she'd wished for ever since she was five years old had finally come true, and she didn't want to blow it.

"I guess he does," she said and felt like she was going to throw up.

ꝏ ꝏ

Midnight called home for the third time in the last ten minutes but her dad didn't answer. She assumed he was out running errands. Luckily, Mrs. Carmichael offered to drive her, but when she got home, the car was in the driveway.

"I guess he's home after all," Midnight said. "Sorry you had to drive me."

"I don't mind," Tracy Carmichael said. "Say hi to your dad." She paused. "And remind him I'm still waiting for that dinner."

Midnight was about to question that but decided to leave it alone. "I will. Thanks again."

She watched Samantha's mom drive away and then let herself into the house. Her dad wasn't in the family room nor the kitchen. She called him but he didn't answer back.

She headed up the stairs, peeked into his room, and was about to walk away when she noticed a foot in the walk-in closet. She let her chin fall against her chest and closed her eyes just for a second, and then took a few hesitant steps.

"Dad?" Her eyes bulged out and she covered her mouth as the smell of vomit curled itself inside her nostrils. She leaned down on her knees. "Dad! Dad, wake up!"

She put two fingers against his neck and felt a pulse. That made her breathe easier. Then she spotted the empty bottle of Crown Royal and shook her head.

"Shit," she mumbled.

She picked up the hundreds of pieces of paper he'd ripped, and she realized what they were. Pictures, reminders really, of his life, of his love, of her mother.

"Goddamnit Mom," she said. "Can't you leave him alone? He's hurt long enough. Let him go."

Suddenly, what Mrs. Carmichael had said to her came to mind. Maybe her dad having dinner with Samantha's mom wouldn't be a bad idea. Anything was better than this torture.

Midnight forgot about her newly found happiness and did what she'd been doing for a long time. She took care of her dad.

TWELVE

~ August 1991 ~

The three kids were playing in Midnight's backyard, Midnight on the swing, Tyler hanging upside down on the monkey bars, and Jake in the sandbox with a couple of rusting construction vehicles in hand: a backhoe and a dump truck. Using his lips, he tried to mimic the noises his equipment would make for real.

"We're moving next week," Tyler said.

"I don't want you to move," Midnight said, probably for the hundredth time. "You're my best friend in the whole world."

"You're my best friend too," Tyler said and flipped off the monkey bars to land on his feet. "I like doing that. Hope we have a play structure at our new house."

"Do you know who bought your house? Do they have kids?"

Tyler shrugged. "Not sure."

"Mommy said it's an old couple with a dog," Jake said. "And they don't speak good English."

Midnight made a face, then got off the swing and walked up to Tyler. She put her two hands up on his shoulders and kissed his cheek.

"Why'd you do that for?"

"For good luck," she said. "And so you don't forget me."

Tyler shoved his hands into his pockets and stared at his feet. His fair complexion turned a shade of red. He seemed to be thinking about something.

Then he kissed her back on the cheek.

"So you won't forget me either," he said.

The two of them sort of stood there, avoiding each other's eyes, not sure what to do now. They both understood that soon they wouldn't be living beside each other, but it also didn't seem real, like it was really going to happen. Midnight made a heavy sigh and Tyler made a strange I-don't-know-what-to-do-now sort of face.

"Let's play soccer," Tyler said after a minute.

Midnight nodded. "I was thinking that too."

They asked Jake, but he didn't want to. He was too busy digging and loading the dumb truck. An hour later, sweating and out of breath, they got Jim to give them juice and a snack. The three kids sat on the edge of the deck, their feet dangling over and nearly touching the ground.

"I'm going to miss playing with you and Jake."

"What about that new friend you made camping?"

Midnight shrugged. "Samantha?"

"Yeah, her."

"I guess," she said, not sounding sure. "I don't really know her that much. Maybe she'll be fun. But it won't be the same."

Midnight shoved the rest of her cookie into her mouth and downed her juice. Her eyes were fixed on a flock of birds perched in the oak tree at the end of the yard. They were chirping so loudly it drowned out everything else, but then they went quiet, and suddenly the entire flock exploded out of the tree and they chased one another across the sky.

"Birds are lucky," she said.

"Why?"

"Because they can go anywhere and come back anytime."

"Yeah."

"If we were birds, we could go away together" she said, looking at him. "I think that would be fun. Just fly up in the sky."

"Yeah," Tyler said. "But I think I'd be afraid to fall."

"If you were a bird you'd have wings, you wouldn't fall, silly."

"Yeah, I guess."

"Could I come too?" Jake said.

"No," Tyler said.

"Of course he could," Midnight said. "We'd all be birds."

"But he's still a baby."

"Am not. I'm three," Jake said, shoving three fingers in Tyler's face for good measure. "Dad says I'm a big boy now."

Tyler just shook his head.

"Birds can fly almost after they're born," Midnight said. "I saw a show on TV that showed a mommy bird having babies, and the babies grow fast and were flying like after a few weeks."

"See?" Jake said. "I could fly too."

"Whatever," Tyler said with a shrug. "This is dumb 'cause we're not birds."

"It's just pretend," Midnight said.

Tyler shrugged again and finished his juice.

"What we doing now?" Jake said.

"We could ride our bikes," Midnight said.

"I don't want to," Tyler said.

"What do you want to do?" Midnight said.

"Dunno," Tyler said. "I think I just want to go home."

Midnight went all quiet and found something on her thumb worth picking.

"We only have a week to play," she said, her voice low. "Then we won't see each other anymore."

"I'm tired."

"But you can't go home," she said, her voice rising and sounding a little panicky. "You can't."

"I can if I want to," he said and stood. "You're not the boss of me."

Midnight folded her arms; a scowl crossed her face. She didn't want to get angry with Tyler. Not today. They had so little time to spend together.

"Come on, Jake. We're going home."

Jake glanced at Midnight. "But I wanna stay and play."

"Well you can't. Mom said you had to come with me."

"Why can't you stay?" Midnight said quietly.

"I just don't."

"Fine!" she shouted. "Go home!"

She hadn't wanted to get angry with him, but he was making her sad. What had she done wrong? Why didn't he want to play with her?

"I will," Tyler said in a snarly way.

She just looked at him, close to tears. He stared off to the left, a big scowl on his face. It was like a standoff, to see who would move first. After a minute, Tyler grabbed his brother's arm and pulled him along, and as soon as the boys were gone, Midnight rushed into the house, her face wet with tears.

She could just scream.

Boys!

☙ ❧

Jim was talking on the phone with a client when Midnight came bursting in through the patio doors, in tears. He tried to tell her to be quiet for just a minute, so he could finish up, but the more he wanted her to be quiet, the louder she cried. Finally, he had to cut his phone call short.

"What happened? Are you hurt?"

She shook her head. "T-Tyler," she managed to say.

"Did you two have a fight?"

Midnight pumped her head up and down so hard Jim thought it might snap right off her shoulders.

"Come here," he said and pulled her into the fold of his arms, a hand caressing her back in a soothing pattern. Maybe they were starting to feel the coming separation, and maybe if they were mad at each other it wouldn't hurt so much when Tyler moved. Maybe this was the first of many heartbreaks. "I'm sure you guys will play again later."

"B-but h-he's l-leaving s-soon."

Jim reached for a tissue from the box on the kitchen counter by the phone, and helped Midnight blow her nose. She finally calmed down.

"I know, honey." He could definitely empathise with his daughter. Losing her best friend was a traumatic event. "And I wish I could make it easier for you, but I can't."

"I know, Daddy," Midnight said, looking into his eyes. "I just wanted to play some more today, but he wanted to go home."

"You've been playing all afternoon. He was probably just tired, needed a little downtime. Maybe after dinner, he'll be in a better mood."

Midnight perked up a bit. She broke away from his hold. "Can I watch TV?"

"Sure," he said, amazed how quickly she had recovered. "Until dinner is ready."

He watched her go into the family room and wished he could be like that: a kid living in the moment. One moment you're upset and feel the world is ending, and the next moment everything is just fine.

He should try and do the same.

ଔ ଓ

Midnight and Tyler were playing golf on the Murphys' front lawn using Tyler's Easy Hit Golf Set that just about every kid got at some point. The late summer sun was sinking slowly into the horizon, and the days were already getting shorter and a touch cooler—hard to believe but school was just around the corner.

Jim and Roger Murphy were sitting in the two Adirondack chairs on the Murphys' front porch, watching the kids and reminiscing a bit.

Midnight hit her golf ball.

"Did you see that?" Midnight said when her ball went straight into the yellow all-surface "hole" on her first try. "I've never done that before."

"Lucky shot," Tyler said.

"Was not."

"Uh, yeah, it was."

Midnight stomped over to the all-surface "hole" and took her ball. She eyed Tyler. "Why do you have to be mean all the time?"

Tyler shrugged. "Maybe because you bug me sometimes."

"I don't like you anymore!" She threw her golf club to the ground and headed home.

"Hey, what's going on you two?" Jim said while standing up and heading their way. "Midnight, stop."

Midnight froze where she was in the middle of the driveway. She turned and folded her arms. She meant business. "Tyler always has to be mean to me."

"No," Tyler said in his defence. "I just said it was a lucky shot."

"It wasn't," Midnight said.

"Okay, okay," Jim said, placing himself between them, in the line of fire. "You only have a few more days to play with each other. Do you really want to be fighting about whether a shot was lucky or not?"

He looked at both kids, trying to get one of them to call a truce. He knew his daughter. She could be stubborn. Tyler, as sweet as he was, could be clueless. They made a great couple.

"Guys?" Jim said.

"Maybe it wasn't a lucky shot," Tyler said to his feet.

"I think Tyler just apologized," Jim said, winking at Roger Murphy, who was standing, beer in hand, on the porch and observing.

"I think he did," Roger said.

"Midnight?" Jim looked at his daughter. "What do you have

to say?"

"He doesn't mean it."

"Midnight Madison!"

"But Daddy—"

"No buts," Jim said. "Tyler apologized, and now you apologize for saying he's always mean to you."

Midnight glared at her father, her lips pursed.

"Midnight, *now*," Jim said.

"Fine," she said sharply. "I'm sorry I said you were mean."

Jim eyed his daughter. "Now say it like you mean it."

"Arrggggg . . ." Midnight said. "I'm sorry, okay?"

And before Jim could say anything more, Midnight was running toward the front door of their house, her grief growing louder.

"What's gotten into her?"

"Don't worry," Roger Murphy said. "It's getting late anyway. I'm sure they're both tired and tomorrow is another day."

"You're right," Jim said and went home to console his daughter.

ଓ ଛ

"I wasn't very nice to Tyler," Midnight said.

She was in bed, her hair still wet from her bath, her stuffed teddy bear secured in the nook of her left arm. In her other hand, she held her blanket.

"No. You weren't," Jim said, his hand brushing a stray strand of hair from her face. "Want to tell me why?"

She pulled Teddy tighter against her chest. "Because I don't want him to leave too."

Too.

That's the word that mattered. Midnight had been abandoned once, and now it was going to happen again. Other people in her life were gone too. His mother had died of breast cancer when Midnight was only one, and his father had a heart attack just a few months before Midnight got sick and had died soon after. Karen's mother had passed away about ten months after Karen left and Jim had never met her dad.

"You'll always have me and Octavia."

"Do you promise?"

Jim held her cheek in his hand. "I promise, honey. You're never getting rid of me."

Midnight dropped Teddy and her blanket so she could wrap her arms around her father's neck. She held him so tightly, he could barely breathe.

"I love you, Daddy."

☙ ❧

It was raining.

Hard.

Seemed very fitting.

It was a sad day.

Today was moving day.

"I don't feel good." Midnight was lying in bed with the blankets up to her neck, her pretty green eyes filled with sadness. "I don't want to get up."

Jim felt her cheeks, her forehead, and they weren't warm. Her tonsils weren't swollen. It didn't seem like there was anything physically wrong with her.

She simply had a bad case of Tyler-is-leaving-today-so-there-is-no-reason-to-get-up blues.

Jim tried to tickle her, to no avail. He told her he'd make his world-famous waffles, the ones Midnight absolutely loved, but that failed too. A trip to *Toys R Us* almost did it, but then she said she wouldn't have anyone to play with, so why bother?

"Do you really want to hide here until he's gone?"

She nodded.

"You know, if you do that, you're going to be so angry with yourself later. You'll have missed your chance to say goodbye. Do you really want that?"

Her grief was heartbreaking.

"Hey kiddo," Octavia said as she walked into Midnight's room. "There's a little boy downstairs who's looking for a special little girl to say goodbye to."

"I'm not feeling good," Midnight said.

Octavia came closer to the bed and kneeled. She took Midnight's hands in hers. "You know, if I were you, the last thing I'd want is to waste the last few hours I had left with the boy that I love."

"Who said I love Tyler?"

"Why would you say he's your boyfriend if you didn't?" Octavia said.

Midnight looked at her sister. "He's not going to be my boyfriend anymore," she said in a cheerless whisper. "Because he won't be here anymore."

"You know," Octavia said. "When I was in grade four, I really liked this boy named Nick. He moved away at Christmas time that year, and even though I couldn't see him anymore, in my heart, I knew I would always like him. Still do."

Midnight sat up. "You do?"

Octavia nodded. "No one can change what's in your heart. Just because someone isn't here anymore doesn't mean you have to stop loving them. You think about them and keep loving them, and somehow they know that you still care about them."

Midnight seemed to think it over. She really didn't want to let Tyler leave without saying goodbye. She kicked back the blankets and rushed down the stairs, leaving Octavia and Jim grinning.

"That did it," Jim said. "It's funny, I don't remember a Nick."

"I made him up."

☙ ❧

"There's a big truck in our driveway," Tyler told Midnight when she came down to greet him. "It takes the whole driveway."

Midnight stepped out onto the covered front porch. It protected her from the downpour.

"That's a big truck," she said.

"All our stuff is gonna go in there, and then the driver is gonna drive it to our new house."

Midnight's lower lip wrapped itself over her upper lip in a pout. She looked at Tyler, on the verge of tears. "Too bad your dad had to get a new job so far away."

"Yeah, too bad."

"It's not fair."

Tyler shoved his hands into his pockets and stared at his feet. He kicked at something invisible with his right foot. "My dad said they have soccer teams over there, so I'll be able to play. He's not sure about hockey. I was gonna play this year, but now I dunno."

Midnight wiped her nose with the back of her hand. "I should get dressed."

"Okay, I'll wait."

Midnight rushed inside, leaving Tyler out on the porch. She slipped into a pair of jeans and a pink t-shirt, and was heading back down the stairs when Jim stopped her.

"Hey, not so fast. What about breakfast?"

Midnight looked toward the front door and back to her dad. "Tyler is waiting outside."

"Well, go get him, and I'll give him something too if he's hungry."

Jim made peanut butter on toast and gave them each a glass of milk. He sat at the kitchen table to finish his coffee and read the morning paper. Octavia was taking a shower.

No one spoke.

"So," Jim said. "Today is the big day."

Midnight and Tyler looked at him, frowns on their faces.

"You're moving, Tyler."

"Oh! Yeah." He took another bite of his toast. "It's gonna take all morning to fill the truck. I think we're leaving after lunch. My dad said it's a long drive to Wash . . ."

"Washington," Jim said.

"Yeah, that's where we're moving," he said with a mouthful of toast. "I still have trouble saying it. It's kinda weird word."

Jim smiled. "I guess it is."

"Maybe we can go visit Tyler," Midnight said.

"We might just do that," Jim said. "I've never been to Washington and it would be neat to see the White House."

Again, both kids frowned.

"It's where the President of the United States lives."

Midnight and Tyler thought it over for a second, and then moved on. Some things weren't all that important.

"Daddy?"

Jim moved his eyes from the newspaper to his daughter.

"Can we move to United States?"

"We can, but it's not that simple. I'd need to apply to get a work visa and if they gave me one, then I'd have to find a job, and then we could move."

Midnight perked up.

"But the United States is a big country and we could end up living just as far from Tyler as we are in Ottawa. Besides, I like our home here, honey."

The kids finished eating and scooted off to Tyler's house to see what was going on there. The basement was nearly empty already, and a few boxes had been taken from Tyler's room. Mr. and Mrs. Murphy were busy cleaning as rooms became empty.

The morning pressed on.

Midnight and Tyler watched as the moving men packed the truck. At first it was sort of neat to see the rooms going from cluttered to completely empty, and it was fun the way the empty rooms echoed, but as the last few boxes were placed into the back of the truck, and then when the truck drove away, it all became too real for Midnight.

Tyler was going away and she wouldn't see him for a long time. Maybe never.

"Well," Mr. Murphy said after looking the house over to make sure nothing was left behind. "I guess we're just about ready to head off."

Midnight and Tyler were standing in the middle of the empty living room, facing each other, not sure what to say.

"You kids had some good fun in this house," Tyler's mother said from where she was standing, in the kitchen doorway. "Remember when you guys camped out in the living room here when Tyler got his Mutant Ninja Turtle tent? It was like your headquarters for fighting the bad guys."

"Yeah," Tyler said. "We battled so many bad guys. And what about the time I wasn't feeling good and I threw up all over the floor, and Midnight stepped in it because she was running after me, and then she threw up too."

Midnight smiled but there was no happiness in her troubled green eyes.

"Oh honey," Mrs. Murphy said and took Midnight into her arms. "I know it's not easy for you, but we'll write, and we'll be back to visit I'm sure, and maybe you and your dad and Octavia can come and see us."

Midnight nodded against the comfort of Mrs. Murphy's belly. Tyler's mom had always been there to help her, like when she scraped a knee or bonked her head, Tyler's mom always knew what to do. And now Midnight was losing her too.

It wasn't fair.

People kept leaving her.

"Come," Mrs. Murphy said, and she led the children out of the house. The rain had almost stopped, having turned into a sprinkle. "We'll go say goodbye to your dad and sister."

They chatted for a few minutes and exchanged pleasantries, promises to keep in touch and get together next summer. The Murphys gave them an open invitation to come visit any time, and when it seemed that everything had been said, the Murphys began to get in the car.

Octavia gave something to Midnight.

"Tyler?" Midnight said and grabbed his arm.

She hugged him.

He hugged her back.

When she'd had enough, Midnight pulled away reluctantly, but not before kissing Tyler on the cheek. A few tears streaked down her face.

"I'll miss you," she said and handed him a small envelope. "You're my best friend forever."

She ran off toward her house before Tyler could say anything, her chest aching from a broken heart.

THIRTEEN

~ January 2002 ~

Midnight settled beside her dad on the couch and knew there was little sense in being angry with him. After today, she understood why after all these years the love for her mother still consumed him.

Hadn't she done the same with Tyler?

Maybe not to her dad's extreme, but the five-year-old in her had definitely held on to the little boy Tyler had been, hoping that someday he would return.

And now that he had?

There was no doubt that he'd grown into a great-looking guy, but who *was* he? Was he still the Tyler she had known? Would she feel the same about him?

Realistically, there was no way that she could. They'd been little kids, had known nothing about love—*real* love. Tyler had been the boy next door with whom she'd played.

But she'd held on to those memories as if nothing that good could ever happen to her again. Even her friendship with Samantha hadn't always felt as special, but she knew that wasn't true. It was just different.

"You okay, Dad?"

Jim couldn't look at her. "I'm sorry. I wish you hadn't found me that way."

"I'm just glad you didn't have a heart attack or a stroke."

A shamed snort escaped him. "At least that would have been acceptable. What I did today . . . what I did today was sink about as low as I can go. I think I need help."

Midnight reached over and hugged him.

"I think that's a great idea," she said after pulling away. "I know there's someone out there for you, someone who will love you back."

"You're not talking about Samantha's mom?"

Midnight shook her head and then shrugged. "It's not my place to say who you date. I just want you to be happy. By the way, she says hi."

Jim gave her a perplexed look.

"She drove me home when I couldn't get hold of you."

"Right."

"You're still young and have a lot to offer. You don't have to worry about me or Octavia anymore. It's time for you to have a life of your own."

"When did you become so wise?"

"If only that were true." She told her dad about Tyler's return and how she'd completely sabotaged the long-awaited moment. "So not so wise after all."

"Don't beat yourself up," he said. "You'll see him tomorrow and you can try again."

Midnight saw the pain in her father's face as he uttered the last two words. She could sense that he still wished he could try again. It was obvious, no matter what he'd just said about getting help.

"Dad—"

"I'm fine, honey." He stood and walked over to the front window. "I'm really happy for you. If anyone deserves a little happiness, it's my precious little girl."

Midnight came to stand beside him. Outside, a light snow was falling, adding itself to the two-plus feet of snow that had already fallen this winter. The wind had picked up too and whistled past the aging windows.

"Old Man Winter is not done, it sounds like," he said.

"Old man Madison is not done either," she said and gave him an elbow to the ribs. "Right?"

Jim kept looking out the window.

"Dad!" she said. "You can't go back on your promise to get help. Please."

"I won't. Today will not happen again." They stood in silence for a minute. "So, what are you going to do about Tyler?"

"He's really just a new boy in school," she said. "One no one really knows, not even me."

"But there's history between you two."

Midnight thought about that. "And history is in the past. It doesn't mean that we'll just pick up where we left off ten years ago, doesn't mean we're still friends, doesn't mean we'll even like each other. History doesn't guarantee anything."

"Yes, but—"

"There's no but," she said. "I think I said that as much for you as for me."

He didn't say anything.

"Let's leave history where it belongs," she said.

"You sure you want to do that?"

"I think it's best not to have preconceived expectations." She paused. "That way I won't be disappointed."

"Sort of put up the wall before it's needed."

"It's not putting up a wall," she said. "I'm not going to hide from him, I'm just not going to expect that he feels about me the way I thought I felt about him."

"So, you don't think you have the same feelings?"

"How can I?" she said. "I'm not the little girl he left behind. Seeing him made me realize that, made me jump back to the present. We are two different people. Plain and simple."

Jim glanced at her. "I suppose that makes sense. We've all changed. Time is the great robber of everything that we once were."

"And time can be a great healer too," she said. "Someone told me that a long time ago."

☙ ❧

Tyler moved passed his mom without saying a word to her and took the stairs up to his room by twos. He rummaged through his boxes—he hadn't bothered to unpack everything from the move yet—searching for something that he'd kept all these years without really knowing why until now.

"Did something happen at school?" Veronica Murphy said as she stood just outside Tyler's bedroom door. "Tyler, everything okay?"

Tyler turned to his mother, a card in his hands. "I saw

Midnight today," he said and flung himself onto his bed, feet crossed at the ankles. He opened the card, and out fell a small photo. The glue that had kept it in place all these years had dried and no longer did its job. Tyler picked the picture off of his chest and stared at two five-year-old kids who were beaming big wide grins. "So you don't forget me."

"Pardon?"

"That's what she wrote," Tyler said, sitting up. "Midnight gave me this when we moved and wrote 'So you don't forget me.'"

Veronica came and sat beside him.

"But I had forgotten," Tyler said. "Sort of. I mean, I never threw this out, but I never really looked at it much. Not in a long time. But today, when I saw her, it was like I had never left."

"I'm so happy you two got to spend some time together."

"Actually, we didn't. I saw her, but it was too late when I realized who she was, and I didn't get a chance to talk to her at all."

"Why didn't you recognize her?"

Tyler described Midnight.

"My, she *does* sound different," Veronica said. "But remember that looks can be deceiving. I'm sure she's just as sweet as ever."

"Remember that day we went to Mooney's Bay, and Midnight totally freaked out when she saw the dead fish? She wouldn't go in the water even though it was so hot."

"You remember that?" she said. "That was so long ago."

"Suddenly, I seem to remember all kinds of things we did," he said. "Like the time she fainted and an ambulance came."

"Yes it did."

"Jake was so excited when he saw it."

Veronica Murphy smiled, the smile of someone remembering something pleasant. "He was such a sweet boy back then."

"That's because *you* didn't have to play with him all the time," Tyler said. "You made me do it."

"He looked up to you."

"Yeah, well. Guess that changed."

Her features darkened. "We all changed."

"You didn't like Washington."

"At first, I did, but after a while I missed the simplicity and safety of Ottawa. I know you probably don't remember much about living here, and Jake doesn't remember any of it, really. Maybe if Midnight came over, it would do him some good."

"Don't get your hopes up."

She patted his knee. "I won't. But it might be nice to see them all again. Maybe I'll invite them over for dinner."

"Seriously, Mom. If you think that's going to get Midnight and me together—"

She stood. "That's not my intention. We used to be close and I'm sure your father would love to catch up with Jim. My goodness, Octavia is twenty-something now. It just would be nice to see them."

"As long as that's all."

"But if it does . . ." she said and walked out of his room.

"Mo-oomm!"

"Dinner will be ready soon," she called back as she headed down the stairs.

Tyler shook his head. But he didn't entirely hate the idea. Especially if Midnight kept avoiding him at school. When he'd first seen the girl with the short purple hair, he'd been drawn to her because of the way she looked, dressed like no one else. And he could tell she had a pretty face even though she didn't wear any makeup. Monica, his girlfriend in Washington, wouldn't have gone out of the house without her layers of makeup. Her looks, the latest fashion, even the latest lingo in Hollywood—these things were all that seemed to matter to Monica. She'd been shallow, he knew, but she'd also been a knockout.

At least, with her makeup on.

He realized that Monica had been very insecure, always needing him to pamper her, tell her how beautiful she was, how much he loved her.

And when he'd told her he was moving, she had turned cold, mean, like he was doing this to punish her. Not like he could do anything about it.

They had broken up a few days later and she'd found a new boyfriend in less than a week. So much for love.

His thoughts returned to Midnight. A stupid grin pulled the corners of his mouth. His mom had taken them to the Museum of Nature one time and Midnight had been grossed out when they'd gotten to the spiders' section. He'd thought they were so cool. They had both loved the dinosaurs and had spent most of the time in that area.

And the time they'd gone to the Kanata wave pool and she'd been swept by a wave and had nearly drowned. His mother had been frantic and had had to console a hysterical Midnight.

And all the times they'd gone to Cosmic Adventures. Those had been the best.

Mostly, he simply remembered playing with Midnight at his house or her house, or the park. She really had been his best friend.

It saddened him to realize he'd forgotten all his years with her.

But he was pretty sure she hadn't. She had known who he was. It had been obvious by the way she kept looking at him, and how she'd asked about Jake.

It didn't mean anything. Probably just that she was glad to see him and thought maybe they could catch up.

Nothing more, he was sure.

Just old friends.

☙ ❧

Jim typed into Google *psychotherapist in Ottawa* and a list popped up. He'd made a promise to Midnight that he'd get help, and he planned on keeping that promise. She'd been telling him for a long time, probably years, that he should move on, and after today, the worst day of his life, he'd run out of excuses.

It was time to bury the past before it buried him.

Jim found the perfect therapist and noted her name and phone number. He'd call in the morning and make an appointment. Maybe, hopefully, this Dr. Godsafe—yes, he'd picked her because of her name—would be able to help him put his life back together.

Because it wasn't right that his fifteen-year-old daughter should be the one taking care of him. She was still a kid, he was the parent, and he should be looking after her.

Shame was a great motivator.

So was nearly drinking himself to death. Maybe there was some truth in what Midnight kept telling him, that he was still young enough to find someone else to build the rest of his life with. It was a scary thought, but the alternative had not been kind to him.

FOURTEEN

~ August 1991 ~

Midnight sat on the front step, her hands holding her face, her elbows resting on her knees. The late summer day was perfect, endless blue sky, birds chirping, temperature warm and void of sticky humidity.

Midnight didn't see the blue sky, she didn't hear the birds singing, and she didn't feel the warmth of the early morning sun. Her world was grey, cold, and silent.

The house next door was empty.

A desperate and pained breath escaped between her lips. She had walked over earlier and looked through the front window. She had seen nothing in the house. Everything was gone; no evidence that Tyler had ever lived there remained.

She had rung the bell.

The sound reverberated loudly in the empty shell.

No one had answered.

That's when it had become real to her that Tyler didn't live next door, that she probably wouldn't see him ever again.

She wanted to scream.

But instead, she whispered his name.

He had been more than a neighbour.

He had been more than a playmate.

He had been the first person she thought of when waking up in the morning and the last person she thought of before falling asleep at night. He had been more than a best friend.

It wasn't fair.

A stream of mucus ran down her nose and covered her upper lip.

She didn't care.

Tyler had only left yesterday, but she already missed him terribly and felt so lost without him. If this was the way her life was going to be from now on—boring, lonely, no one to play with—then that would really suck.

She'd heard Octavia say that many times and now she understood what it meant. Suck! It meant there was no one to play with. Suck! It meant you were alone. Suck! It meant no one was your friend.

Suck! Suck! Suck!

She looked around, afraid her dad would read her thoughts. She'd said a bad word in her head and even though no one could have heard her, she didn't want to get in trouble. Midnight didn't think her dad would be happy to hear her say it.

But Tyler moving really did suck.

Absentmindedly, she wiped the snot from her lip with the back of her hand and then rubbed her hand on her shorts. She looked up and down the street and there were no other kids outside, no one to play with.

She was so bored.

An army of ants marched passed her feet and Midnight examined them as if she had never seen ants before. They seemed so busy, moving about at breakneck speed, like an army with purpose. Midnight wondered how they felt when their best friend moved.

There were too many of them to notice one missing, she guessed.

With nothing better to do, she watched them for what seemed forever, occasionally glancing up to see if by some small miracle Tyler might be there, staring at her, not saying anything.

Not like he'd never done that before.

More snot ran down her nose while her shoulders bounced up and down like a wild horse bucking a rider. After a few minutes, she grew tired and her grief petered out.

Midnight trudged back into the house.

The new school year couldn't arrive fast enough.

Grade one.

Big time.

Big time worry, too.

It had seemed less scary when she'd known that Tyler would be there with her, on the first day. And even though she knew a lot of the kids that would be in her class—many of them had been in kindergarten with her—she was sort of afraid of all the other grades. They were going to be all mixed up with the big kids now and she wasn't sure she liked that.

Bradley Eriksson was one of those bigger kids and now that Tyler wasn't here to protect her—well, he never really did protect her from Bradley, but she still would have preferred that he be there with her—she felt a bit vulnerable.

Maybe she wasn't looking forward to school after all.

ଔ ଓ

"Hi," the girl with the golden locks said. She was sitting beside Midnight. "We met camping, Remember? I'm Samantha."

Midnight smiled politely. "I remember."

"We were supposed to play."

Since Tyler had left, she'd spent her days moping around, lying on her bed or watching TV. Her heart hadn't been into doing anything with anyone else, so when her dad had asked if she wanted to call Samantha to see if she wanted to play, Midnight had said no.

Same with her other kindergarten friends, Emma, Jill, and Becca. She just hadn't felt like it. Those friends were fine to play with at school, but at home, Tyler was the only one she wanted to play with. Thinking of him made her eyes watery and she fought to keep them under control.

"Are you going to cry?" Samantha said.

"No," Midnight said in a voice that betrayed her. "I just don't feel well."

"I wasn't feeling good this morning too," Samantha said. "Kinda scared of grade one. And homework. I don't want homework."

Midnight shook her head. "That's not why."

"Oh," Samantha said. "What is it?"

Midnight looked at Samantha for a good long time before deciding to tell her. "My best friend moved away just before school."

"That boy you talked about at camping?"

She nodded.

"Why did he move?"

"His dad got a better job far away, in the United States."

"Is that far?" Samantha said.

"Takes hours to drive there," Midnight said in a bummed-out tone. "Like almost a whole day."

"That sucks."

Midnight's eyes nearly bulged out of their sockets and she looked around to see who might have heard.

"What?" Samantha said.

"You said a bad word," Midnight whispered.

"Suck?"

Midnight nodded.

"It's not really a bad word," Samantha said. "My mom says it all the time."

"Oh!" Midnight said. "My sister Tavia says it sometimes, but never around my dad. I think he'd get mad at her."

"Really?"

"I think so," she said. "He doesn't like us to say bad words."

"What about your m—" Samantha said and stopped. "You don't have a mom, right?"

Midnight shook her head. "She left when I got sick with cancer."

"You told me at camping, but I forgot," Samantha said. "That sucks too."

Midnight giggled quietly. "You sure like saying that word."

"You say it?"

"I can't."

"Why?"

"Told you," Midnight said, sounding a little exasperated. "My dad doesn't want us to say bad word."

"But he's not here. He won't know."

Midnight pondered that.

"I'll say it with you."

"I don't know."

"You'll feel better."

"How is saying that word going to make me feel better?" Midnight said with a big frown on her face. "It won't bring Tyler back home. Or my mom."

"No. But you'll feel better anyway."

"That's silly."

"Trust me."

If Tyler had told her this, she would have believed him. But she barely knew Samantha. She seemed nice enough, and maybe they'd become good friends, but today she was just a girl she'd met once while camping.

Besides, just because her dad wouldn't hear her, didn't mean it was okay to say. She'd thought the word the day after Tyler moved and that hadn't made her feel better, so saying it out loud probably wouldn't either.

Or maybe it would.

What if it did?

It sure would be better than feeling sad all the time. And lonely. And bored.

What if it made all of that go away?

"Okay," she said.

"Really?" Samantha said.

"Yes," she said. "Our teacher is coming so we better hurry."

"Let's say it together on three," Samantha said. "One, two, three."

"Sucks!" they said.

Their teacher, who had been standing just outside the classroom door to guide the kids into the proper room, just happened to walk in then. "Girls? We won't be saying that again in my class, right?"

Midnight and Samantha stared at each other.

"Right?' their teacher said.

"Yes, ma'am," they said.

"Good," she said. "Class, settle down. Welcome to grade one. My name is Mrs. Hood, and I'll be your teacher this year."

Midnight felt horrible. Not only had saying *sucks* not helped, they'd also been caught by Mrs. Hood. Midnight wondered if her teacher was going to call her dad now and tell him. Why had she listened to Samantha?

Tyler wouldn't have gotten her into trouble.

Midnight wondered if Tyler would have been in her class or in the other grade one class. That wouldn't have been as good as being in the same class, but it would have been better than not being here at all.

Midnight listened to Mrs. Hood tell them about the things they were going to learn this year. Mrs. Hood reminded Midnight of Octavia with her long silky strawberry blond hair—before her sister had cut it—and fair features. She looked like a mannequin. Not that Octavia looked that fragile, because she didn't. Octavia was beautiful and so was Mrs. Hood.

Would she be beautiful too?

Her dad told her so all the time, but that didn't count. Octavia also said it but that didn't count either. Strangers had to say it, people who didn't know you. If they thought you were beautiful, like Midnight thought Mrs. Hood was, then it must be true.

Tyler had never said she was beautiful.

Midnight looked at Samantha.

At her long, wavy blond hair.

Samantha was going to be beautiful, Midnight was sure of that. But right now, she was mad at her and if she had a pair of scissors, she'd cut off Samantha's long blond hair.

Maybe *that* would make her feel better.

As soon as the thought popped into her head, Midnight felt bad. Cutting off Samantha's hair wouldn't make her feel better, she knew that, and worse, she'd probably lose a friend before they had a chance at becoming good friends.

Maybe even best friends.

Tyler would always be her best friend, but Octavia had told her that you could have more than one best friend. That didn't make sense to Midnight. There can't be more than one winner in a game, so how can you have more than one best friend? Then Octavia had said that Tyler had been her best boy friend and there was no reason why she couldn't have a best girl friend.

After thinking about it, Midnight had sort of understood.

So it was possible that Samantha could become her best girl friend. Or Emma, or Jill, or Becca. But none of them were in her class this year.

So maybe Samantha could become her new best friend. They'd be together more often, so that might help.

At morning recess, Midnight and Samantha headed off toward the play structure and after a few minutes, Midnight realized her other friends hadn't joined them. Then she spotted them over on the paved part of the yard, playing hopscotch, but before she could ask Samantha if she wanted to go play with them, the bell rang and they all headed back in.

"That was short," Samantha said.

"Way too short," Midnight said. "But I think lunch recess is longer."

"I hope so," Samantha said. "Grade one sure doesn't feel like kindergarten. I think it's gonna be much harder."

"That sucks," Midnight said and both girls exploded with laughter.

☙ ❧

"What are you doing?"

Midnight and Samantha were on the play structure again. It was becoming their favourite place to play at recess. It was Friday, the end of their first week of grade one.

"Hi Becca," she said. "Me and Sam are just playing."

"Can I play too?"

Midnight looked at Samantha, who gave her a non-committal shrug.

"Sure," she said. "Why aren't you with Emma and Jill?"

Becca looked down. "Emma isn't here and Jill was being mean. She said I cheated at hopscotch but I didn't."

Becca joined them and they played for a bit without saying much.

"Do you like your teacher?" Becca said.

"Mrs. Hood is fun," Midnight said. "Who's your teacher?"

"Miss Foster. She didn't let me and Emma or Jill sit together.

She didn't let anyone sit with a friend."

"Mrs. Hood let me and Sam sit together. But I guess we weren't really friends yet," Midnight said and looked at Sam.

"We're best friends," Samantha said with a big smile on her face.

Had they really become best friends in just one week? She did like Sam a lot, and they laughed a lot when playing together, and she didn't think of Tyler too much when she was with Sam.

"Yeah, me and Sam are best friends."

"Can't I be your best friend too?" Becca said.

"I can only have one best girl friend," Midnight said. "But you can be my friend."

"Can I be Sam's friend too?"

Midnight looked at Sam.

"Sure," Samantha said. "We can all be friends."

"Sweet," Becca said. "My older brother says that all the time when he likes something."

"My sister Tavia does too."

"I only have a younger sister, and she's mostly annoying," Samantha said. "She's always telling on me when I don't want to play with her or watch her shows like Dora. That show is *sooooo* boring. I'm not a baby anymore."

"I still like to watch it," Becca said.

"I do too," Midnight said. "I like Boots. He's funny."

After a pause, Samantha said, "Yeah, Boots is kinda fun."

Just then the bell rang to signal the end of afternoon recess and Samantha reached out and took Midnight's hand and started walking back toward the school. Quickly, Midnight grabbed Becca's hand and the three of them trotted across the yard to the doors.

On the bus ride home, Midnight and Samantha sat together, chatting and laughing the way best friends did. Midnight asked Samantha if she wanted to come over to her house on Saturday to play and she said yes. Samantha was nice and they liked to play the same things, and having a new best friend made it much easier for Midnight not to miss her old best friend.

FIFTEEN

~ January 2002 ~

Tyler was standing in front of the school entrance, the frigid winter air biting his face. Washington winters weren't this harsh, something he had obviously forgotten. As everyone approached, he checked them out.

No sign of Midnight.

A group of boys walked by, grade nines, trying to act like they were today's hotshots, and Tyler chuckled. He thought of his buddies back in Washington and how they'd been just as stupid. High school was just some big popularity competition—who knew who, who was the coolest, who you shouldn't mess with. Just who, who, who, all the time.

High school life.

It was all bad. Or wouldn't be if he could find Midnight. Crazy but he'd been unable to stop thinking about her since he'd seen her yesterday. It was weird. He hadn't thought of her in years, hadn't even realized he'd be going to the same school as her, even after his parents had told him they were moving back not just to Ottawa, but to Bridgehaven, and now he desperately needed to talk to her.

A silver minivan pulled up, Midnight climbed out, and the van pulled away. Tyler took a step toward her and stopped when he saw the look of horror on her face.

☙ ❧

Midnight said goodbye to Mrs. Carmichael—it still felt a bit strange that Mrs. Carmichael insisted on driving Midnight to school without Samantha—and when she turned around, she froze. What was Tyler doing? Stalking her? She hadn't expected him to be waiting for her. She wasn't ready to talk to him.

Really?

Well . . . maybe like, later, but not first thing in the morning.

Really?

Well . . . maybe she'd been ready for like ten years, but it had been easier to want something when she hadn't expected it to happen.

Really?

Well . . . okay, maybe she was ready but the way her stomach was flip-flopping was a bit of a distraction. Last thing she wanted to do was throw up on him.

That would not make a good impression.

"Tyler?"

He gave her an uneasy smile. "I . . . I didn't mean to crowd your space or anything. I just thought that maybe you'd like to talk after yesterday. You know?"

She stopped a couple of feet in front of him. "Yeah, I know."

"I'm sorry I didn't recognize you."

"Don't worry about."

"But you recognized me."

She smiled. "You're just an older version of the boy that moved away."

"Ouch! Not sure how to take that."

"I didn't mean it in a bad way," she said. "You just look a lot like you used to, but in a more mature way."

"I guess that's good?"

"I think so," she said and bit her lower lip.

He seemed tongue-tied for a moment and stared at her. His blue eyes were full of depth, and warmth, something she definitely couldn't have noticed all those years ago. In fact, now that she was really looking at him, his hair wasn't as red, and the freckles that had run across the bridge of his nose and the top of his cheeks were a lot less noticeable than back then.

He really was handsome.

Okay, hot!

But she wasn't about to tell him that. Not today, anyway.

"Whose van was that?"

"My friend Samantha's mom," she said. "I met her camping just before you moved. We've been friends since."

"So where is she?"

"She was in a car accident," Midnight said. "Pretty bad. Spent a few months in the hospital and now she's home recuperating."

"What happened?"

"Let's go in before we freeze," she said. They started walking toward the doors. "The accident happened back in September. She broke her pelvis, leg, ankle. I think that's right. Anyway, she was a mess. But she's better than the driver. He died."

"Ah, that sucks," he said and opened the door for her. "Was

he her boyfriend?"

"No, just friends. She liked him though, so who knows if anything would have happened. They were going to a party."

"That's too bad," he said. "But she's okay? When is she coming back to school?"

"Hopefully soon," she said, the heat feeling good against her face. "She pretty much has to learn to walk again."

"I'm sorry."

"Thanks," she said. "So, you're back?"

"I'm back."

The bell rang and they both looked annoyed. "We're late. What's your first class?"

"Chemistry. You?" he said.

"Psychology."

"Really?"

"Yeah. Why?"

He shrugged. "I have no idea why I said it that way. I guess I don't really know much about you anymore." The principal urged them on. "I'll see you in English class after lunch."

"Maybe we can have lunch together?"

"Yeah. I'll see you there."

☙ ❧

"Tyler and I talked today."

Jim was standing by the kitchen counter, waiting for the kettle to boil so he could make hot chocolate. He was red-faced from his walk. He'd decided that losing a few pounds—okay, maybe more than a few—was in his best interest, and that walking every day was a good way to start, but he hadn't counted on the temperature being near twenty below.

"You did?" he said.

"Yeah," Midnight said "What were you doing?"

"I went for a walk."

"You?" She stifled the urge to laugh.

"Yes. Me," he said and poured boiling water into a cup. "I've decided to take your advice."

"About seeing a therapist?"

Jim turned, holding the cup in both hands, his fingers slowly thawing. "About losing weight."

"When did I say that?"

"It was a while ago."

"And the therapist?"

"I've made an appointment for next Monday. Soonest I could get in."

Midnight hugged her dad. "I'm proud of you."

"Thanks, honey."

He took a sip and burned his tongue. "Damn. That's hot."

"Language," Midnight said, imitating her dad's voice. "Maybe you should get one of those stationary bikes for the winter."

"Maybe," he said and took another sip. "So, what about you and Tyler?"

"We met up today when we first got to school." Midnight walked over to the fruit bowl and pulled out a tangerine. She peeled it. "It was weird at first, didn't seem real."

"I guess it would seem kind of strange."

She tore the tangerine apart and stuffed a couple of pieces into her mouth. "It was like going back in time," she said after swallowing. "I could see us running around in the backyard, playing like we used to. And then I'd see him for who he is now and . . ." She shrugged.

"And what?" Jim said.

"I don't really know. It was like, *do I really know you*? Weird, huh?"

Jim rinsed his empty cup and placed it in the sink. "Not really, honey. You're comfortable with the five-year-old part of the life you shared with Tyler, but you don't have anything to share with the fifteen-year-old Tyler. Give it time and you will."

Midnight popped the last piece of tangerine into her mouth. "So you're on a diet?"

"An exercise plan," Jim said.

Midnight smiled. That was her dad, leaving his options open. Oh well, at least he was doing something to take care of himself. Plus, he was going to see a psychologist. If the exercise plan didn't pan out, she hoped that the therapy would.

It was a start.

☙ ❧

Every day, the conversations between Midnight and Tyler became easier, longer, more personal. They had ten years of catching up to do, and Midnight was surprised by how much she looked forward to each new day, knowing that she would learn a bit more about him. It was like reading a good book, each chapter revealing a bit more, each chapter making you want to keep turning the pages.

What came next?

She didn't know.

But she sure wanted to keep turning the pages.

It didn't take long for rumours to start spreading about them, that somehow the weird girl had snatched the hot new guy so it must be because of sex, it had to be.

They hadn't even been on a date.

They were just old friends.

Most people didn't know that. Fact is, if there was something to gossip about, nothing moved faster through the hallways of a high school than a good old-fashioned rumour, and the juicier the better.

Midnight didn't care, but she noticed that Tyler was bothered by it.

"I've been here less than a week and people I don't even know are asking me how I managed to score with you so fast."

"I wouldn't pay much attention to them."

"I've noticed you don't really have many friends, or at least when I'm around."

"Samantha is my best friend, but since she's not back at school yet, I'm sort of flying solo."

"Why don't you have other friends?"

Midnight took a deep breath. "Some people think I'm . . . *different* . . . because of the way I dress, the way I seem not to care, the way I'm standoffish."

"Is that deliberate?"

She shrugged. "I don't think I ever planned it. It just sort of happened. I just don't really care about the things most teenagers care about. Seems so meaningless to worry about wearing the latest fashion, the best makeup, who your circle of friends is. Like, really, it will not make my life any better. In two more years we're all out of here and all of this will mean nothing. What will matter is what we do afterward, and I don't plan on being some dumb housewife depending on a husband to take care of me."

Tyler laughed. "Oh yeah. That's the Midnight I know. You're still the same girl I lo—"

He stopped himself, his cheeks suddenly a slightly rosier colour.

Midnight pretended she hadn't heard.

A moment passed.

"So, want to hang out Saturday?" he said.

"Can't," she said with a hint of disappointment. "I volunteer at the Children's Hospital."

He nodded. "I'm not surprised. But what about when you get home? Or are you planning on sleeping there too?"

"I'll be home around seven."

"So let's do something then."

She didn't have to think twice. "I'd like that."

☙ ❧

Her name was Lily, and she was just three—a cute little girl with soft caramel skin and dimples that wouldn't quit. The chemo had taken all of her hair, but not her spirit.

Midnight had found out that Lily had leukemia and had been going through a heavy dosage of chemo all week. If all went well, she would be going home middle of next week.

"Hey," Midnight said as she sat down on the edge of the bed. "My name is Midnight, and you're Lily."

The little girl nodded, after glancing at her parents to make sure it was okay to talk to this stranger.

"I asked your mommy and daddy if I could spend a bit of

time with you while they take a lunch break. Is that okay with you?"

Again, Lily nodded after glancing at her parents.

"I had cancer too, when I was your age," Midnight said and immediately Lily relaxed. "So if you want to ask me anything, *anything,* I'll do my best to answer your questions. And if you don't want to ask me anything, then maybe we can play a game, or make a puzzle, or read a story."

Lily smiled, those dimples grabbing hold of Midnight's heart. "A story," she said.

When Midnight began reading, Lily's parents left quietly. She read a couple of Franklin stories and then Lily became quiet. She looked up at Midnight with the same coloured eyes as Midnight and asked a question that was just too tragic for a three-year-old to ask, but one Midnight had asked her own father.

"Am I going to die?"

Midnight caught her lip in her teeth, wondering how much truth she should tell. This was the part she disliked the most about volunteering: getting to know the kids, putting a life to the face, falling in love. She wanted so much for all of them to be all right, to get better and go home and live a happy life. Like her.

"I don't really know," she said. "It really depends on how strong you are, and if God is really ready for you."

Lily nodded. "That's what my mommy and daddy said."

Midnight put on a brave face and leaned in to hug Lily. She didn't want the little girl to see her fighting back tears.

"You just need to keep fighting," Midnight said as she pulled away, her eyes dry but burning. "Don't ever give up."

"I won't," Lily said. "You didn't die."

"That's right. I fought real hard."

Lily's dimples returned. "I'll fight too. Just like you." She paused and took Midnight's hand. "And when I'm older like you, I can come visit sick kids and talk and read to them."

Midnight smiled. "Yes. You can do that."

"I like you," Lily said.

"I like you too."

After a while, Lily's parents returned, and Midnight got up to leave. The little girl grabbed her hand. "Come back to see me?"

"I'll come back before I leave," she said. "Okay?"

"Okay."

☙ ❧

Midnight ended up having a full, emotional-rollercoaster day at the hospital, and when she got home she didn't feel angry or depressed; instead she felt calm and hopeful. Those kids, sick as some were, had so much love and life in them that it was impossible not to feel their energy and get excited about their chances. Those beautiful, innocent faces made you believe in small miracles.

Borrowed time made you appreciate the little things.

She saw it in the parents' eyes, heard it in their words, lived it with their actions. Nothing was more important than the moment, and for those few hours she was there, that's exactly what she did. Each moment she spent with a child was a moment that was changing her, making her a better person. It put things in her life into perspective.

Which made it difficult to have to turn down Samantha's invitation to hangout because she'd already agreed to see Tyler tonight. All of a sudden, she had to share herself with her two best friends, a dilemma she'd never dealt with before.

"I'm sorry," she said for the third time.

"So, is it like a date? It better be a date if you're going to blow me off."

"I . . . I don't think it is," she said.

"And what does he think?"

Midnight was silent.

"Hello?" Samantha said. "You still there?"

"Yeah," she said. "Do you think he thinks we're going on a date?"

"Probably," she said. "What are you doing?"

Midnight couldn't remember if they'd actually made any sort of plan. "I have no idea."

"So you left it up to him?"

"I guess," she said. "I told him I was busy all-day volunteering at the hospital, so he just said maybe we could do something after I got home."

Just then her dad called out that dinner was ready.

"My dad just—"

"I heard," Samantha said. "You'd better call me and tell me all about your date with boyfriend-from-the-past."

"It's not a date."

"Uh-huh," Samantha said with obvious glee. "You tell yourself that. It's a date, trust me."

"It's not a date."

"You'd better look good," Samantha said. "Put some makeup on and wear some nice jeans and top. Impress him."

"Will you stop? It's *not* a date."

"Call me."

"It might be late."

"Call me tomorrow then."

"Got to go." She hung up and raced down to eat whatever dinner her dad had concocted in the few minutes they'd been home. "Spaghetti! Looks good. I'm starving."

"Dig in."

"You and Samantha hanging out?"

"No," she said between mouthfuls. "Remember, I'm hanging out with Tyler."

"Oh, right. What are you doing?"

"No idea. Got to call him after."

The phone rang.

"Or he'll be calling you," her dad said.

Midnight grabbed the cordless phone and headed out of the kitchen into the living room. Her heart was beating a little faster than she would have expected if all she was doing was hanging out with Tyler.

"Hey," she said. "Everyone's asking me what we're doing and I have no idea what to say."

"Who's everyone?"

"My dad. Sam."

"Oh," he said. "So I thought maybe we could catch a movie. Unless you don't want to?"

"Which one?"

"There's the *Lord of the Rings* or that *Harry Potter* movie which seems to be all the rage," he said. "Unless you'd prefer some romantic comedy or something?"

"Either one would be fine," she said casually, but in her head, she was screaming, *Crap crap crap, this is a date, crap crap crap!*

"Maybe we can decide when we get there."

"Sure."

"My mom is going to drive us," he said. "And she'll probably talk your ear off. She's so excited to see you."

"I liked your mom," Midnight said. "It'll be nice to see her again."

"We'll pick you up in about fifteen minutes."

"I'll be ready."

☙ ❧

Midnight heard the doorbell ring but she wasn't quite ready. She'd slipped into a pair of tight blue jeans that she hardly ever wore, put on a bit of mascara and eyeliner, taken out all but two earrings per ear, leaving a couple of diamond studs in each lobe, and she'd put on a bit of lipstick too. She just wanted to put a little gel in her purple hair, to spike it up.

"Hey Mr. Madison," she heard Tyler say.

"Come in," her dad said. "It's freezing out there."

"I'd forgotten how cold winter is in Ottawa," Tyler said. "My mom wanted to come in and say hello but I told her we didn't have time because the movie starts in forty minutes."

"Which movie you guys going to see?"

"*The Lord of the Rings.*"

"I've heard great things about it. The imageries are supposed to be outstanding."

Midnight finished setting her hair and hurried down the stairs, before the conversation between her dad and Tyler ran out. "Hey Tyler."

Tyler stared. "Wow! I mean, you look really nice."

"Thanks," she said and slid her feet into her black combat boots, and then her dad held her winter coat. "Where's your mom?"

"I insisted she stay in the car because she'd probably talk to your dad all night if she came in."

"Well, you say hi to your parents for me," Jim said. "We'll get together soon."

"I think she wants to have all of you over for dinner," Tyler said.

"Sounds good," Jim said.

"We better go," Tyler said. "Nice to see you again, Mr. Madison."

"You two have a good time."

"No need to stay up, Dad," Midnight said. "I think the movie is over two hours long."

"It's actually just under three hours," he said. "If I'm up, I'm up. Don't worry about me."

Tyler and Midnight walked out into the cold and hurried to the car. The snow crunched under their feet and the cold nipped at their cheeks.

"Hi Mrs. Murphy," Midnight said. "Nice to see you again."

Veronica Murphy smiled a smile that was filled with warmth and something else, something that was almost motherly. "It's nice to see you again, Midnight."

"Mom," Tyler said in a voice that reminded Midnight of the boy she knew. "We really need to get going if we're going to make the movie. Maybe we can talk later."

"I'm on it," Veronica said and backed out of the driveway.

"My dad says hi."

"Let him know I'll have you guys over for dinner soon."

"I did already," Tyler said. "Let's go."

Veronica Murphy had a smile that only mothers could get away with. "My, my, someone's a little uptight."

"Mo-oom!"

"We're fine," Midnight said.

Less than five minutes later, while in line to buy their tickets, Tyler laced his fingers together with Midnight's, giving her heart a jolt that wasn't unpleasant.

Samantha had been right.

This was definitely a date.

SIXTEEN

~ April 1994 ~

It was just after midnight and Jim was sitting in the dark on the couch, waiting for Octavia to come home. Her behavior had become more erratic and defiant, and he was lost as to what to do. This wasn't her, at least not the her he wanted his daughter to be. She had turned fifteen a few weeks ago and he felt like he was losing her, that she was heading in the wrong direction.

A direction he was familiar with.

He took a drink of his beer, his third since he'd put Midnight to bed, and maybe it wasn't the best thing to do considering his annoyance with Octavia, but it had become a habit that seemed to own him.

It dulled the pain of the last five years.

Five years.

Had it really been that long?

How many times could he replay the days, weeks, months leading up to that day? Nothing was going to change what happened no matter how guilty he felt, how much blame he put on his shoulders, how much disappointment filled him for having failed his family. Maybe that's the one feeling that really left him raw, the one that held him back, the big roadblock he couldn't get past.

He did the best that he could, he really believed that. Every day he wondered if he was good enough for his girls. Did he do enough to help them get on with their lives? Or was he messing things up so badly that he was forced to sit in the dark on a Friday night waiting for his eldest daughter to come home?

Was she getting herself into trouble?

That would be *his* biggest failure, not hers, and the dad in him couldn't in good conscience allow that to happen. She shouldn't have to pay for his mistakes; those were on him and him alone.

He heard the key in the lock.

☙ ❧

Octavia dropped her keys, picked them up, swore, couldn't find the keyhole, swore again, then finally unlocked the front door. Her brain felt way too big inside her skull, the electrical pulses firing as if a madman lived inside her head. Plus, she felt like throwing up.

What an awesome party.

She'd met a cute boy. His name was Trevor. He was a high school senior but she didn't care. He'd made her feel like she was the most important person in the world. They had kissed and messed around a bit. Not too much. She knew where to draw the line, even in her inebriated stupor. Still, it had felt good to be wanted for a while, to forget her home obligations, to act like a fifteen-year-old. Whatever that was, she had no idea, but she knew it wasn't what was expected of her from her dad or sister. Not that she minded, most of the time. Midnight needed her and she took care of her. And her dad.

However, that sometimes got under her skin, the way he couldn't get his shit together. Like, come on, enough already. But she knew better than to bring that up. Maybe someday, if she got her heart broken, she'd understand better, but she also hoped that her heart wouldn't ever be that broken. She never wanted to be the wreck that her dad was.

He wasn't a bad—

"Where have you been?" Jim said.

Octavia screamed. What the—! Her eyes couldn't see him but she knew he was there in the family room, waiting for her. She should have expected that, but it had totally escaped her. She was just fifteen, after all, so of course he'd be waiting. Like duh!

"Octavia," he said. "You were supposed to be home by eleven thirty."

"Do you have to be sitting in the dark?" she said. "Kind of creepy to have you yell at me where I can't see you."

"I'm not yelling," he said. "I haven't even raised my voice."

He had sounded so loud in her head, like he was using one of those bullhorns three inches from her ears. And she wished the damn room would stop spinning. Why the hell was the entire house on a merry-go-round?

She cupped her mouth with her hand, but it didn't stop the evening's overindulgence of alcohol from gushing out onto the hardwood floor and splashing against the wall. The smell hit her instantly and the rest of tonight's awesomeness joined the rest of the party on the family room floor.

"Jesus Christ!" Jim said loudly through gritted teeth as he shot to his feet. "Is this who you are now? What kind of friends do you hang out with that they get a fifteen-year-old girl to drink herself sick? Octavia, what's going on with you?"

She wiped her mouth with the back of her hand. "You! *You're* the problem! You think you're the only one that's allowed to hurt, that's allowed to drink to forget how shitty your life is? I'm so sorry that Midnight and I fucked things up for you. I'm sorry I was ever born because then you'd still be with her instead of stuck with us. I'm sorry . . ."

She let her words hang in the air between them like a toxic cloud.

"Don't say that."

"Why, Dad?" she said. "It's the truth. Midnight is too young to see what I see, and I don't like what I see."

"I get what you're saying," he said. "But you're still only fifteen and you shouldn't be drinking. It's not just illegal, it's wrong."

"It might not be illegal for you," she said, trying hard to keep the room straight. "But it's also wrong that you drink so much. I hate it. You know why? Because then I'm responsible for everyone. After all, I'm only fifteen."

☙ ❧

Jim ran a slightly trembling hand across his lips. The anger he'd let ferment while he waited for Octavia to come home had festered and turned poisonous, and she had turned it against him, given him a well-deserved kick in the gut. To be honest, Octavia had just stomped on his pride—the little bit he'd had left—and he couldn't even blame her. But damn it, he needed a little help to get through the lonely hours of the night. That's all. Wasn't it? He knew the answer to that, of course he did, but knowing something was a lot easier than doing something about it. It was easy to hide truths under a haze of drunkenness.

Damn it!

He needed to do better, or at least hide it better, so his daughters didn't feel the need to be looking after him. They both had beautiful times ahead, he felt sure of that, beautiful days without the baggage of yesterday. It was his job to relieve them of that baggage.

He wanted them to find happiness even if he never did. When he looked into Octavia's eyes, he saw way too much grief weighed down by a burden that he'd unloaded onto her. She was right, she was just fifteen and shouldn't be seeking to escape as he'd done. It wasn't right.

"You go to bed," he said, all the fight in him gone. He touched the side of her face with his hand, the softness of her skin pulling him back to the first time he'd done that the day she was born. "I'll clean this up."

"Goodnight, Daddy."

ೞ ೞ

Midnight was lying on her stomach on her bed; Samantha, who had come over just after lunch, was on her back on the floor, her head propped up on a pillow against the wall. Outside, a cool April rain fell hard against the window, sounding a little hollow and full of melancholy.

"He's been gone a long time," Samantha said. "So why do you

still have his picture on your wall?"

Midnight twisted her neck to look up at her wall to see what Sam was talking about, and then let out a loud sigh. "I have lots of pictures. My dad took them just before Tyler moved away so I wouldn't miss him."

"But that was three years ago."

"So?"

"We're eight and he's five in that picture," Samantha said. "It's kind of weird."

"I don't have new ones," Midnight said, stating the obvious that Samantha seemed to have missed. "So, I can't put a new one up on my wall."

"But *I'm* your best friend now."

Midnight was getting annoyed. Her mood matched the weather, and she really didn't feel like talking about Tyler's picture on her wall. Why did it bug Samantha so much? Tyler had been Midnight's friend, not Samantha's. If she wanted to leave his picture on her wall, she should be able to. The Christmas picture on her night table was even older and that didn't seem to bug Samantha.

"I'm bored," Midnight finally said. "I hate rain. Why did it have to rain today? I want to go play at the park."

Samantha pulled herself up and stared out the window. "I can barely see across the street."

Midnight stood beside her. She and Sam had been friends for three years so maybe she should put Tyler's picture away. Maybe she would feel the same as Sam if *she'd* had the picture of an old best friend on her bedroom wall. Maybe it would bug Midnight too.

"We're really best friends now," Midnight said and put her arm around Samantha's shoulder. "Best friends forever."

Samantha put her arm over Midnight's shoulder. "Best friends forever. Promise."

ꕥ

Jim just happened to be staring out the front window when Tracy Carmichael's car pulled into the driveway. Things had been quiet between him and Octavia, mostly because she'd stayed in her room all day, probably feeling like roadkill after last night, and he'd worked at the kitchen table all afternoon so that Midnight and Samantha could play in the basement. They were now upstairs in Midnight's room.

"Come in," he said after opening the door. "I saw you drive in," he added when he saw the look of surprise on her face.

"I hope the girls were good?" Tracy said.

"They got a little loud when they were playing in the basement, but they're quiet now. Sometimes that's worse."

"I recall my girls making a mess with paint they'd found in a jar in the basement a couple years ago. They were going to repaint the wall because it had marks on it, they said." She laughed and Jim thought it was a beautiful sound. "The fact that it was blue and the wall was beige didn't quite faze them. They were so proud when they showed me."

"I bet you were proud too."

"I was proud all right."

She laughed again and Jim felt his entire face smile. "How's Dave?"

Her features seemed to darken just a little. "He's fine.

Working lots. Still complains about being so far from downtown, from the office, but I'm glad to be out of that apartment. It had become way too small for the four of us. Nice to be back in the old neighbourhood. Even better for Sam and Midnight that we live so close."

"She's been a good friend," Jim said. "Midnight needed that."

"She's such a sweet girl," Tracy said. "She always includes Emily into their play when she comes over, even when Sam complains. I think she's been a positive influence on her."

Jim felt a tiny hand inside of him do a high five.

"I should call them down," he finally said, unable to take his eyes off of Tracy. He remembered her from school, back in the dark ages. She had been pretty, too pretty for him. And Dave had been the quarterback of the football team. They'd been the biggest cliché of high school. "I'll be right back."

"I'll be here."

He went to the bottom of the stairs and called up to the girls. A moment later, two pairs of feet raced down, sounding like a hundred elephants. The girls said goodbye, and Jim noticed Tracy looking at him a moment longer than necessary.

He didn't exactly hate the extra attention.

He gave her a little wave before closing the door.

SEVENTEEN

~ January 2002 ~

Tyler stared at his wrists. If he looked carefully, he could see a couple of tiny scars from his worst two cuts. Life in Washington had not always been pleasant, and at thirteen he'd thought that everything just sucked. Puberty hadn't been kind—his face had become a minefield of acne housing a mouthful of metal wires and tiny elastics. His highs and lows had been polar extremities that'd left him feeling confused, angry, and completely drained. He'd hated school, hated his teachers, hated his parents. He'd worn only black, dyed his hair black, and walked around in a black funk.

His world had been without light.

He'd heard about other kids cutting themselves and had decided to try it. But it had done nothing to ease his pain, and his anger and loneliness had gotten worse. Until that day just before he turned fifteen and thought he'd crossed the line. He'd needed stitches. His parents had freaked out on him, told him he was going to see a psychiatrist, and he'd fought with them about it. His first visit didn't do much, it seemed, but by his seventh, he began to notice that his moods weren't as dire. Actually talking to someone who didn't judge him but actually listened and made him feel like his problems mattered, slowly eased his despondency.

He'd started to feel less moody.

Less angry.

Less lonely.

Almost like a miracle—at least, to him it had felt that way—sprinkles of cheerfulness began to drop into his life as if out of nowhere, like a stranger that wasn't quite welcomed at first but soon became a best friend.

Tyler washed his hands, looked at himself in the mirror, and went to meet Midnight. She was still in the women's washroom so he waited. Not much else he could do. He checked his watched. They still had ten minutes.

Midnight came out of the washroom and a smile spread across his face and he felt something deep inside of him, something that he'd never felt for Monica.

Was that what real love felt like?

Could he be falling in love with Midnight so quickly? It wasn't like he'd just met her. They had a past together. Maybe he was just remembering that time they'd shared. Maybe it wasn't love . . . but if not that, then what was this burning sensation he felt running through him?

"That grin on your face is creeping me out," she said. "You okay?"

He didn't answer right away. He wondered if he deserved someone like Midnight. He didn't want to let her down. That must be love, real love. It just had to be.

"Tyler?"

"You're beautiful, Midnight."

And before she could say anything, he leaned in and pressed his lips against hers, and promised himself that he would do everything that he could to make sure he never disappointed her.

ℭ ℘

At first Midnight wasn't sure what was happening. Tyler was just standing there grinning at her, looking a bit weird, and then he was kissing her. It had happened so unexpectedly that her initial instinct was to pull away, but then she liked the taste of his lips—sort of minty, like the gum he'd been chewing—and she pressed her lips harder against his.

They parted and stood in the middle of the aisle, people having to go around them. She looked up into his penetrating blue eyes, and her entire face lit up.

"That was nice," she said.

"You have no idea."

"Well, duh, I was sort of there."

He made a gesture with his upper body that seemed to indicate how relieved he was. "I meant, you have no idea how nervous I've been all day about tonight. I've wanted to kiss you like, for days, but wasn't sure if I was going to be able to do it."

"And you did it just fine."

Neither was able to look away.

"Guess we should go," he finally said. "The movie is about to start and we'll probably have crappy seats."

"Probably but you're forgetting the most important thing about going to the movies," she said.

He looked at her with a frown.

"Popcorn," she said. "We need a large bag of popcorn and drinks."

"Oh crap!" he said. "How dumb can I be? Of course we need popcorn. What drink do you want?"

"Diet Coke," she said. "You get those and I'll get seats."

Tyler headed to the concession stand while Midnight grabbed a couple of seats. She was able to find two in the third row from the top, and Tyler joined her just as the lights were dimming.

"Good seats," he said. "I was sure we'd be stuck down in the front row."

"I got a couple people to move and voilà, two seats with our names on them."

"Midnight Madison, you're something else," he said.

She popped a few kernels into her mouth. "Glad you noticed, finally."

☙ ❧

The movie ended just after midnight and they stood in the lobby, lost in a sea of teenagers. Some headed to the games area to get in a few turns before the theater closed. Others were gathering to make plans, call for rides, say goodnight. Tyler and Midnight weren't quite ready for that. They wanted to talk about the movie, talk about what was happening between them, just talk about anything and everything.

"I can't wait to drive," Tyler said. "Kind of sucks that I have to call my parents to come and get us."

"We could walk over to Tim's first and get something to eat," she said. "I'm sort of hungry."

"After you practically ate that entire bag of popcorn by yourself?"

She jabbed him in the ribs with her elbow. "I let you have some."

"I thought you were going to eat my hand every time I tried to get some."

"I like my popcorn."

"Next time, I'm getting two bags."

"That'll be nice."

"Yeah, it will be," he said. "Ready? It's cold outside."

Midnight pulled her dad's Ottawa Senator's hat from her pocket and put it on, then slipped her hands into leather gloves. "Ready."

"You look so cute."

"And warm. Where's your hat?"

"Kind of don't have one," he said. "Didn't need one in Washington."

"You'll need one here," Midnight said and took his hand. "Let's go before they kick us out of this place."

Three minutes later they were inside the Tim Hortons, and had ordered two hot chocolates, a carrot cake muffin for Midnight and a giant double chocolate chip cookie for Tyler.

"I'll call home and tell them to pick us up here," Tyler said and pulled a cell phone from his pocket.

"Seems like everyone is getting cell phones these days," Midnight said and took a bite of her muffin.

"My mom wanted to know where I was at all times back in Washington," Tyler said and popped a piece of cookie into his mouth. "I kind of feel lost without it now."

Midnight finished her muffin while Tyler phoned home.

"Guess my dad was sleeping," he said. "He'll be here in fifteen or so."

Midnight took a sip of her drink. "How's your cookie?"

"Oh no you don't."

She made a pouty face.

"That is so not you," he said. "You're just not one of those girls."

"So what sort am I?"

He bit a chunk off. "I don't know, but you're not the sucky kind or the princess diva. You're just a lot better."

"Was your old girlfriend one of those girls?"

"She could be," he said. "A lot of the times when she wasn't getting her way. It really annoyed me sometimes now that I think about it."

"Just sometimes?"

"It doesn't matter because she's ancient history," he said, holding her gaze. "I'd rather concentrate on you."

"You would, huh?"

Tyler tore the remainder of his cookie in two, popped half in his mouth and then went to give Midnight the rest but she shook her head.

"I don't want to be one of those needy girlfriends," she said. "Besides, I'm full and probably don't need more sugar."

"Girlfriend?"

She bit the inside of her mouth and looked away. There were just a few people inside the fast food place—a group of five girls at one end, three guys sitting nearby and getting nowhere with them, and another couple in their twenties three tables over.

Tim's closed at one a.m. Tyler's dad would be here soon.

"You know what I meant."

"So you *don't* want to be my girlfriend?"

A twinkle filled her eyes. "Do you want me to be?"

"So we're going to play that game."

"What game is that?"

He laughed quietly. "I've missed you. I never realized it until now. So yeah, I'd like you to be my girlfriend if you want."

Midnight took another sip of hot chocolate. Apparently, the boys had scored now and joined the group of girls. That had never been her thing. Even when she did go out with Samantha, she never got into the group flirting thing.

But she seemed to be flirting just fine tonight. Maybe it was a matter of finding the right boy to flirt with.

The boy she'd lost.

The boy she'd been waiting for.

The boy she'd loved always.

"My dad is here," Tyler said.

They stood. Midnight grabbed his hand and moved in close. She kissed him softly.

"Yes, I'd like that," she said.

ଓ ஐ

Tyler lay in bed, wide awake, the clock inching closer to two in the morning. He couldn't settle down, his thoughts revisiting each moment of his date with Midnight. Every time they'd held hands he'd felt a little jolt, every time he'd heard her laugh his heart had swelled with desire, and every time their lips had touched . . . well, he could just do that all day. More than once, he'd been totally lost staring into her eyes, like he was looking at two priceless gems that had the power to destroy him.

It was a little scary.

He got up and paced. Had she had as great a time as him? What if she hadn't? What if she didn't feel the same about him as he did about her? What if, what if, what if?

Get a grip.

She had said yes, hadn't she? She wanted to be his girlfriend, and they had kissed like they were a couple. She made him feel completely vulnerable. God! He couldn't wait to see her again. Is this what falling in love was like?

No.

This was what falling off a cliff must feel like. It was bloody terrifying, heart-pounding exhilarating, and mind-blowing insane.

He was falling in love so *hard*.

☙ ❧

Midnight started up the stairs and saw the light in her dad's room turn off. A tiny smile appeared on her lips. No matter what demons he fought every day, he was a dad with a golden heart.

"Goodnight, Dad."

"Night sweetie."

She washed up, brushed her teeth, and did a quick test. With everything they'd just eaten, she was relieved when her reading showed her blood glucose was higher than it should be, but still below where she would need insulin. Content, she turned off the bathroom light and slipped into the warm comfort of her bed. She was tired. It had been a long day, first at the hospital and then out with Tyler.

Her face ached she was smiling so much.

When's the last time she'd had a day like today? Couldn't really remember one. This was what being really happy felt like. She was sure of that. It was so new to her.

That was sort of sad.

She knew it was her fault for turning everyone, almost everyone, away. It was difficult sometimes to let people in, to ignore the fear of the potential disappointment. Samantha had seen through her shield, obviously, and for that she loved her.

And tonight, another person had penetrated her shield; tonight had reminded her that something else had been missing in her life, a void she hadn't realized was there. It had taken the boy she'd once loved to come back into her life to awaken her, the same boy she knew she was falling in love with all over again.

Her heart felt so big inside her chest that she was afraid it might rupture. *Not yet*, she thought. *I want to kiss him a few million times more.*

At least.

EIGHTEEN

~ May 1996 ~

Samantha could hear them arguing again. Her room shared a wall with her parents' room, and even though they were trying to keep it down, she could tell that her dad was pissed off with her mom. She didn't understand everything that was being said—some words were muffled, others were lost in her mom's sobs—but most she heard as if she was in the room with them.

She couldn't remember them fighting when they lived in the small apartment. Her mom and dad seemed happy then, laughing and kissing all the time, spending lots of time playing with her and Emily. Now her dad was always working and when he came home he was always too tired to play. That was one thing her mom was telling him right now, how he never had time for anyone, especially the girls. They weren't going to stay little forever, Samantha was already ten and in a few more years she probably wouldn't want to spend any time with her parents.

Samantha heard a door slam, probably the door to the bathroom in her parents' room, and then the shower was running and she couldn't hear anything except for the water rushing through the pipes inside her wall.

And her mom crying.

She looked at the clock on her night table: 10:03 pm. She should be asleep, and she probably had been until she got woken up by their shouting. She slipped out from under the blankets, grabbed her glasses, and knocked on her mom's door. It was locked so she couldn't just walk in.

"Hey honey," her mom said while still wiping her eyes. "You should be sleeping."

"I had a bad dream," Samantha lied. She didn't want her mom to know she'd heard them. "Did you have a bad dream too?"

"No," Tracy said after hesitating just for a second. "Let me tuck you back in."

☙ ❧

After putting Samantha back to bed and checking on Emily, Tracy Carmichael went down to the kitchen, found a bottle of whiskey in the cupboard, poured herself three fingers worth, and knocked it back. She took a cigarette from her purse that was on the counter and went out onto the deck to smoke. She should quit these damn things, but right now wasn't a good time. Right now, she needed the nicotine to calm her. She and Dave were having way too many fights. Where had all the love they'd had gone? Where was the man she'd married?

To be truthful, that man hadn't seemed to have moved with them. She couldn't pinpoint exactly when things had started to go astray, but maybe it was after Emily was born and she'd started to suggest that they should find a house to move to, that it would be nice for the girls to have a back yard to play in. She'd grown tired of living downtown where it was loud and busy almost all the time.

Tracy had grown up. High school was too far back to actually remember, and her daughters had become her life. She loved being a mother, loved taking care of them, loved to see the little challenges they conquered every day. It brought joy to her heart when she saw them succeed, but more so, when the delight on their faces glowed with that triumph. She could never have guessed that motherhood would be so rewarding and fulfilling, and although Dave had hinted that if she got a job then they'd probably have a better standard of living, she hadn't wanted to give up her children's upbringing to a stranger.

Dave didn't understand that. He'd become obsessed with money, with the idea that they needed more of it, that somehow he'd find his happiness again if he could just make a few more dollars. The fact that childcare would be expensive and might take most if not all that she earned didn't stop him from thinking that they'd still be ahead of the game; even if they were left with just a few thousand dollars more a year, it was a few more than they had now.

She finished her cigarette and dropped it into the sand-filled aluminum can that she kept out on the deck railing. It probably once had diced tomatoes in it, or maybe red kidney beans. It was now full of butts—too many. She would have to empty it.

The evening was warm for the middle of May. She could hear the rushing of traffic out on Greenfield Road, people coming and going, people with happier lives. Her eyes wandered into the night, aimed in a certain direction.

Maybe not everyone had happier lives.

The kids' bathing suits were hanging over the railing along with towels. The day had been hot enough for Samantha and Emily to want to run through the sprinkler. Remembering them play in the water brought a smile back to her lips. Midnight had come over and the three girls had had fun. She sometimes wished she'd had another child, but she knew that wouldn't happen now. Dave had made sure of that.

Midnight was such a sweet girl.

Again her eyes wandered in the direction of their house, and her thoughts started to go where they shouldn't be going. She had her own family to care for, her own marriage to fix. After all, she and Dave had been voted the most likely to marry and live happily ever after.

I guess it depends on your definition of happily ever after.

ശ ഇ

Samantha was old enough to ride her bike over to Midnight's now, not needing her mom to drive her. It was really just a couple of streets away, but her mom made her call her as soon as she got to her friend's house.

Which she did.

Then she and Midnight went over to the park to play on the play structure. Lately they'd taken to climbing on top of the roof of the little playhouse, just like all the big kids did. The first time, Samantha had been pretty scared, but now she did it with barely a second thought.

"What do you think being a teenager will be like?" she said.

Midnight gave it some thought. "Octavia goes out a lot and

can come home late. She has a new boyfriend now and my dad likes him. His name is Mark. He said Octavia has settled down since she met him." She looked at Samantha. "I don't know what he means."

Samantha shrugged. "Does she kiss him?"

"I've seen them, when they're sitting on the couch watching TV and don't notice me." She rolled her eyes. "They French-kiss."

"What's that?"

Midnight explained it.

"Sounds kind of gross," Samantha said. "I don't think I'd let a boy do that."

"Me either."

They sat on top of the playhouse in silence for a bit. Out in the field a group of boys played soccer, a man threw a Frisbee for his dog to fetch, and a girl and a boy a little younger than them were riding their bikes.

"My parents were fighting again last night."

Midnight looked at Samantha, squinting because the sun was behind Sam and blinded her. "Grownups do that. My dad and Octavia used to fight too."

"But they stopped?"

"Yeah," Midnight said. "Maybe that's what my dad meant."

"Octavia isn't a grownup yet, and she's not married to your dad," Samantha said. "It's not the same as my mom and dad fighting."

"I suppose," she said. "What do they fight about?"

"Money. Work. Never spending time with me and Emily."

"Oh."

Again they sat in silence, watching the world unfold below. Toddlers were playing in the sandbox and a mom was pushing a young girl on the baby swing.

"Did your mom and dad fight a lot?"

Midnight shook her head. "I don't know. I don't remember her."

"What if my mom leaves too?" Samantha said with obvious concern. "I don't want my mom to leave."

☙ ❧

Midnight watched Samantha ride away, glanced at the house next door and saw Snow run up to her. She crouched down and patted the dog before Mrs. Petrovich came to retrieve her.

"I figured she'd be with you," Mrs. Petrovich said in her thick accent. "She likes you very much."

"She's cute," Midnight said. "I like her too. Her tongue feels funny when she licks my fingers. Sort of tickles."

Mrs. Petrovich gathered the small dog into her hands and gave Midnight a sweet smile. "Goodbye, dear."

"Bye."

Midnight looked the other way, the way Samantha had gone, a hint of sadness in her heart. She hoped that Samantha's mom wouldn't leave either. She liked Samantha's mom. She was always so nice to her, and Midnight liked that she was nice to her.

NINETEEN

~ February 2002 ~

The first Monday of February was a wonderful day, sunny and not too cold, in complete contrast to how Midnight and Tyler's relationship was going: definitely heating up. She'd never been happier, so when she saw Samantha in the minivan when Mrs. Carmichael picked her up, it felt like things couldn't get any better.

"You little sneak," Midnight said. "Why didn't you tell me you were coming to school today?"

"I wanted to surprise you," Samantha said, sitting in the seat behind her mom instead of her usual spot in the front passenger seat. "I was getting bored at home."

"I think she chose school over another week of physiotherapy," Mrs. Carmichael said.

"Another week with Drill Sergeant Michel wasn't happening," Samantha said.

"He wanted you to get back on your feet," Mrs. Carmichael said. "Which he did."

"He didn't need to try and kill me," Samantha said.

"Oh, stop whining," Emily said, turning to look at her sister. "You had such a crush on him. *Oh Michel please, I can't. Oh Michel please, I'm so tired. Oh Michel please*, blah, blah, blah," Emily said, pretending to shove a finger down her throat.

"You're such a pain," Samantha said.

"*You're* such a pain," Emily said.

"Girls," Mrs. Carmichael said.

"But it's so true," Emily said.

"Sweetheart," Mrs. Carmichael said, "just let it be."

"Ever since her stupid accident, you treat her like a baby,"

"Emily, that's enough."

She folded her arms and faced forward.

"So how was your latest date?" Samantha said to Midnight. "How many has it been? Three? Four?"

"Four," she said and blushed a little. "And it's been really nice."

"You are so done," Samantha said, obviously relishing what was happening to her friend. "You're glowing, like, big time."

Midnight couldn't say anything.

"So, what did you and Tyler do Saturday night?" Samantha said.

"Not much really," she said and her face seemed to saddened. "We grabbed a pizza and hung out at my place, watching movies."

"Really?"

Midnight nodded. "I was too tired after my day at the hospital. It wasn't a good day. Remember little Lily?"

Samantha put a hand to her mouth. "I'm so sorry. I know you'd become close to her."

Midnight had a hard time swallowing. "She took a turn for the worse after getting a cold the week before last." Tears stung her eyes. "And she was gone when I got there Saturday. It was hard to be cheerful for the other kids. I almost cancelled on Tyler, but he really got what I was going through and hanging out together helped."

Silence filled the minivan.

"I'm sorry," Mrs. Carmichael said eventually.

"Thank you," Midnight said. "She was so young. It doesn't seem very fair. We should all try to enjoy every day because we just never know."

Samantha reached over and took hold of Midnight's hand. "After my accident, when I thought I would never walk, I wanted to die. But I'm glad I didn't. I understand how precious life is. How precious our friendship is."

Midnight returned Samantha's gaze. "Yes, it is."

"You know, I haven't seen Julie and Kim in months. Haven't spoken to them on the phone. I really don't miss them. You, I miss a lot when we don't talk every day. Almost called you yesterday, but since I'd decided I'd be back at school today, I figured we'd catch up then. Just don't ditch me because of Tyler."

"He's looking forward to meeting you."

"Right," Samantha said. "I've actually never met him, yet I feel like I've known him all my life."

They dropped off Emily and a few minutes later arrived at school. There was a big crowd of kids but Midnight managed to spot Tyler and immediately she felt better.

"Need any help?" Mrs. Carmichael said.

Samantha shook her head. "I can manage."

"Don't forget your cane."

"Seriously, Mom, I can't use that."

"I'll bring it," Midnight said. "Just in case."

"Thanks, Midnight," Mrs. Carmichael said.

"I'm not going to use that."

"Probably not," Midnight said and stepped out of the minivan. "Let me help you out."

Samantha took hold of Midnight's hand and climbed down. "Well, this place hasn't changed a bit."

"It's only been four months," Midnight said and grabbed her backpack and Samantha's, along with the cane. "Thanks, Mrs. Carmichael."

"All good?"

"All good."

With a final concerned glance at her daughter, Mrs. Carmichael drove away. "It'll be nice to be away from my mom a bit. As much for her as for me. She's been a bit clingy."

"She's a mom and she loves you."

"I know, but I'm fine," Samantha said trying to find her balance. "It stills hurts to put too much weight on my leg, but it's better than it was."

"Ready then?"

She looked around. "Not surprised to see those two hanging back. Wait until they see me walk. That should clear them out."

"Don't worry about Kim and Julie," Midnight said. She looked Tyler's way and gave him an eye signal that it was fine to come over. "You'll be back to yourself soon."

They started walking toward the school entrance, Samantha wincing as she got going. Although she was mobile, she didn't have the same fluid stride as before. She didn't look unsteady, like a toddler learning to walk, but it was going to be a little while before she got back to normal.

"Can I help?" Tyler said when he came up behind them and stood to Samantha's left.

"No," Samantha said. "We're fine."

"Hey Tyler," Midnight said, sounding as if she hadn't seen him already. "This is my friend Samantha. Samantha, this is Tyler."

"Oh, so you're *Tyler*," Samantha said, then looked at Midnight and mouthed *OMG!*

ꕥ

The three of them stood out in the cold for a moment as they got acquainted, but the frigid temperature moved them along. Tyler took Samantha's backpack from Midnight, and then offered his arm to Samantha.

"Wow! Such a gentleman," Samantha said.

"Since when do you speak that way?"

"I've been watching a lot of old movies lately," she said with a fake flip of her hair. "After my physiotherapist leaves for the day. Those old black and white films are pretty good. Men were gentlemen back then."

"I hate to say this," Midnight said, "but that accident might have been the best thing that happened to you."

A confused look spread across Tyler's face.

"Samantha had become a bit of a rich snot."

A denial died on Samantha's tongue. "I guess you're probably right. I think it was the new lifestyle."

Again, Tyler looked confused.

"Her dad made a lot of money a few years ago and they moved to this mansion out on Cedarview."

"Oh," he said.

Samantha reached over and grabbed Midnight's hand. "But with everything that's happened, we're better then ever. Like sisters."

The two girls laughed.

"My mom has a thing for her dad, I think," Samantha said. "My parents are separated."

"I think Midnight told me that," he said.

Midnight couldn't remember what she'd told him about Samantha. But Sam had been a big part of their conversation. She'd wanted him to like her. She'd wanted her two best friends to really like each other.

"My mom still hopes your dad will take her up on dinner," Samantha said. "What do you think, sis?"

Midnight pulled the door open and Tyler led the way with Samantha at his arm.

"We have plenty of rooms," Samantha said without missing a beat. "I think it would be cool to have you as a sister."

"Don't pay attention to her," Midnight said. "I think she took too many painkillers this morning."

"They do make me a bit woozy," Samantha said. "I guess we should make our way to the office so I can get my schedule."

"Good idea," Midnight said. "I'll hang with her if you want to head to class," she said to Tyler.

"Sure," he said and leaned in for a kiss before heading away.

"Tyler?" Samantha said.

He turned.

"I've never seen Midnight this happy in all the years I've known her, so whatever you're doing, keep doing it. My best friend deserves it."

Tyler smiled. "I'll see you two at lunch."

"I like him," Samantha said when he was gone. "He's good for you."

Midnight watched Tyler climb the stairs. "Yeah, I like him too. A lot more than I could have imagined. It still seems surreal that he's back. I sometimes think I'll wake up from this dream and he'll be gone. Ouch! Why'd you do that?"

"You're not dreaming," Samantha said. "It's all real."

"Let's get your schedule before we're late."

☙ ❧

When Midnight got home, her dad and sister were sitting at the kitchen table, which was sort of strange since Octavia should have been at work. Midnight took a cautious step.

"What's going on?" she said.

"Your sister decided to drop by and say hello."

"Shouldn't you be at work?"

There was a glow in Octavia's eyes that Midnight had never seen before. She frowned, dropped her backpack on the floor, and took a seat. She sat on the edge. Something was up.

"I had a doctor's appointment."

"Are you all right?" Midnight said, the fear rising in her throat instantly. "You're not sick, are you?"

"No, I'm fine."

"Relax, sweetie," Jim said. "Octavia has some really good

news."

She chewed the inside of her mouth. "So?"

"How do you like the idea of becoming an aunt?"

Midnight stared at Octavia, then glanced at her dad, who had the biggest grin she'd ever seen, then looked at her sister again. The middle of her forehead had that crease she got when thinking deeply. And then it hit her.

"You're pregnant?"

Octavia nodded. "Eight weeks."

"And you're just telling us now?"

"I wanted to make sure," Octavia said. "We haven't even told Mark's parents yet, but after today, I couldn't keep it a secret from you two any longer."

"Wow!" Midnight said and jumped to her feet and wrapped her arms around her sister. "Does this mean you'll get married?"

"No," Octavia said. "It's not in our immediate plans. We know we love each other."

"Wow!" Midnight said again and straightened up. "You're going to be a mom! You're going to make a great mom. I should know."

"Thanks," Octavia said. "It wasn't quite planned, but I'm really happy nonetheless."

Jim put a hand over Octavia's. "You are going to be a wonderful mother. I have no doubt."

"So, Grandpa," Midnight said. "How's that sound?"

"Pretty darn good," he said.

"What's Mark say?"

"He's really thrilled," Octavia said. "He wants a big family. Being an only child, he wants four kids."

Midnight was standing in the middle of the kitchen, her hands clasped, practically jumping on the spot like a little kid. "First Tyler comes back, and now I'm going to be an aunt. This is awesome."

"This family has earned a bit of happiness," Jim said.

"Speaking of which," Midnight said, "Mrs. Carmichael is still waiting for that dinner date."

"Isn't that your friend's mom?" Octavia said.

Midnight nodded.

"Dad? A date?" Octavia said. "That's great."

"Just hold on, you two," he said. "I never agreed to any dinner date. Did I?"

"Remember at Christmas when we went over to their place?"

Jim scratched his chin. "Well, Tracy and I talked about a lot of things. I do remember we joked about going out to dinner but I assumed . . . did I assumed wrong?"

"What's the harm?" Octavia said. "It's just dinner. Nothing wrong with an evening out. It'll do you good."

"I have no idea how you two do this, but we were celebrating you being pregnant and now you've got me going on a date with Tracy Carmichael."

"It's not like you don't know her," Midnight said. "You did go to school with her. And from what I've found out from Sam, she had an eye on you back then."

Jim shook his head. "I doubt that. Her and Dave—" He paused. "Well, guess that didn't work out, now did it? Besides, won't this be weird for you and Samantha?"

Midnight shrugged. "It's just dinner, Dad. Think of it as part of your therapy."

"Therapy?" Octavia said.

"Dad's been seeing a psychologist now for a few weeks and doing really great." She gave her sister a look that they both understood. "And he's lost a few pounds and cut back a lot on drinking too."

"Wow!" Octavia said. "This year *is* looking good for the Madison family."

"Don't blow Mrs. Carmichael off because of me and Samantha," Midnight said. "She's actually a really nice person."

"I did enjoy her company at Christmas." Jim scratched the back of his neck and gave a nervous laugh. "It's a little scary, you know? Dating at my age."

"You're not old," Midnight said.

"You've got a lot to offer," Octavia added.

They all looked at each other.

"I understand what you're both saying," Jim said, looking as uncomfortable as a grown man could while having this sort of discussion with his daughters. "I know it's long overdue. I'm getting there."

"*There* has arrived," Octavia said. "Seize it."

"Look who's the parent now," Jim said. "Gosh! You're going to be a mother."

"And I'm going to be an aunt. I've got to tell Tyler and Samantha." Midnight grabbed the cordless phone and headed out of the kitchen.

"Guess she's thrilled," Octavia said.

"I know I am," Jim said. "I'm going to be a grandfather. Seems not that long ago you fit in the crook of my arm. It'll be nice to get to hold a baby again."

"I can't wait."

TWENTY

~ June 1998 ~

Midnight looked at Samantha, then at the cigarettes in her hand, then at Samantha again. The features of her face turned hard. "Are you insane?"

"I took them from my mom's purse," Samantha said, sounding like she'd found gold. "Wanna try?"

"Hello!" Midnight said, the anger in her voice like a runaway train. "You do remember that I was very sick when I was young, before I met you, right?"

"But you're fine now."

"And I want to stay fine." Midnight crossed her arms and froze her friend with her glare. They were out in the school yard, as far away from anyone as they could be and still be on school property. The early June sun beat down on them as the last days of grade six drew nearer.

"God! You're becoming really boring. You never want to have fun anymore."

"I like to have fun," Midnight said in her defence. "But not *that* kind of fun. What's fun about smoking anyway? Just last year you used to complain how you hated it when your mom smoked because she stunk."

"Yeah, well . . . that was last year. Cool kids smoke."

Midnight pressed her lips into a thin, disapproving line. "*Dumb* kids smoke."

"Vicky Barnes. Justine Lemieux. Hilary Webley."

"And I should care about those stupid girls why?" Midnight said. "Don't tell me you think they're cool."

"All the guys hang with them," Samantha said and pushed her glasses up her nose. "I hate these stupid things. I've got to get contacts."

"Why all the concern about how you look all of a sudden?"

"Look at me. I'm skinny, I have zero curves, I wear glasses, and have metal in my mouth. I would like to have guys look at me someday and not gross them out. Don't you?"

Midnight simply shrugged.

"You know that he's never coming back," she said.

"You don't know that."

"And even if he does, do you really think you two would be friends again? He's probably changed. He's not five years old anymore and neither are you. You should be looking at hot guys like Kim's brother Derek."

Midnight rolled her eyes. "He's in high school."

"We'll be in high school next year too," Samantha said. "I'm friends with Kim now and I've been over to her place a few times."

"Really?"

"I like her. She's fun."

"You never used to think so."

"Well . . . I do now."

Midnight scoffed. "Whatever. I'm sure he's not interested in you anyway."

"Maybe not," Samantha said and pushed her glasses up her nose again, "but at least he's here, not a million miles away."

"Tyler's not—"

"You're hopeless," Samantha said. "Tyler moved away. He's probably never coming back. Move on and have some fun."

"So we should act stupid now? That's your idea of fun?"

"You're so annoying," Samantha said. "They're just cigarettes. Smoking one cigarette won't kill you."

"Do what you want, but I'm not smoking those."

"Whatever."

Samantha stuck one of the cigarettes into her mouth and lit it with the lighter she had also taken from her mom's purse. There'd been two in there, so Samantha figured her mom wouldn't miss this one.

"Are you a complete idiot?" Midnight said and attempted to swat the cigarettes from Samantha's mouth but missed. "If you get caught, you'll be expelled."

Samantha snorted as she inhaled and began coughing. "We have like a week left, so who cares? We're never coming back to this school. Next year we're in high school."

She took a long drag and this time held her own. This wasn't the first cigarette she'd taken from her mom.

"We're just going into grade seven."

"Still, I can't wait," Samantha said. "Finally, we'll be teenagers. Teenage boys are so much better, more mature than those." She pointed at a group of boys playing touch football.

Midnight rolled her eyes again. "First off, we're still gonna be just twelve. Not teenagers."

"Blah, blah, blah."

"And second, who says any teenage boy is gonna want to hang with us?"

"If you put out they will," Samantha said as she finished the cigarette and crushed it underneath her foot. "I've made out before. Have you?"

Midnight had nothing to say.

"We French-kissed and everything," Samantha said, trying to make herself sound like she'd done it a bunch of times, like every twelve-year-old should know how to do that.

"What exactly is *everything*?"

"You know," Samantha said and let her hands air-touch her non-existent breasts. "Everything."

"Who are you?" Midnight said in disgust. "What have you done with my friend?"

"Oh come on, Midnight," Samantha said with a flare of superiority. "Grow up, why don't you. We're going to be in high school in September and if you want to fit in, you gotta do what the older kids do. Simple as that."

Midnight shook her head. "If that's what I have to do, then maybe I don't care if I fit in or not. I'm not going to become a smoking slut just to show I belong. That's just dumb. D-U-M-B."

"I know how to spell," Samantha said. "And I'm not dumb."

"Could have fooled me."

"Arggg . . ." Samantha said. "Maybe I'll just hang out with Julie and Kim. They look like they'd be fun."

Midnight scoffed again. "D-U-M-B is spelled J-U-L-I-E."

"Oh, you're acting like a total B," Samantha said.

"So are *you*."

The two friends stood no more than a couple feet apart, eyeing each other. It was a beautiful sunny afternoon with the birds flying high above and the promise of a wonderful summer just on the horizon, but neither noticed.

"I didn't know you were so stuck up."

"And I thought you had some common sense."

"I do. I'm not the Virgin Mary, is all."

Midnight's jaw dropped. "You've had sex?"

Samantha didn't say anything.

"I really don't know you anymore." Midnight turned and walked away. "I thought you were my best friend."

"And I thought you were *my* best friend," Samantha said.

Midnight stopped and glanced back at Sam. "You *were*. This Samantha, I don't care to be friends with."

"Whatever," Samantha said. "Just go hang with the losers."

Midnight walked away and didn't turn. She didn't want Samantha to see the pain in her eyes and the disappointment on her face. Why did everyone she cared about leave her? Was it her fault? Did she push them away? Was she too hard, her expectations too high?

Was she not worth their friendship, their love?

TWENTY-ONE

~ February 2002 ~

Midnight woke up around five on the second Monday of February, her bones and joints aching in places she hadn't known she had, and a chill covering her like a sheet of ice. She felt her tonsils and she was sure they were the size of baseballs.

Nausea rose up and down her throat like crashing ocean waves.

She kicked back the blankets and hurried to the bathroom, barely making it to the toilet before last night's dinner was given its eviction notice. The back of her throat was coated with burning bile that caused her to vomit a second time.

The third time was a gut-wrenching dry heave that took the last of her strength. She wiped her mouth with toilet paper and flushed the whole mess away. Her watery legs gave out and she grabbed the counter edge.

"Oh, honey, let me help you." Jim steadied her by taking her upper arm, and walked her back to bed. "I'll call the school and Sam's mom in a couple of hours. You just get some rest."

"Thanks," Midnight said quietly. "I was feeling fine last night."

"Every winter you get the flu at least once. I remember the first few times you got sick after your battle. Off to the hospital we went each time, like the paranoid dad I'd become." He felt her forehead. "You probably pushed yourself a bit too much between Tyler, school, and the hospital. You might have caught the flu there. Let's hope you get over it quickly."

He went to the linen closet to grab an extra blanket and took a small plastic bucket from under the bathroom sink. When he returned, Midnight was already asleep.

He covered her with the blanket and put the bucket on the floor, within arm's reach.

Around 7:00 a.m., Jim phoned the school and left a message that Midnight would be off a few days, and then he called Tracy Carmichael. As routine as the call should be, he had to take a breath before dialing.

"It's Jim," he said, certain his voice sounded like he was going through puberty again. "I just want to tell you that Midnight is sick with the flu so you don't need to pick her up."

"Oh no! Poor thing."

"I'm sure a few days of rest is all she needs," he said. "She usually bounces back fairly quickly, considering . . ."

"Yes, she does," Tracy said. "I'm sure she'll be back on her feet in no time."

There was a silence between them, not uncomfortable, more of a pause before moving on to something else.

"I had a really good time Saturday night," he said. "I . . . I haven't laughed like that since Christmas. Must be the company."

"It was good to hear you laugh," she said. "And I'm glad I didn't scare you off."

"I was a little uneasy at first." He paused. "I'm a little rusty, and I didn't know if . . . well, I hope I wasn't a bad date."

"I was little nervous too," she said. "And you were quite a nice date. A real gentleman."

Jim felt the tightness in his chest ease. "I'd better let you go. I'm sure you need to get ready to drive the girls."

"If you need anything, don't hesitate to call," Tracy said. "I can come over any time if you want. I've had a bit of practice with sick kids."

"Unfortunately, so have I."

Another silence followed, as if neither wanted the conversation to end. Jim hadn't felt like a schoolboy in decades, and he didn't exactly hate the awkwardness. Well, maybe a little, but it was also exhilarating.

"Let me know how she's doing," Tracy finally said.

"I will," Jim said. "I'll call you later."

☙ ❧

In her dream, Tyler had never moved. But their friendship had dwindled over time and now they barely spoke. Their troubles had started around the age of ten, when Tyler had needed to play with other boys because playing with Midnight no longer challenged him. Playing with her had become a bore and he'd told her so. It was time for her to find new friends. Girl friends.

At school, he totally ignored her, pretending he didn't even know her. On the bus, they no longer sat together. In fact, Tyler now sat with their old nemesis, Bradley Eriksson. And when Bradley ridiculed her, Tyler didn't try to stop him.

He just looked away.

What had she done?

Why had he become so aloof?

It hurt.

A lot.

Not in a physical sense, but much worse. A broken heart was like nothing she had experienced before. She could barely breathe, think, eat.

She wanted to die.

She felt ill.

Something rose in her throat.

God! She was going to throw up . . .

Midnight grabbed the bucket her father had left on the floor by her bed and retched. Not much came out. She'd pretty much emptied her stomach earlier.

Everything ached.

Her eyes seemed to roll as she tried to focus on the clock beside her bed. The red numbers glowed. 7:17. Was it morning or evening? How long had she slept? Her pyjamas were drenched and clung to her like a cold wet film, giving her the shivers. She needed to change but didn't have the energy to get out of bed.

She was so thirsty.

Something came into her room but she couldn't see what it was until a cat jumped on the end of her bed and meowed. Bugs the second. The first Bugs had died when Midnight was ten. After a little coaxing and promises that she would take care of a new cat, her dad had caved.

"Bugs," she said. "You never come upstairs."

The cat meowed again, jumped off the bed, and waited by the door.

"You hungry?"

Another meow.

Reluctantly she pulled back the blankets and shuffled across her room. She stood at the top of the stairs and held on to the railing while a dizzy spell passed.

"Dad," she called down.

She heard him make his way to the bottom of the stairs. "How are you feeling?"

"Tired, but I think my fever broke." Her mouth was pasty. "Bugs needs to be fed. Can you do it? And check his litter."

"Right," he said. "Slipped my mind. Hadn't seen him all day."

"I'm going to take a hot shower," she said

"Probably do you good," Jim said. "And I'll take care of Bugs."

Midnight stood under the nearly scalding water for a good fifteen minutes, and as she stepped out of the tub, her dad knocked on the bathroom door.

"Someone on the phone for you."

Midnight wrapped herself in a towel and opened the door a bit, letting steam out. "Samantha? Tell her I'll call her back."

Jim handed her the phone. "Tyler."

The smile that normally lit her face died before it reached her lips. The shower had felt good but had done little to remove her weariness. She closed the door and sat on the toilet seat lid. "Hey Tyler."

"How are you feeling?"

"Achy and tired."

"I missed you today," he said. "I felt a little lost without you."

"Good," she said. "I've missed you too."

"You sound exhausted," he said. "I just wanted to hear your voice. I'll let you go so you can rest." He paused. "I love you."

She started to shake. "I love you too."

☙ ❧

After she hung up, Midnight put the phone down on the counter and had she felt better, she would have danced. Instead, she sat on the toilet seat lid feeling a little numb.

I love you.

Tyler had really said those words to her, and she'd said them back. Too bad she was sick. The moment didn't quite have the fireworks it deserved. Had she felt better, she'd be getting her dad to drive her to Tyler's house so she could jump into his arms and kiss him.

A tiny smile pulled itself from her weariness. They were a couple, a real couple in love. Wow! It had happened so suddenly that she wasn't sure if it had really happened.

Ten years.

That's how long she'd waited to fall in love. Ten long years. She needed to get better fast. No more time to waste. Her heart ached from his absence, her lips hungered to feel his lips pressed against them, her cold body longed to feel the warmth of his arms around her.

I love you.

Those three little words gave her the boost of energy she

needed to dry off and slip into a fresh pair of pyjamas. As quickly as it had come, it was gone. Her congestion returned, the effects of the hot shower faded, and she felt weak again. The bathroom seemed to be spinning and she waited for the moment to pass. Then she dragged herself back to bed.

"Hey honey," Jim said and put a bowl of chicken noodle soup on her night table. "Not sure if you feel up to it but you haven't eaten anything since last night."

Midnight looked at the soup. "I wish I could."

"I'll leave it here." He felt her forehead. "A little warm, but not horrible."

She wanted to tell her dad what Tyler had said, share her moment, but she was falling asleep. "Tired."

"Just rest," he said and left her room.

Midnight woke up the next morning not feeling any better and her fever had returned overnight. She stayed home. Wednesday seemed worse and she had her first nosebleed in two months, long enough that she'd forgotten about them. Or conveniently dismissed. She couldn't be bothered to change her pillow case so she flipped it over and slipped back into fevered sleep.

Thursday morning came and she was feeling awful.

"I'm really concerned," Jim said, sitting on the edge of her bed, his hand on her forehead. "Maybe we should go see your doctor. I know you've been sick before, it's just you look so pale right now. You normally bounce back quickly and I find it strange that your fever came back."

"Give me another day or two," she said. "Like you said earlier, I probably pushed myself too much with everything. Besides, rest is the best medicine for the flu."

"I know," he said and frowned. "But we need to be smart."

"It's just a bad flu, Dad," she said, pleading. "Hospitals get backlogged with worried parents. I've seen it a lot volunteering."

He caressed her face. "It's our job to worry about our kids. I'll give you another day and if we don't see any improvements, we're going to see your doctor."

"I want to get better soon, trust me," she said. "This wasn't the way I wanted to spend Valentine's Day."

☙ ❧

Saturday morning, Midnight woke up around eleven intending to do her volunteering but by the time she got out of the shower, she knew there was no way she could go. But because she'd missed Valentine's Day and felt guilty, when Tyler called to see how she was feeling and wondered if she might feel up to going out later, she lied and said sure, going out would be nice.

When she went to make her bed, she saw the bloodstain on her pillowcase and instinctively turned to see if her dad was standing behind her, arms folded, angry eyes—no, *disappointed* eyes—glaring at her. Yes, she'd promised to tell him if she wasn't feeling any better, but she wasn't feeling any worse, so wasn't that a good thing? And if she told him about the nosebleeds, he'd freak and she was sure they'd be on their way to the hospital.

Midnight pulled the dirty pillowcase off her pillow, shoved it into her hamper, and got a clean one. They were just nosebleeds. It didn't mean she had brain cancer or anything. Maybe she'd been blowing her nose too hard these last few days. That was probably it. Nothing more.

She really wanted to see Tyler.

Samantha came over around two and they caught up on what she'd been missing at school. Then she helped Midnight get ready for her date. They chose black jeans and a white blouse, some nice diamond stud earrings her dad had bought her a couple of Christmases ago, and then Samantha helped with the makeup.

"I look so washed out," Midnight said. "Maybe I should cancel."

"You look gorgeous," Samantha said in a fake British accent. "And there's no way you're cancelling."

Midnight looked at the mirror and touched her hair.

"Just leave it alone," Samantha said. "You look great. He's going to love you."

Midnight caught her lower lip in her teeth. "He's already told me he did."

"Really? When? Why didn't you tell me?"

"I think it was Monday."

"You think."

"Sorry, but this week is a bit of a blur."

"I'm sure," Samantha said. "So go out and try to enjoy yourself."

Midnight looked at her friend. "Not sure if I can. I still feel very tired and sort of sick, but I also feel kind of weird, like, you know?"

"Lustful?"

Midnight gave Samantha a look. "I guess that's the polite way of describing it. But I've been sick all week, so how can I be feeling like this?"

"You're in love, honey. But don't worry, I'm sure he's feeling the same."

"Great," Midnight said. "I can't go now. We're only fifteen and there's no way anything like that is happening."

"I'm sure he's not expecting anything like that anyway."

Midnight hesitated. She rung her hands in her lap. "What was it like?"

"What was what like?"

"You know, when you did it the first time." There was a bit of fear in her eyes. "Unlike you, I'm still a virgin."

Samantha looked at Midnight, confused.

"Remember back in grade six when you told me you'd done it."

Samantha took a moment to pull the memory out of the past. "You really believed me?"

"You mean you were lying?"

"God, yeah." She laughed. "We were twelve. I was an ugly duckling back then. Sorry to disappoint, but you're not the only V in here."

"Really? Even after all your boyfriends?"

"Second base is as far as I've been," Samantha said, quite serious. "When they want more, it's time to move on. That's why I've had so many boyfriends. Better to leave them wanting more, right?"

"Really?"

"Really. I just talk a big game."

Midnight was relieved.

"But tell anyone, and I'll tell them you're lying and that you're the one who is still a virgin. I still have a reputation."

Midnight raised a skeptical eyebrow. "Really?"

Samantha shrugged. "Okay. Maybe my reputation isn't what

it used to be. No one wants the crippled girl with the ugly scar."

"You're not crippled and soon you'll be walking just fine." Midnight hugged her. "And you're anything but ugly."

"You're my best friend. You have to say that."

"I said it because it's true and because I love you."

☙ ❧

When Tyler came to pick her up, Midnight new that she couldn't handle a night out no matter how badly she wanted to, so she asked him if they could just stay home.

"You sure you don't mind if we stay here?" she said.

"As long as I'm with you, I don't care where we are," he said. "Let me tell my dad so he doesn't wait for us."

"Thank you," she said when he returned, and after he'd hung his coat in the closet, she led him to the couch. "My dad is making us dinner."

"He doesn't have to. My dad gave me some money so we could order a pizza."

"I'm making Midnight's favourite," Jim said from the kitchen.

Tyler glanced at Midnight.

"I love tacos," she said. "And since I haven't eaten much all week . . . maybe it'll do me good."

"Maybe I shouldn't be here," Tyler said. "You still look very tired."

She took his hand. It felt nice and warm compared to hers. "I want you to stay."

They sat side by side, Midnight leaned her head on his shoulder, and they stayed quiet for a few minutes, until Jim called them in for dinner.

"This looks great," Tyler said.

"You two enjoy your dinner together," he said and then started to leave the kitchen with his plate.

"You're not eating with us?" Midnight said.

"I've got work I need to finish."

"I think he didn't want to be a third wheel," Tyler said. "Your house feels so familiar, like I've been here before, lots of times, eating snacks or lunches. Feels like home, more so than our new house does."

"I can't imagine not living here," she said.

They each took mouthfuls of their tacos.

"So, what does Tyler Murphy want to be when he grows up?" she said.

"What everyone wants. To be rich and famous. Seriously, I want to be happy sharing my life with the person I love." He held her gaze for a few seconds. "You?"

"That sounds wonderful," she said. "Professionally, I'd love to be a doctor and cure people of cancer, but I don't think I'm cut out for that. Academically, I'm a straight-A student, but I hate biology. And I can't see myself going to school until I'm like thirty. And the hours new doctors must put in."

"Research."

"What?"

"You don't want to be a doctor, you want to be a research scientist."

"I do?"

He nodded.

"Just like that, you know what I want."

He nodded again and sipped his cola.

"Have you ever seen a purple-haired scientist?"

He laughed so hard that he snorted some of his drink. Embarrassed, he wiped his nose with a napkin. "Way to go, Murphy," he mumbled.

"That was too funny," Midnight said.

"Only because it wasn't you with Coke coming out of your nose," he said. "Man, that hurts too."

"I've done that before and it does hurt the sinuses," she said. "Anyway, I'm not sure about the scientist thing."

"You'll probably grow tired of the purple hair by then anyway."

"Probably." She washed down her food with a long gulp of her drink. "Do you miss Washington?"

"Not really," he said, the look on his face distant. "There was a lot of crap there, a lot of violence. I didn't realize how tense life was there until we moved back here."

"What did you mean by a lot of crap?"

Tyler looked away for a moment. "I went through a tough time when I was thirteen. You know what cutting is?"

She nodded.

And then he told her all about those two dark years. When he was done, Midnight had tears in her eyes.

"I didn't mean to upset you," he said. "I just felt like you should know."

"I wish I'd been there for you," she said and reached for his hand.

"It's like I've never lived there," he said. "I used to think that living in Bridgehaven had been a dream, but now I think living in Washington was the dream. This is my *real* home." He stared into her eyes as he said those last words.

"I'm so glad you're back."

"Me too."

ଔ ଓ

After dinner, they settled on the couch and watched Notting Hill, one of Midnight's favourite movies. She was a big fan of Julia Roberts, and Hugh Grant wasn't bad to look at.

About halfway through the movie, she went to the kitchen to make popcorn and she got a paper cut on her finger trying to open the new box. It didn't bleed, just stung. Three minutes later, she returned with a bowl of popcorn and a couple of Cokes, hers diet.

"I love that movie," she said when it ended. "I know there weren't explosion and guns and car chases. . ."

"As long as I'm with you," he said, "I'm good."

She leaned into him and felt like she belonged there, her head adjusting to the contour of his shoulder and chest. They stayed that way while the credits rolled by on the TV and when she went to get the remote, Tyler put a hand to her face and leaned in, pressing his kips against hers.

Midnight closed her eyes to enjoy the moment.

When he pulled away, the sweetness of his lips lingered on hers, and nonchalantly she licked her lips. She tasted the Coke and salty popcorn he'd had during the movie.

"Maybe kissing me wasn't a good idea," she said. "You might get sick."

He shrugged. "Small price to pay for those lips."

Tyler kissed her again and she felt it—those butterflies

everyone talks about. It was really nice to be loved by someone.

"It's almost eleven thirty," he said. "I guess I should call my dad to come and get me."

Midnight pouted. "I wish I was feeling better so you could stay a bit longer."

"Me too, but you look really tired."

She yawned, while Tyler called his dad.

Ten minutes later, his ride arrived. She walked him to the front door and waited as he put his jacket on.

They kissed.

She let him out.

"Wow," Tyler said, looking up at the stars. "What a beautiful night." He turned and kissed her again. "Love you, *beautiful* Midnight."

TWENTY-TWO

~ December 1988 ~

Christmas morning. Outside, fat snowflakes fell from the sky in sporadic patterns, whipped by the wintery wind and looking like drunken partygoers going home after a night of celebration. The white ground looked pure and soft and foreboding.

Winter had never been Karen's favourite season. It was cold, unforgiving, and lonely.

She pulled herself away from the family room window and sat on the floor amidst a mess of boxes, torn Christmas wrapping papers, and toys.

Jim had bought too much again. She wondered how they were going to pay for all of that. It wasn't like the kids needed that many toys. How many Barbies did Midnight need? How many games did Octavia need?

A shudder rolled over her and made her feel like she was trapped in a bad B-movie.

The Christmas tree, which they'd gotten on the first of December at a little place about twenty kilometres west of

Bridgehaven where they went each year, had looked majestic an hour ago with its overabundance of gifts embarrassingly tucked all along the base, but it now looked naked, frail, and out of place. Christmas season was always filled with promises, hopes, and dreams, but in a matter of an hour or less, it was done, gone—just a moment that could never quite live up to all the expectations.

Karen wrapped her arms around herself.

Jim had bought her a beautiful long-sleeve striped cardigan, black and white, her two favourite colours, and she felt cozy wearing it, but she also felt like she was wearing a straightjacket.

"I love Christmas," Jim said and got up to get a garbage bag. "It's the best time of year."

Karen leaned her head against the couch and closed her eyes. The girls had woken them up at six, which was way too early for her, even for Christmas Day. She could feel herself fall asleep. Her warm comfy bed called to her. She could sleep all day. That would suit her just fine. Get this day over with. It was nonsense anyway. As if some guy named Jesus had died for mankind some two thousand years ago. If he had, he'd made one colossal mistake.

Mankind wasn't worth it.

She could use a drink.

And a bit of pot.

Now *that* would make her Christmas Day worth it. Damn straight it would. But she knew Jim wouldn't partake. He had changed. He'd bought into this suburban life.

She opened her eyes and looked around. So this was her life? This wasn't what she'd expected when she'd hooked up with Jim back in high school. There had been something about him that had dared her to pick him, and she had not been wrong.

The nerdy kid had been badass once she'd given him the right motivation. And she could motivate even the dead.

Karen caught her bottom lip between her teeth.

She loved her girls, but she also didn't. Seemed like her life had been sucked dry by them, all her hopes, her dreams, gone. She felt like an empty shell of who she'd been.

What had happened to her dreams?

Their dreams?

Midnight's birth had been intolerable. The contractions had felt like a gigantic vise crushing Karen's body, wave after crashing wave of such excruciating pain that she'd screamed to just take the fucking baby out of her before it killed her.

She'd told Jim that there would be no more babies.

Midnight came over to her mother and showed Karen one of her many toys. Karen faked a smile, the pressure at the back of her neck a forewarning of a coming migraine.

Stress. It was just stress. The sort you got when raising a family. The sort you got when your life was in constant chaos. When everything was too loud. When your world moved so fast it left you dizzy.

So damn busy all the time.

She pulled herself up and headed for the kitchen to make coffee. Maybe she could sneak a little Baileys into it. After all, it was Christmas.

She waited for the coffee to brew and thought how wonderful it would be to take Jim upstairs and spend quality time between the sheets. They just never seemed to do that anymore. Or when they did, it was rushed, in case the girls needed them.

"Merry Christmas," he said into her ear. "You okay?"

She nodded but didn't speak. Her head felt like it would explode. She leaned back into Jim and let quiet tears streak down her cheeks.

☙ ❧

Karen simply told Jim that she wasn't feeling well and that maybe a nap might help get rid of her headache. She apologized to the girls for not being much fun on Christmas Day and hoped that later she would feel better and want to do something with them.

Karen looked outside her bedroom window and felt the weight of winter suffocate her spirit. She and Jim had once had a dream: hitting the road and making a name for themselves playing venues across Canada, cutting an album, getting some airplay on the radio. Maybe a few college stations would pick them up, and before long mainstream radio would discover them too. Maybe some big-name recording industry executives would be beating down their door to sign them to a multi-million-dollar deal. Yes, she and Jim had spoken of this dream many times back in high school, back before this life had stolen it.

Now, nothing changed. Same old scenery day after day. Get Octavia ready for school every morning, constantly on her to get up, get dressed, eat, brush her teeth, the bus is coming, hurry, hurry, hurry. And then endless hours alone with Midnight. Jim could easily get down on all fours to play with her, but Karen found so little enjoyment or fulfillment in doing so. And then her knees and hips would ache.

She held her forehead in her hand.

Finding out that she was pregnant with Octavia at the age of eighteen had changed everything. She'd thought of giving her up for adoption, but Jim had been against it. And getting an abortion hadn't been an option back in 1978.

Thankfully, Octavia's delivery had been quick and nearly painless.

And now here she was, nine years later and nine years older, as far from her dream life as she could be, feeling alone and trapped on Christmas Day of all days. It should be a time to be happy with her family, but instead she found herself ill and wanting no part of the holiday.

Karen slipped underneath the blankets and began to cry—to cry for the life she'd lost, cry for the dream that would never be, cry for the horrible mother that she had become.

Her kids deserved better.

Jim deserved better.

☙ ❧

"Mommy?" Octavia said quietly after tugging at her. "Mommy?"

"Is Mommy okay?" Midnight asked Octavia.

Octavia looked down at her sister and shrugged. She poked her mom's arm again. "Mommy?"

Karen peeled an eye open and forced a smile. Her room was much darker than when she'd gone back to bed. She glanced at the clock on the night table: 4:13.

In December, the sun was setting already. She had slept the day away.

She didn't know what to do, what to say. She should be feeling bad, she supposed, since she'd turned this special day into a very ordinary day, and part of her felt somewhat guilty, but not the sort of guilt that made her feel sorry for her kids. She felt sorry for herself, for having to pretend that all was fine while she swung her legs over the edge of the bed and wrapped her kids in her arms and told them how much better she felt and boy, wait until she got into that kitchen and whipped a Christmas dinner together that they would talk about years from now.

With another empty smile, she shooed them away while she went to the bathroom. She splashed her face with cold water, hoping to get rid of the dark circles beneath her eyes. She applied a bit of makeup, fixed her hair, made herself look somewhat presentable. She slipped into a pair of jeans and a long-sleeve sweater, and headed down the stairs, filling her nostrils with the mouth-watering aroma of a cooked turkey, knowing that Jim had been hard at work all day and that if a Christmas dinner to remember was going to be served tonight, it wouldn't be of her doing but of her husband's.

Her family deserved more than she could give them.

☙ ❧

"Maybe you should see a doctor," Jim said as he joined Karen in bed. "You've been getting headaches a lot lately."

"I'm fine," she said in a clipped tone. "I don't like winter. It brings me down."

Jim wanted to suggest that maybe she was suffering from depression—not that he was a doctor—and maybe she could get something prescribed that might help. But in the state she was in, he decided to say nothing. She wasn't wrong, winters in Ottawa could be long and cold, but so far December hadn't been too bad. The real nasty weather didn't really hit until January.

"The kids missed you today," he said, trying not to sound like he was blaming her. "All day, they asked when you were going to come down and play, and I just kept telling them soon. Even they must have realized that I wasn't telling the truth."

She turned to him. "I'm sorry, Jim. But I'm exhausted, so can we just forget about it and get some sleep? Maybe I can make it up to them tomorrow."

Part irritation and part defeat flashed across his face. He understood his wife, had realized for some time now that Karen felt like a mouse trapped in a cage—safe and sound in her surroundings, but so bored. It must be difficult for her to live the life she'd made fun of when they'd been young and foolish, but that was it: they'd been young and foolish. Teenagers were supposed to be young and foolish and think that they were never going to be like their parents, that their lives were going to be epic, like the best goddamned trip ever.

But they weren't kids anymore. They had a house, kids, responsibilities. They'd had to grow up.

He didn't mind.

He was happy.

He had two great kids that he couldn't imagine not having in his life, and a wife that he loved. It was enough.

But he knew it wasn't for Karen. And that scared him a little.

But what was he supposed to do? All he could do was love her as much as he could and hope that in time it would be enough for her too.

"Merry Christmas," he said and pulled her into the comfort and safety of his arms. "You are the most wonderful person I know. We are so lucky to have you."

Jim waited for her to say something, but soon he heard the deep, even breathing of someone who has found peace in the tranquility that only sleep can offer.

☙ ❧

Karen woke up two hours later and went to Octavia's room, tucked the blankets that Octavia had kicked back, kissed her on the forehead, and went to check on Midnight. Her baby girl was sleeping soundly. She kneeled and watched her, almost overwhelmed by Midnight's beauty. She brushed a strand of hair away from Midnight's face and kissed her cheek.

"I don't know why," she whispered, "but loving you scares the life out of me. You are so precious, so fragile, and you own my heart. And that horrifies me. You are my child, I am your mother, and I would die if anything ever happened to you or your sister. I think that is what drains me—the love, this absolute motherly love. It's all-consuming."

Karen kissed Midnight again and walked out of the room, wondering what in the world had made her say these things, and where they'd come from.

She woke Jim and they made love as if it were their last night together.

TWENTY-THREE

~ February 2002 ~

Love is a funny thing. Some seek it and never seem to find it, while others try to hide from it but keep stumbling into its arms. Love can hit unannounced and make you feel like you've been run over by a truck, or it simply taps you on the shoulder like a friendly reminder. Love can make your knees weak, your stomach roll, your head throb. And love can turn your world into a downward spiral when it suddenly dies.

And even with all that it seems to have going against it, everyone wants a piece of love.

And why not?

When your heart finds that other special heart, well, it feels like the most beautiful and warm spring day after a long harsh winter, like scoring the winning goal in overtime, like finding that special pair of earrings that you'd lost and happen to find on the one night you desperately needed to wear them.

Love is what makes life worth living.

Love is life itself. Someone without love is someone with a

dead soul. It's no wonder that everyone is willing to risk everything to have a taste of it. The possibility of finding it at any given moment is what keeps us strong during those times that it escapes us.

When Midnight didn't show up again on Monday morning, Tyler felt off balance, this being the second Monday in a row that she wasn't at school. He'd enjoyed seeing her Saturday night and when he'd called Sunday, she'd said she wasn't feeling great, really tired actually, but she'd told him she was hoping that tomorrow she'd see him at school.

He had looked forward to seeing her.

It was selfish of him and he knew it. He understood she wasn't over whatever it was she was sick with, but damn it, he missed her.

His chest felt tight, like a squeeze around his heart, a squeeze that made him realize how much he loved her and how hopelessly and totally vulnerable he'd become.

Wanting someone this much was the best feeling he'd ever known.

☙ ❧

Midnight was sleeping soundly when Jim came into her room to check up on her. He hesitated a moment, not sure that he should wake her up. She still looked pale. Too pale. He'd listened to her, but enough was enough. He had to get her to her doctors.

"Hey, sleepy-head," Jim said while rubbing her arm gently to wake her. "Midnight, honey."

"I don't feel well," she finally said after waking up. "It hurts everywhere. Especially my paper-cut."

Jim sat on the edge of the bed and took her hand. "When did you do that? Didn't you use Polysporin?"

"Forgot, I guess," she said and winced. "Happened Saturday night, when I made popcorn. I had trouble opening the new box and slid my finger under the flap and that's how I got the cut. Just a tiny bit."

"Looks infected. What about the bruise?"

"Where?"

The sleeve of her pyjama top was pulled up and he pointed to her left forearm, by the elbow. "Here."

She looked at her arm. "I have no idea how that happened. Must have banged it against something."

"We've waited too long," he said. "I'm calling your doctor's office and if they can't see you, we're going to the hospital."

Midnight bit her lower lip. "There's more."

Something in her tone he didn't like, and he could see the three-year-old she had once been, sick and vulnerable.

"Please don't be angry with me," she said.

"Midnight," he said, unable to hide the fear in his voice. "What is it?"

"I've been having nosebleeds," she said. "For a while."

"How long?" His mind started to fill with dark thoughts. "How many?"

Midnight started to cry. "I don't remember. The first one was about the time I started to volunteer. It didn't happen again until before Christmas, so I sort of forgot about it. And then you seemed so happy with Mrs. Carmichael. I didn't want to . . ." She moved her head from the pillow and he saw the red stain. "I'm sorry I didn't tell you before. I just thought it was the flu, but—

”

Jim took her into his arms and rubbed her back like he did when she was little. “It’ll be fine. Get dressed. We’re going to the hospital.”

Out in the hallway, Jim put a hand on the wall to steady himself. He’d been irresponsible. He’d wanted so much to believe his daughter was like everyone else. He’d been negligent and had missed the signs. There had been too many.

He’d never forgive himself if something happened to her.

☙ ❧

Samantha and Tyler were at his locker, getting books for first class. Their friendship had grown quickly, bound by Midnight. Tyler could see why Samantha and Midnight had become best friends after he’d left; they were a lot alike. Midnight had told him everything about the ups and downs of her friendship with Samantha, and he was sure it was true, but the Samantha standing with him at his locker right now cared and loved Midnight as much as he did.

“Has she been sick like this before?” he said.

“I don’t remember anything this bad since I’ve known her.”

“I’m really lost without her,” he said, chewing his lower lip. “I guess when I was a kid, I didn’t realize how special she was. She makes me want to be better. Weird, huh?”

“Not really,” she said. “I’ve learned over the last few months that Midnight seems to bring out the best in me. I don’t know what it is. I’ve known her a long time, but I feel like I’ve only gotten to know her for real since my accident.”

“When we were kids,” he said, “she used to say we were best

friends all the time, and it never hit me how true that was, and is now, until this weekend. I felt so bad for her and wished I could have made her better somehow. I wonder how things would have been with Midnight had we never moved away. All the years I lost without her."

"Maybe the fact that the two of you were apart for that time is what is making this special."

He closed his locker door and fastened the lock. "I guess you could be right. All I know is that I just want to make Midnight happy."

"You have no idea how happy you've already made her," Samantha said as they headed down the hall slowly so she could follow without needing her cane. "You've always been part of her, all those years you were away. If she didn't talk about you, that look in her eyes as she stared out into space gave her away. I remember when we became good friends in grade one, how she talked about you all the time. It drove me nuts. I was so jealous."

"Why?"

"Because you weren't there but I was and she still wanted to be with you more than with me. I was six. I didn't understand about love."

Tyler stopped. "You really think she's been in love with me for that long?"

"Yeah. In some way or another. Midnight has loved you a very long time. I have no idea what she would have done if you hadn't come back."

"What do you mean?"

"I don't think she would have given anyone else a chance," Samantha said. "Ever."

ઉ ઈ

Class was long. Too long. Tyler didn't want to be here. All he could think of was Midnight. Midnight Madison. He said her name over and over in his head, liking the sound of it, loving the way she made him feel. He wanted to hold her so badly that he was ready to ditch school and head over to her place. He just had to see her, touch her, kiss her.

This was love with a capital L.

This was what people meant when they talked about finding The One—their soulmate. He suddenly understood the thrill of having found the person that mattered more than anything, the person he wanted to spend every waking hour with, the person he would surely die for.

He looked at the other students and they all seemed to be looking at him. He knew they weren't, but still he wondered what they were thinking, and realized he didn't really care. He knew Midnight better than any of them, and even though she wasn't part of the in-crowd, it didn't matter to him. He didn't know these people, so who cared what they thought about him dating Midnight? He loved her and that was all that mattered.

She was better than all of them.

Class finally ended and he grabbed his books and headed out the door.

"Hey Murphy?"

Tyler turned to find Bradley Eriksson coming after him, a big fat grin on his pimple-infested face. Puberty wasn't being kind to him.

Tyler said, "I got to get to my next class."

"Sooooo, you're dating Madison. You desperate?"

Tyler looked at him as if to say *what's it to you*? "Her name is Midnight."

"She's not gonna put out for you, man." He laughed, sounding like a seal on steroids. "But I heard her little friend sure does . . . or did, before her little accident."

Tyler wanted to reach down Bradley's throat and pull out his intestines and smother his ugly fat face with them.

"Does your mother regret giving birth to such an idiot?" Tyler said and walked away.

ᘓ ᘐ

Midnight drove up to the house on the hill. It had a barn, and corn fields as far as the eye could see. She climbed out of the car, ran her hands over her dress to straighten it out—strange, because she never wore dresses—and walked toward the front door. She heard a dog bark but couldn't see it.

She stopped, her right hand inches from the door, ready to knock. What was she going to say to her when she came to the door? Would she even recognize her own mother? It had been over twenty years since she'd abandoned them.

Midnight turned and began to walk away. The door creaked opened.

"Can I help you?" the woman's voice said.

Midnight stopped, hesitated, and turned.

The woman looking back at her was old. Her long hair was grey. Her face was leathery and lined. Dark circles shadowed her eyes. But those eyes . . . Yes, those eyes she recognized. They were just like Octavia's.

"I'm sorry," Midnight said and turned toward her car. She ran. "I shouldn't have come here. I shouldn't have troubled you."

"Midnight?" The woman took a step forward. Then another. Tears streaked her face. "Midnight, please stay. Please."

Midnight looked back at the woman. Her hand was on the car door handle. Her inner voice was telling her to get in the car and go, that this had been a bad idea, that she really didn't know this woman. "I'm not sure why I'm here," she said. "I don't know what I expected to find. I'm sorry, but I should go."

"I don't blame you," the woman said, stepping closer.

"I'm not even sure if you are her," Midnight said, her hand falling to her side. "You could be. It's been so long since the last time I saw you."

The woman stopped ten feet away.

Midnight stared at her, catching her lower lip between her teeth. Her heart hammered in her chest. The rolling in her stomach wasn't very pleasant.

"Are you her?" Midnight said. "Are you my mother, Karen?"

The woman took a hesitant step forward. Then another. She closed the gap until she was within arm's reach.

They looked into each other's eyes.

The woman said, "My name is Karen Madison, and I am your mother."

Midnight didn't say anything. She couldn't. Her knees had turned to water and she wanted to vomit. There was the beginning of a headache just behind her eyes. Her nerves were wound so tight they could snap. This broken-down woman was not who she had expected to find. She didn't know what she had expected to find, but not this. Maybe in her dreams she had always hoped to find her mother still young and beautiful. Successful. Rich and famous. Instead, she was a poor, lost soul. Midnight couldn't believe that this woman had given her up for this miserable existence.

Midnight began to cry. The truth hurt.

"Let me," the woman said and pulled Midnight into her arms. "Let me chase your pain away like I should have done all those years ago."

Midnight began to scream.

☙ ❧

"Midnight! Midnight, it's Dad."

Midnight snapped her eyes open but couldn't make out where she was. She had the feeling of movement, and her stomach turned. *Don't throw up, don't throw up, don't throw up.* A dream. Just a weird, sad dream that had left the image of her mother seared into her mind, a scar from the past that had reopened.

"Midnight, you okay?" Jim said. "Honey?"

"I'm okay, Dad," Midnight said. "I'm okay. Why are we in the car?"

"Because—"

"I know why," she said, cutting him off. "I remember now. I'm so sorry I didn't tell you sooner. I just wanted to . . . I don't want to be sick again, Dad. I'm finally feeling like a normal teenager. I'm finally happy. I'm finally in *love.*"

"I know, honey." He ran a hand across his face and returned it to the steering wheel. "Maybe it's nothing. Probably it's nothing. We're just making sure by going to the hospital. They'll check you over and send us home, I'm sure."

"But—"

"Let's wait and see," he said. "We don't know that it's not just the flu. Let's wait and see."

Midnight heard the fear in her father's voice, the same fear she was feeling. It wasn't something that he wanted to think about right now and neither did she. But she could also sense the lie that it was, the lie they both wanted to ignore as long as they could.

A shiver grabbed her and wouldn't let go.

It was a lie so big it filled the entire car with cold, chilling dread.

TWENTY-FOUR

~ August 1990 ~

Midnight and Tyler were in the back yard playing on the play structure, with Jim watching them, thankful that his little girl was alive and healthy once again. He wasn't a religious man, but he couldn't ignore that it must have been some sort of miracle that had saved her.

For how long?

That question kept popping into his mind. How much time had she bought herself? A year? Five? Ten?

A lifetime?

That's the only answer that would satisfy him. He wanted Midnight to attend his funeral some forty years from now, not the other way around. Parents shouldn't bury their children.

Jim stepped out onto the deck and felt the late summer sunshine on his face. It had been a very long year. A very lonely year trying to take care of two kids. A draining year that he felt deep in his weary bones.

He'd heard nothing from Karen.

Now that things had settled, he'd started to think about her more and more, what they'd had, what they could be having now. At night, lying in bed alone, he'd really started to miss her.

"Daddy, watch me!" Midnight said and jumped off the swing as her momentum pushed her forward, giving the illusion that she was flying. "That was fun."

The smile that spread across his face wasn't like any other smile he'd ever had. This one, he felt through his entire being. Just a few months ago, he'd been wondering whether he was going to have to plan his daughter's funeral, and today he was watching her jump off the swing.

Today, he could breathe again.

Tyler was now showing her how to throw a football, and Jim noticed that Midnight wasn't looking at Tyler the same way as she'd always looked at him. Those two were something. They seemed to fit like a pair of mittens, meant to be together. Tyler had waited patiently while Midnight received her treatment over several months, coming to see her when he knew she was home, to say hi, to wish her get well soon. Most of the times, she was asleep, so he'd simply stare at her for a few minutes, and then leave with his hands stuffed in his pockets, sadness in his eyes, his head tucked between his shoulders, looking so lonely.

But today, Tyler looked like the happiest kid around.

And so was Jim.

☙ ❧

Jim tucked Midnight into bed that night and sat on the edge facing her. He touched her cheek gently, feeling his eyes water. That had been happening more and more, sometimes because he was so grateful, other times because he couldn't believe that she was really still there. He grabbed a Franklin book.

"Is Mommy coming back now?"

"I don't know."

He could have lied, but to what end? He didn't want Midnight to get her hopes up. She'd been through enough. They'd all been through a lot. And he didn't want to get his hopes up either.

"Mommy doesn't know that you're all better now," he said. "And that is something she must live with. I know you must miss her, and that it must not seem fair to you for her to be gone, but grownups don't always do the right thing. We think we do, and we try to, but we don't always."

He looked at the longing in his daughter's eyes and pulled her into him. He knew how she felt because that's the way he felt too.

"You miss her, don't you?"

Midnight didn't answer right away. She looked at the things in her room. "I'd miss my Teddy if he was missing, or my barbies." She looked at Jim, apologetic. "I don't really remember Mommy. Is that bad?"

"No, sweetie, it's not."

It wasn't bad.

It was sad.

Jim kissed Midnight on the forehead. He then opened the Franklin book he'd started the night before and began to read.

Their lives moved on.

☙ ❧

After finishing the story, Jim bent down to kiss Midnight goodnight and she wrapped her arms around his neck and wouldn't let go.

"You're the best Daddy ever."

"And you're the best little munchkin ever," he said and kissed her cheek again. "I love you to the moon and back."

"I love you to infinity and back." Infinity was her new favourite word lately. "So I love you more." She beamed.

"Not possible," he said as Midnight finally let go of him and he straightened up. "How about we love each other the same?"

Midnight nodded, sleep already dragging her away as her eyes closed. Jim put Teddy into the nook of her arm. Karen had bought the stuffed animal when she'd been pregnant with Midnight, which he recalled had seemed out of character.

That's something *he'd* normally thought of doing, not Karen.

Jim left Midnight's bedroom, leaving the door ajar. Just a little. He looked in on Octavia and she was flat on her bed, talking on the phone with a friend. She had just turned eleven and had begun to show signs of becoming a teenager.

Normalcy would be so nice after the past year.

TWENTY-FIVE

~ February 2002 ~

They'd been waiting for hours to get news about Midnight, but so far no one had come to talk to them. Jim sat on the hospital couch with his face buried in his hands, oblivious to the chaos around him, memories of 1989 slamming into his brain faster than he cared to remember.

Why had it taken him so long to notice she wasn't getting better?

Because she'd been fine for years and after a while you start to believe that she's paid her dues, that nothing bad was ever going to come again. Because when your child survives such an ordeal, you want to believe that she's special and was saved for a reason. Because believing otherwise would drive you insane.

Jim pulled his face from his hands and looked around. Roger and Veronica Murphy, along with Jake, sat in uncomfortable chairs across from him, their fear-filled eyes avoiding his. Samantha sat stone cold in a far corner of the waiting area with Emily at her side. He saw Tyler pacing, the agony on his face breaking his heart. Jim buried his face in his hands again and shook his head. Then he felt a hand on his back, a touch that somehow felt familiar and soothing. He looked at Tracy Carmichael sitting beside him. Just having her here with him allowed him to breathe.

They were all suffering.

That's how much Midnight meant to everyone.

"They won't tell me anything," Octavia said as she came back from the nurses' station and sat down beside him. "I need to know that she'll be all right."

Jim put a hand on hers. "I know. We all do. Don't get yourself all worked up. My grandchild is in there and you must stay healthy. That includes mental health."

"I know, I know. Wish Mark would get here."

"He'll be here as soon as he can."

"I'm so worried, Dad," Octavia said. "My little sister . . . she can't be . . . she just . . . you don't think she's . . .?"

Jim didn't say anything.

༄ ༄

The doctor that examined Midnight was of Asian descent, somewhere in his fifties, with a touch of grey at the temples. His English was that of someone who had lived in Ottawa a very long time but hadn't been born in Canada.

He came out a few minutes after nine and asked to speak to Jim privately, but Jim insisted that Octavia come with him. The three of them stood just outside Midnight's room, far enough from the others that their conversation wouldn't be overheard.

"Midnight is very sick," Dr. Ishiguro said to Jim and Octavia. "We've run all the tests that we could, to be sure. Her prognosis isn't very good."

Jim felt like someone had just kicked him in the gut. He could feel himself losing it, had a hard time focusing. He wanted to hit something, anything.

"She's got cancer again," he whispered. "Is that it? It's come back, right?"

Dr. Ishiguro lowered his gaze for the briefest of moments, but it was long enough for Jim to know that it wasn't good.

"Midnight has what is called Acute Myeloid Leukemia, a form of leukemia that strikes quickly, in both adults and children," Dr. Ishiguro said. "We'll start chemo and radiation therapy right away, but a bone marrow aspiration is her best chance for survival."

Everyone volunteered to be tested, including Octavia, who insisted—even though she was pregnant, she couldn't have lived with herself if she were the match Midnight needed and she hadn't done all that she could to save her sister—but none of them were matches for the stem cell transplant that Midnight needed. The one most likely to match, to save her life, had left a long time ago.

The treatment started as soon as they could, and it was extremely aggressive, but Midnight didn't respond. Maybe because her body had already experienced chemo and radiation therapy before, and built some sort of resistance. Maybe the disease was simply too strong for her immune system this time. Maybe it wasn't meant to be.

Jim couldn't accept that and pushed Dr. Ishiguro to find an alternative, anything that could save his daughter. Dr. Ishiguro reiterated that her best chances were with the stem cell transplant.

Each day that passed saw their hopes fade.

Midnight's health was deteriorating rapidly.

ഗ ഉ

Tyler had to stay after school to use the resource centre for an English essay he should have worked on during March Break and now he'd missed the due date. He tried to concentrate but it was impossible. His thoughts were elsewhere, on Midnight, and finally he gave up. To hell with a stupid assignment when the one he loved was . . . was . . . damn it, he couldn't think that. If only he could do something, anything.

Little bits of his heart were being torn by his inability to help.

Walking back to his locker, everything seemed narrower—the walls, the ceiling, even the floor. His world was caving in and his books slipped from his hands. He got on a knee to pick them up but stayed in the position as his shoulders began to shake, and then his whole body. He couldn't breathe and he didn't hear his name being called out.

"Look at the cry-baby," a voice boomed behind him. "So, looks like you're not the big hotshot you think you are. You're just that baby I used to bully."

Tyler stood, wiped his face, and faced Bradley Eriksson. "Just go away."

"Not so tough after all," Bradley said.

Tyler turned and started to walk away.

Then a meaty hand grabbed his shoulder and spun him around, and a fist hit him in the face, momentarily bringing everything to a halt. Tyler touched his nose and blood covered his fingertips.

"What the *fuck*!," he said. "Have you always been mental?"

Bradley took another swing but Tyler managed to duck and step back. "You don't want to do this."

"You come back here after all these years and you act like some fucking shithead who thinks he owns the world," Bradley said. "I got news for you. This is my *turf*."

Tyler managed a snicker. "What movies have you been watching? Are you for real? You were a stupid little bully when I left and now you're just a dumber, older version."

He turned to walk away again.

"That's right," Bradley said. "Run to Mommy. Or maybe it's run to *Midnight*. I hear she's not doing too hot these days. Probably got sick of you." Bradley cackled like he'd said the funniest joke ever told.

Tyler whipped around and charged at Bradley, hitting him like a linebacker and pushing him into a row of lockers. Bradley recovered, shoved Tyler away and swung his right fist, connecting with Tyler's jaw. Instantly, Tyler's Taekwondo training took over and he kicked Bradley in the mid-section, and then he grabbed him and flipped him over onto his back. He was about to drive his fist into Bradley's face when someone grabbed him and pulled him off.

"That's enough," Mr. Langlois, the gym teacher, said. "Tyler, you could have really hurt him."

"But I didn't," Tyler said. "I kept trying to walk away but he kept asking for it. It's been a long time coming, sir. Way too long."

"What's your name?" Mr. Langlois said to the boy lying dazed on the ground.

"Bradley."

"Bradley who?"

"Eriksson."

Mr. Langlois looked at both boys. "I have no choice but to report this. And you'll both probably get a three-day suspension."

"But it's all his fault—" Bradley started to say.

"I'd be quiet if I were you," the gym teacher said. "I probably saved you from a world of hurt. Now let's go to the office."

ღ ჯ

Jim had made phone calls to Karen's family in desperation, doubting that any of them knew were Karen might be, and he'd been right. Her brother Tom apologized a million times, but he hadn't heard from his sister in years. He agreed to get tested to see if he might be a match, and his two kids as well, but a few days later Jim's doctor had gotten negative results from their tests.

A month had passed already, and Midnight wasn't getting any better. She had no appetite, no energy, and her skin was pasty white with grey undertones. She had bruises on her arms and red spots on her neck, chest, and thighs. She slept almost all the time.

Jim looked up when he heard a knock on the door.

"Hey, Mr. Madison."

"Come in, Tyler." Jim stood, noticed the cut on Tyler's nose and the half-closed left eye, but said nothing. "She's been out for about two hours now."

Tyler approached the bed, hesitated a moment, then grabbed the safety bar that ran parallel to the bed, let go, crossed his arms, and then simply let them drop to his sides. He turned to Jim, glassy-eyed.

"Is she—?"

"She's just sleeping," he said. "I'll give you some privacy. I need to get a coffee anyway."

ᴓᴕ

Tyler hadn't been able to say the word. That word was too painful, too final, too permanent. How could it all end when it had just begun for them? He didn't want to sound like a whining baby, but it wasn't fair. Midnight was just about the nicest, most giving person he'd ever known, and for all her kindness, her life was being taken away. That was just wrong.

Mean.

Unforgiveable.

What could he do?

Tyler reached for Midnight's hand and was surprised at how lifeless it felt. He even thought he'd seen her wince at his touch. He didn't want to hurt her. But he needed to touch her, to feel her, to know that she was still there. He had to make sure that she was still alive, fighting.

Not dying.

There were bruises everywhere on her body, unwelcome reminders that she was losing the battle. Her face looked drained of life, emaciated, her eyes sunken dark marbles. Tyler couldn't believe how much weight she'd lost, how quickly her body had turned on her. This was Midnight lying in this hospital bed—*his* Midnight, the Midnight he had loved when he was five and the Midnight that he'd found again at fifteen and fallen in love with for real this time.

His stomach tightened and he couldn't catch his breath. This wasn't how it was supposed to go for them. They were just getting started. He wanted the fairy tale love story with the fairy tale ending. He wanted Midnight to get up and walk out of here with him. He wanted to marry her and have a bunch of kids. She would be a wonderful mother. Better than wonderful, like the best goddamned mother that ever lived.

Better than Mother Teresa.

Tyler bent over and kissed Midnight's fragile hand. The coldness of her skin brought fresh tears to his eyes. He blinked them away and then stared at her chest to make sure it was still rising. Her breaths were quick and shallow.

The breaths of the dying.

As soon as he thought it, he wanted to take it back. He couldn't accept that she was dying. She *couldn't* be dying. How could she be dying?

He recalled their first date just a few weeks ago, and how alive he had felt being with her, the electricity rushing through him as he'd kissed her, really kissed her, for the first time. Her lips had felt like soft heavenly clouds, full of sweetness and innocence and love, and he had known at that very moment that his heart would always belong to her. Ten years of separation had not pulled them apart, but instead had made their feelings for one another that much stronger.

She couldn't leave him now.

Tyler did not want to think about moving on without her; he did not want to imagine going to school and not meeting up with her between classes or at lunch; he did not see the point in ever being happy again when all he wanted was right here in front of him. He would trade places with her if it were possible.

Midnight was too good to die.

Tyler moved closer to her and feathered her face with the back of his fingers. She looked so peaceful to him, angelic. He now understood what real love was. What he had shared with Monica had never been real love. He had cared for her, but he wouldn't have traded his life for hers. Love was not selfish. Love was hurting when the other was hurting. Love was feeling a part of you die when the one you loved was taken away from you.

Love made life worth living.

"Hi," Midnight whispered.

Tyler nearly jumped backward. Her eyes were still closed, yet she seemed to know it was him here with her.

"Are you in pain?" he said, knowing that she was. "I hate seeing you suffer so much."

Midnight licked her parched lips and opened her eyes. "What happened to your face?"

Tyler felt the power of her eyes, like precious gemstones that somehow reached inside his heart and managed to appease his sorrow, like a soft caress that could magically chase away his grief.

"It's something I should have done ten years ago," he said.

Midnight tried to raise her hand, but she couldn't. "You were always my hero."

"Your hero would fix this."

"No one can fix this," she said.

"Are you afraid?" he said. "Because I am."

Her smile, as weak as it was, reassured him. He should be the one to reassure her, not the other way around.

"Yes," was all she could say.

"D'you think there's a God?" Tyler could see that Midnight

was struggling to find the strength to answer. "I'm just babbling. You rest. You need to keep fighting. I need you to keep fighting. I'm the one that needs to answer that question for myself. I mean, does anyone even believe anymore? I don't think I know anyone who goes to church. Have we all given up on God? Have we all grown so cynical? Yeah, I know a few big words."

He laughed nervously.

"Yes," she managed to say.

Tyler looked at her, a frown in his brow. He'd forgotten what he'd been saying. Midnight glanced up at him, her eyes doing what her mouth couldn't: smile.

"I think there's a God," she said.

"Oh!"

Neither said a word for a long time. He stroked her hair and tried to keep his tears away. Maybe he was the cynical one. Just a few years ago he'd been cutting himself; a part of him had wanted to die. He was glad he hadn't. He wouldn't have ever known real love.

Real love hurt like hell, but it was so worth it.

"You don't need to start believing," Midnight said. "I'm not sure I always did. But you're here now, and I want to believe that God made sure that you came back in time for us to have this last bit of time together."

She closed her eyes.

Tyler wanted to tell her that if God could do that, then He could definitely make her better. So why wasn't He? "Maybe I should leave," he said instead. "Talking is exhausting you."

Midnight shook her head. "I need you to stay."

Tyler closed his eyes, fresh tears fighting the back of his

eyelids. When he opened them, wet streaks rushed down his face like silver streams.

"I don't know what to do for you." He wiped his tears with the back of his hand and winced when he touched his nose. "I hate that you are in such pain. I hate that this is happening to you. I hate that no one seems able to save you. It's not fair."

"It's not fair for any of the kids here either," she said. "I'm not alone."

"Your dad told me that many of them have come by to see you," he said. "Some remember you visiting with them."

"My kindness is being rewarded."

"You're driving me insane," he said, a pained smile crossing his face. "Stop seeing the good in this craziness. I don't want you to be here. I want to take you out again, maybe see a concert or something. Then this summer we can go to the beach out at Mooney's Bay. Remember when we were there last time?"

"That was a very long time ago."

"I stepped on your castle because you'd made one better than mine and I was so pissed off with you. I called it stupid, as if a sand castle can be stupid."

She half smiled.

"I want to build the greatest castle with you. Only with you," he said. "Please get better so we can."

Midnight didn't answer. For a second, Tyler thought she had fallen asleep. Maybe that was best. He wasn't making it easy on her, feeling sorry for himself. But this was so hard.

"I love you," he whispered and kissed her forehead. "I think I always have, and I know I always will."

He turned to walk away, but felt her hand give a very light pull on his. He turned, and she was staring at him.

"I've always loved you too."

ও ঌ

Tyler had never read the Bible his grandparents had given him when he was born. It was one of those Bibles written for kids, the Discoverer's Bible. The language it was written in was simpler and made God's message easier to understand. When he got home from the hospital, he went straight to his room and pulled the Bible from his shelf, sat on the edge of his bed, and held the book in his lap, closed.

His hands were shaking.

Tyler opened the Bible randomly and came across page 695. Nothing grabbed him, so he turned the pages until he came across Psalm 6. It did nothing to drive away his grief. He continued until he came across Matthew 6:9-13, and to his surprise, he remembered the passage from the few times his family had gone to church in Washington, mostly after the 9/11 attacks. His mother had insisted that they all start going to church on Sundays. Of course, he had not wanted to, but now he wondered whether it was coincidence or whether there had been a purpose for him to learn the Lord's Prayer.

He recited it, but once he was done, he still felt just as lost and angry. He closed the Bible and put it down beside him on the bed and stared at nothing. When his mother knocked on his bedroom door, he was so lost in thought that he didn't hear her.

"You were in a fight?"

He shrugged. "I'm sorry. I tried not to, but no one talks about Midnight that way."

She sat beside him. "Are you okay, honey?"

He turned to her. "I love her."

"And you're angry." She paused. "Is that why you had the fight?"

Another shrug. "Maybe."

"I know this hurts."

"Why her? I keep asking, why Midnight? It always seems like someone doesn't like her and just wants her to suffer."

"And that someone would be?"

Tyler hung his head low. He picked at the nail on his right thumb.

"I see you were reading the Bible."

He said nothing. His mother caressed his back.

"It's hard to understand why things happen sometimes," she said. "We live in a world that no longer believes. I'm as guilty of it as the next person. Don't be afraid to believe, to reach out to God."

"But I don't think He's listening," he said.

"Maybe He is."

"Midnight is sick, dying," he said bitterly. "I don't call that listening."

"You're expecting a miracle, honey. I'm not sure God is in the miracle business anymore."

"The Bible is full of them."

"That was a different era. Some of those miracles might be explainable today."

He looked at her. "So you don't believe in miracles?"

"I'm just saying that the world is much different today. I don't think it's God's way to dish out miracles to everyone who wants one. He'd be doing it all the time."

Tyler said nothing.

"Do you want to know what I think?" she said.

After a moment, he nodded.

"Now don't laugh, but I think that God is like comfort food."

Tyler looked at his mother as if she had gone mad.

"That's right. Comfort food makes us feel good. Reaching out to God can also make us feel good. We shouldn't just do it because we want something from Him, but because we need to give something to Him. And that something that we give to Him is our faith, our love. And by giving to Him, we get His strength back to help us get through what it is that we need to get through."

Tyler looked at the Bible beside him. His left hand touched it. He wanted Midnight to get better. He wanted a miracle that he knew would probably not come true. Losing her would be like losing his heart. He didn't want God to give him the strength to watch her die; he wanted God to make her well.

"This is difficult," he said. "Is this what being a grownup is like?"

"Being an adult is not always easy," she said. "Kids are always in such a hurry to get there because they think they'll be able to do whatever they want, but it really isn't so. With that freedom comes responsibilities, and many, many hurdles."

"You mean pain."

"That is one of the hurdles. Being an adult means that you're aware of your world, and our world has many pains."

"You're not really making this easy, Mom."

"No. I'm not."

"Is this how I'm supposed to cross over and become a man?"

A sad smile shadowed her face. "You're going to have to answer that one, honey," she said. "Love is a wonderful thing, and a cruel thing. But either way, it sure tests our strength."

Tyler licked his lips. "You know I would trade places with her if I could. I know that would be hard for you and Dad, but that's how much I love her."

His mother kissed the side of his head and held him against her.

"You don't need to worry about becoming a man," she said. "You already are."

ᴖᴗ

Samantha stood in the doorway, feeling small, timid, and scared. She was leaning on her cane because her leg hurt more today. It wasn't the only thing hurting. Looking in at Midnight, her eyes became watery. She was so tired of crying every time she saw her friend, but what else was she supposed to do? Laughter wasn't an option.

"Come in," Jim said and stood.

"Is she sleeping?"

"I'm awake," Midnight said in a tiny voice.

"I'll leave you two alone," Jim said and left.

Samantha hesitated a moment, a lifetime of friendship stuck in the back of her throat. Her mind relived all the years she had shared with Midnight and couldn't understand how it might end soon. That didn't seem real. None of this seemed real.

"Come closer," Midnight said.

Samantha wanted to touch her but held off. "You look so

fragile. I can't believe this." She caught her bottom lip between her teeth, something she had seen Midnight do for years.

"I won't break," Midnight said and gave Samantha her hand. "See?"

"I miss you at school," Samantha said. "It's weird that you're not there. I'd break my legs all over again if it made you better."

"And I'd let you if it would."

Samantha felt warm tears escape the corner of her eyes as a smile forced itself onto her face. She wanted to crawl into Midnight's bed and hold her.

"I love you," Samantha said. "And I need to sit before my legs give out."

That got a weak chuckle out of Midnight. She motioned for her friend to sit on the edge of the bed. "So, your mom and my dad," she said.

"I never thought I'd be happy about it, but I am."

"Sisters."

Samantha lay down beside Midnight and took her hand. "Sisters."

ଓ ଓ

The phone was ringing. Jim pulled himself up and glanced at the clock on the night table which indicated it was just after eleven. He couldn't remember what time he'd gone to bed. He couldn't remember much lately as all his energy was spent on Midnight. He wasn't even sure what day it was.

"Jim? It's Tom. Did I wake you? I did, didn't I? I forgot about the two-hour time difference. Sorry. I'm really sorry."

Jim was suddenly fully awake. "Did you find her? Did you

find Karen?"

The way Tom hesitated a little too long felt like lead in the bottom of Jim's gut. He didn't think he was going to like the answer.

"Yes," Tom finally said.

The word weighed heavy with hopelessness.

TWENTY-SIX

~ December 1999 ~

Karen looked at the pathetic thirty-nine-year-old that stared back at her from the mirror—lackluster hair that looked more hacked than cut, skin that felt pasty and dry, and red-rimmed eyes tortured by lifelong regrets. All these years, she had followed deadbeat rockers, sucked in by promising dreams—dreams of becoming someone, dreams that she and Jim had shared a lifetime ago.

What a fucking mess she'd made of her life. She was nothing but a broken-down whore. She'd sold herself to these incompetent men and now, about to turn forty in the new millennium, she was a skeleton of what she could have been.

A loving and caring mother.

Her children came to mind more and more lately, but fear kept her from going back. She'd been gone ten years, an entire decade. Her family would never take her back, not after all the pain she'd caused. She wouldn't take her back if she were them.

She didn't even know if Midnight had survived. What kind of mother left her child to die?

A pathetic, selfish bitch.

She was evil. Only someone without a soul could have done what she had. She stared at the woman in the mirror a long time, unable to see who this woman was, what redeeming quality this woman had.

She couldn't forgive herself.

How could anyone else?

Karen walked out of the bathroom, noticing some guy barely out of diapers passed out on the motel bed. There were empty bottles everywhere. She couldn't remember where they were, or what his name was.

If her situation wasn't so dire, she might actually cry. She couldn't bring herself to feel sorry for what life had brought her. It was all her fault. She'd had a chance at something good but had fled in fear of being suffocated by boredom in that suburban life.

That life would have been a million times better than this one.

She looked around. On the night table, a little white baggy. Part of the haze began to clear. That cocaine had been good.

Real good.

Tired and defeated sadness crossed her face.

Karen walked to the night table and scooped up the baggy. She turned to the guy on the bed, wondering if he'd been any good. She didn't notice the dried blood on his upper lip or the stillness of his chest.

She locked herself in the bathroom.

Spread the entire content of the baggy on the counter.

Three days later, after no one had come out of room 6 to pay for an extended stay, the motel manager knocked on the door several times before letting himself in.

He immediately called the cops.

TWENTY-SEVEN

~ March 2002 ~

The drive to the hospital was a battle between what Jim needed to do and what he wanted to do. It would be so easy to aim the car into oncoming traffic; end the nightmare he'd been running from for the last ten years.

But he couldn't.

He had to see this through, for Midnight. And Octavia. And his unborn grandchild.

But how could he accept this? Midnight was too damn young. All he could think of was everything that she would never do. She was never coming back home, she was never going back to school, and she was never going to marry and have a family.

That was a lot of never.

He had called Octavia and told her about Karen being dead for over two years now, and both had cried even after all these years, partly for Karen, but mostly for Midnight.

Jim parked the car and made his way to Midnight's hospital room, wondering how he would tell her about Karen. There wasn't an easy way to do it. No words in the world would change the reality that faced them all. Jim stood in the doorway looking at Midnight, knowing that what mattered now was to make the time they had left last a lifetime. The baby she had been in his arms, the toddler who had been a beacon of light in his life, the hellish years that had tested them in unbelievable ways, the wonderful young woman she had become. It was all there, wrapped in the beautiful Midnight of his life.

He took a breath and entered her room.

Midnight opened her eyes and it made him break a bit more. Her face had no colour, her smile was brave, and her eyes were full of wisdom that he'd probably never have.

"Hi Daddy."

"How did you do last night?" he said as he sat in the chair close to the bed.

The sudden wince on her face answered his question. "Nurse had to increase my medicine."

"I'm sorry, honey," he said, his chest feeling like an elephant was sitting on it. "If Daddy could make it all go away, he would."

"I know, Daddy. I know." She caught her lip between her teeth. "Please don't feel bad. It's not your fault."

"I just . . . I just hate to see you in so much pain," he managed to say. "No father wants to see his little girl suffer so much. You've been so good to me, so good to everyone. You have a good heart. A gentle heart. This world needs more Midnight."

His emotions were so overwhelming and suffocating that for a moment he was like a toddler, that wave building and building and building, until finally the wail exploded out of his lungs and didn't stop until he had emptied himself.

"I'm sorry," he said over and over, resting his forehead on the side of the bed, filled with shame. "I feel so helpless."

Midnight stroked the top of his head. "It's okay," she said, and then waited until a jab of pain faded. "It's okay."

He raised his head just in time to see the pain fade from her face. He'd had almost sixteen wonderful years with her, but that wasn't enough. He wanted more. So much more. What could he possibly do to get more time with her? She was too young.

"Do you remember your first day in grade one?" he said. "You came home, upset with Samantha because she couldn't play the same way as Tyler." He looked at Midnight, and even though her eyes were closed, she smiled at the memory. "You swore that you'd never be able to stay friends with her, and then you asked me when Tyler was going to move back and I had to tell you, for the millionth time, that he had moved away and chances were that he wouldn't be coming back. Well, we were both wrong. You became best friends with Samantha *and* Tyler is back."

"Funny how things turn out," she said, opening her eyes.

"Life is full of surprises." He stroked her hair and stared at her like she was some kind of deity. "None better than the day you were born. You were such a good baby. Barely ever cried. Even during your first fight with cancer, you were a real trooper. You deserve so much better than you've gotten, yet you've never complained. I'm so lucky to be your dad."

"And you've been a great one," she said. "Even when Octavia wasn't easy to deal with, you kept it together. You did a good job of taking care of us."

Jim kissed her on the nose and stared into her eyes—her beautiful green eyes full of serenity. She could probably see the panic in his. He'd never been good at hiding how he felt.

Midnight knew what was coming and somehow, she'd managed to accept it. Through her eyes, he could tell that she was at peace with her fate. He was still at war.

He pulled away. "If you could get out of here right now, what would you like to do more than anything?"

Midnight thought it over. "I'd like to visit France," she said. "And then all of Europe. I think it would be nice to see where our ancestors came from."

"That would be a wonderful trip," he said.

"Maybe you can take that trip," she said and closed her eyes again. She waited a moment. "For me."

"Don't talk like that."

She opened her eyes. "We can't change what is."

"How about we wait until you get better and we both go."

She shook her head.

"Oh, honey," Jim said. "You can beat this."

"I don't think that's going to happen, Dad. The typical treatments aren't working. A donor is what I need, but none have been found."

She closed her eyes again and Jim could see that she was fighting to stay awake for him. He didn't see the point in telling her about her mother. Her words told him that she already knew.

"Get some rest, sweetie," he said. "I'll just sit here."

Midnight was asleep in seconds. He watched her sleep, watched her chest rise and fall, and he thought he could do that forever.

଼ ଼

Samantha and Tyler walked into Midnight's hospital room

together, Samantha's right arm looped around Tyler's left for support. She hadn't brought her cane today.

"Hey guys," Midnight said. "How's the leg?"

"It hurts a bit," Samantha said, "Not sure if my limp will ever go away, but I'm not complaining. I've got this nice young man helping me out."

"Yes he is," Midnight said.

Tyler kissed her. "How are you feeling?"

"I'm okay," she said. "What's it like outside?"

"Beautiful March day," Tyler said. "Looks like winter is over for another year. The sun feels warm again."

"Take me out," Midnight said.

Samantha and Tyler looked at one another.

"Not sure we can do that," Samantha said. "Can we?"

"I haven't been outside in such a long time and I just want to feel the sun on my face one more time."

Tyler went to ask a nurse. Fifteen minutes later, bundled against the cold, Tyler pushed Midnight down the walkway in a wheelchair, and headed out toward where the sun could shine on them.

Midnight shivered when the rays touched her face.

"Are you cold?" Samantha said.

"A little," Midnight said. "But I'll be fine. It feels so good."

"We'll only stay a few minutes," Tyler said. "Let me know if you start to feel pain and we'll go."

Midnight reached for his hand. "I'm okay."

The three friends stood outside for a bit, enjoying the early spring warmth, enjoying each other's company. No one spoke. No one felt the need to. They all knew what this moment meant, a moment that Tyler and Samantha would look back on with the fondest of memories.

Twenty minutes later, Midnight was back in her bed, exhausted but happy.

"I think we're going to go," Tyler said at last. "You look really tired and probably need some rest."

"We'll come back later," Samantha said.

"I'm sorry, you guys."

"Nothing to be sorry about," Samantha said and hugged Midnight as best she could. "I love you. Keep fighting."

Tyler pressed his lips against Midnight's, desperation and fear and pain seeming to flow through his flesh, as if knowing that it would be their last kiss. "I love you so much."

"I love you too."

ଔ ଓ

Samantha was dropped off at home by Tyler's mom and when she entered the house and saw Emily coming down the stairs, she made a beeline for Emily and wrapped her arms around her sister.

"What's wrong with you?" Emily said, trying to break free. "Let go of me, you freak."

Samantha held her a moment longer, and then let go. "I love you."

"Whatever," Emily said. "Mom, I think Sam has taken too many meds."

Tracy Carmichael was in the foyer, putting on her coat. She had a knowing smile on her lips. "Samantha is fine, honey."

"Yeah, well, I don't think so," Emily said. "Where are you

going?"

"Jim's picking me up. We're going to the hospital."

"Oh," Emily said.

"I'll be back in a little while."

"We'll be fine," Samantha said.

Tracy nodded. "I know you will."

☙ ❧

Midnight had fallen asleep immediately after Tyler and Samantha had left and as she was waking up, she saw her dad and Mrs. Carmichael sitting in a couple of chairs, holding hands. That made her smile.

"How long have you two been here?" she said.

"A while," Jim said.

They got up and approached the bed. Jim kissed her forehead and took her hand while Tracy took her other hand.

"Hi sweetie," Tracy said.

Midnight's one regret was that she wasn't going to see her dad be happy but knowing that he'd found someone as nice as Mrs. Carmichael made it a little easier to accept.

"Thank you," Midnight said.

Tracy frowned.

"For everything you've done for me," Midnight said. "I really appreciate it. You were like . . ."

"It was easy," Tracy said. "You're a beautiful person and you've made Samantha a better person, so I'm the one that ought to thank you. Who would have guessed all those years ago when we met camping that you'd change all our lives?"

"He needs you," Midnight said. "Now that I won't be here to

take care of him."

"Don't talk that way," Jim said, his face a mess of sadness. "You're my beautiful baby girl and I can't . . . it's just . . . I . . ."

"It'll be okay, Dad," Midnight said. "You'll be okay."

"This is so . . ."

Just then Octavia entered the room and approached the bed. She put a hand on her father's back and gave him a gentle rub. "Hey, little sister."

"Hey, big sister," Midnight said. "Come closer, I want to feel your belly."

Jim switched position with his eldest daughter so Midnight could reach Octavia's belly. "It's still too early to feel movement."

"That's so cool," Midnight said. "Just knowing a little baby is growing in there."

"You look wonderful," Tracy said. "How are your mornings?"

"So far, not too bad."

"I was sick like a dog with Samantha, and barely anything with Emily."

"Hopefully it stays not too bad," Octavia said.

"We're going to get coffees," Jim said as he reached for Tracy's hand. "You two haven't had a lot of time together lately."

"If you see Mark, give him the room number," Octavia said. "He dropped me off and went to park the car."

"I will," he said and they left.

"I never thought I'd see the day," Octavia said.

"Neither did I." Pain made her wince. "It couldn't happen at a better time."

Octavia took her sister's hand. "So, how are you really, little sis?"

"I'm not doing too good. The pain is constant now, and I had the nurses increase the medicine this morning again. Not sure how much more they can do that."

Octavia drew in a long breath. "I wish I could have been a donor."

"You've done so much for me," Midnight said.

"Not enough," Octavia said.

"I'm ready."

Octavia couldn't talk.

"I'm tired, Octavia. I might have a few more hours or a few more days, but I'm okay with that. Just knowing Dad will have Mrs. Carmichael to get him through it is all I could hope for. I can go with peace in my heart."

Octavia grabbed her sister's hand and squeezed it.

"Remember when I used to sneak into your bed?" Midnight said, her weary face taking on a hint of colour from the memory. "I don't think you told me even once that I couldn't do that or that I needed to go back to my own bed."

"I couldn't do that. You needed me and I probably needed you just as much. All we had was each other." Tears stung Octavia's eyes.

"You took care of me when I was sick. You helped me when Tyler moved away and broke my little five-year-old heart. You showed me how to apply makeup, although I still don't do it very well and needed Samantha's help for my dates with Tyler."

Octavia grabbed a bunch of tissues from the table next to the bed.

"My only regret," Midnight said, "is that I will never get to know your baby. I'll never get to hold or babysit my niece or nephew. I think I would have made an awesome aunt."

"I know you'd be an awesome aunt," Octavia said, sobs choking her words. She pulled out her camera from her purse. "And he or she is going to get to know you. I want to record you. Say whatever you want to say to your future niece or nephew."

Midnight bit her lower lip as she thought of what to say, and Octavia captured her little sister for eternity.

"Hi," Midnight said, looking at the camera. "It's March 25, 2002, and right now your mom, who by the way is a wonderful person, is filming me, your Aunt Midnight. I'm very sick and I probably won't get to know you. I'm very sad about that, but I know that I'll be able to watch over you from heaven."

Midnight stopped, closed her eyes, and waited for the pain to ease which seemed to last forever. When she opened her eyes, her dad, Tracy, Mark, Tyler, Samantha, and Emily, who was holding her sister's hand, were all standing beside Octavia. Everyone that had ever really mattered to her was here.

It was all she needed.

"When you get scared at night," Midnight continued. "Your mom will be there to make all your bad dreams go away, just like she did for me when I was little like you . . ."

Did you enjoy *Beautiful Midnight*?

You can make a big difference. Reviews are incredibly powerful in bringing attention to my books and helping other readers decide to take a chance and read them. I'd be extremely grateful if you could take a few minutes to leave your review on your favourite social media site as well as on any of these sites: Amazon, Kobo, Barnes & Noble, Smashwords, and other online book retailers.

Building a relationship with my readers who have decided to take this journey with me is really awesome, and as a thank you for signing-up to my Readers' Group on my website, you'll get a FREE copy of my novella *We Became Us*. You'll only hear from me periodically when I have something to share with you, and I promise never to spam you. You'll be able to unsubscribe from my Readers' Group anytime you want, but I hope you'll stick around because more stories are coming.

Story behind *Beautiful Midnight*

I wrote the original draft of *Beautiful Midnight* in 2007-2008 after my father passed away. This was the second novel I'd written over two years (writing really helped me get through that tough period in my life) but before I could start to edit it, the idea for *It Happened to Us* came and I wrote it immediately. I ended up publishing that one first but I couldn't ignore *Beautiful Midnight* any longer. So in 2015, I started to edit and rewrite it, and with the help of a wonderful editor, it all came together. I'm extremely happy with how it turned out and I hope you feel the same. If you enjoyed it, why not try one of my other books?

A short excerpt of each follows next.

And if you've read them all, sit tight because more are coming (I just have that full-time job thing getting in the way but until *that* changes, I'll continue to write whenever I can).

As always, happy reading!

Excerpt from

THE LITTLE LIES WE HIDE

ONE

Why are you behaving like a dumbass?"

"I'm not!"

"Of course you are."

Bradley glared at Kate from across the living room, the black leather couch between them acting like a bored arbitrator. Behind him, a wall of windows looked out at the Vancouver skyline from the seventeenth floor.

This was Kate's three-million-dollar condo. He had a tiny apartment about a tenth of the size in the old part of downtown. It was within walking distance of the radio station he worked at as the Program Director, so the location suited him fine.

Besides, Bradley didn't own a car.

Kate, on the other hand, had a brand-new BMW 4 Series Convertible in a gorgeous Melbourne Red Metallic. It complemented her high-powered position as Executive Vice-President of the conglomerate that owned, amongst many things, the radio station Bradley worked at.

"We're going to be late for work," he said. "Can we talk about this later?"

"Well, *you're* going to be late for work as I can pretty much come in as I please, and no, we're going to talk about this right now."

"Oh, pulling the old boss trick on me."

Kate crossed her arms and focused her emerald green eyes on him. He could feel the sharp intensity radiating from them cut him to pieces. He hated it when she pulled rank. Didn't make for fair play.

But damn it if she didn't look beautiful. At forty, she put to shame girls half her age, and in the boardroom, she ate grown men whole with her sharp tongue and sharper intelligence. Why she was with him, he still couldn't quite figure out. And this argument they were having left him even more confused. Had she really just asked him—?

"Whatever it takes," she said.

"Whatever it takes? You make it sound like I'm some deal you need to close before breakfast. And I haven't even had a cup of coffee. Why can't we get a damn coffee machine in here?"

"If that's what you need to say yes, then I'll have one installed this afternoon."

Bradley ran a hand through his longish auburn but slightly greying hair. A few weeks back, he'd told Kate he was thinking of getting his hair cut short, but she hadn't liked the idea. She'd told him the long hair, the goatee, and the earrings fit his radio persona to a T. And then she'd added *makes me weak in the knees.*

Nothing made her weak in the knees, as far as he knew. They had met about three years ago when her company had bought the radio station he'd been working at. The station had gone through different ownerships over the years, changed format a few times to try to cater to new markets, and there had even been rumours of being shut down. But then Kate had showed up one Monday afternoon and gathered the staff and told them they'd been bought. No surprise there for anyone, and of course all the mumbo-jumbo coming out of Kate's mouth about them turning a corner and becoming *the* radio station of Vancouver had fallen on deaf ears. They'd heard it before, including Bradley.

Except that he hadn't been able to keep his eyes off this tall brunette wearing a power suit that probably cost more than his monthly wage, and the faint aroma of her perfume had been just strong enough to make him imagine that her smile was filled with hidden messages and possibilities.

Not the first time he'd been fooled so easily.

And as quickly as she had materialized on that day, he'd barely seen her the next three months. The station still sucked, the format was still awful and dated, and just like before, rumours of being shut down floated through the stale office air like a bad cold.

Then things started to change, and fast. The previous Program Director was shown the door, Bradley was told he was the new PD (he'd sensed he couldn't refuse, unless he viewed being unemployed as a better career move), and Kate became a permanent resident of the station. Three months later, the station had been well on its way to becoming *the* radio station of Vancouver and Bradley had found himself falling hard for Kate.

So why was he freaking out at her marriage proposal?

☙ ❧

He should have known something was up this morning when he found Kate still in bed at five. She never skipped a day to run her

5k before work. He'd thought maybe she was sick, but he'd never known her to be sick. The woman was all about healthy lifestyle. She popped vitamins like they were M&Ms. Probably when they then made love, that should have told him that something was definitely up, but when Kate O'Grady made love to him, she was like a drug that left him completely and utterly in her possession.

He wasn't complaining.

He really did love her.

But why did they need to get married? Hadn't she been the one who had said two years ago that although she wasn't looking for a fly-by-night fling, marriage wasn't on her horizon either? That had suited him just fine. This was 2018 and no one needed a marriage certificate to *seal the deal*. He hadn't needed a piece of paper to confirm his feelings for her, and neither had she.

Until this morning.

"Marriage? Why now? What's changed?"

"Not exactly the response I'd expected," she said and softened her stance. A little. "What's changed? I guess *I* have. I'm not twenty anymore."

"So?"

Kate looked at him as if he were a bad puppy who had just peed on the floor, and she was about to reprimand him. He hated feeling so inferior to her. Maybe that's why he didn't get the marriage thing all of a sudden. She really didn't need him, but he hoped that she still wanted him. Of *course* she did. Why else would she want to marry him?

Well, he knew one person who would be thrilled at the news: his mom. It had been a long time since he'd spoken to her—last Mother's Day, he thought. It was September. Crap, he'd let time fly.

"You here?" Kate said with a flash of annoyance. "Bradley Knighton?"

He was in trouble now. She only used his full name when she was getting pretty pissed with him. "Just thinking about my mother."

"Seriously?" she said, now totally irritated. "I ask you to marry me and your mom is what pops into your head."

"Yeah," he said, getting defensive. "I was thinking that if anyone was going to be thrilled at the news, it will be her."

"Well, that's exactly why I've asked you to marry me," Kate said with a hint of irony. "So I can meet her and the rest of your family."

Bradley became distantly quiet.

"What is it with you and your family?" she said, softening her tone. "You never talk about them. When's the last time you actually went home?"

"A while," he whispered.

"You might need to right whatever is wrong there," she said. "I won't put up with any family ill will at my wedding."

"So, it's a done deal?" he said, sounding like a six-year-old. "I don't even get to say what I want?"

"Jesus, Brad!" She closed the distance between them and stood a foot away. "Do you love me?"

"Of course."

"Then what's the holdup?"

He tried to step away but she grabbed his arm. He looked down at her grasp, a sudden burn churning deep inside of him in a place he couldn't reach. "I don't know. I guess it's not something I ever thought we'd be discussing. I didn't think we needed it to be together."

She let go of his arm. "I didn't think I needed it either before . . . before I met you. You're special to me. No other man has ever made me feel this complete before. I guess . . . I guess I don't want to lose you."

He looked into her eyes, the depth of her love pulling him in and driving it home that he was a fool not to put a ring on her finger. Still, he couldn't silence the nagging burn. "Marriage is no guarantee. We both know that."

She stepped into him and rested her head in the hollow of his shoulder. She was the strongest woman he'd ever known and it always caught him by surprise when she showed that she had fears and insecurities; that, like everyone else, she had vulnerabilities.

He wrapped his arms around her and took in the scent of her perfume. Why couldn't he say yes?

The answer was nineteen years in the past and thousands of miles east.

ଓ ୨

Bradley was standing at the massive kitchen island, a glass of orange juice in hand. He set it down on the granite countertop, his hand running against its smooth surface, not finding any of the chipped edges that were so prominent along the worn laminate countertop at his apartment. The more time he spent in Kate's condo, the more he realized the huge gap between their lifestyles.

When is the last time she's been in my apartment?

"Don't worry about it," Kate said, back from the washroom.

She looked ready to take on the world for another day. "You obviously don't feel the same as I do."

"It's not that," he said in a voice full of regret. "I'm crazy about you."

"But?"

"There's no but," he said, his hand still running across the granite. "Look at this countertop."

Standing on the other side of the island, she crossed her arms. "What about it?"

"It's gorgeous."

She sighed. "Brad, really? And your point?"

"I make about sixty thousand a year. I live in a shabby apartment in a downtown area that's not the safest. You live along the waterfront in this luxurious condo. I know what these condos sell for."

"Again, what is your point?""

He rubbed his goatee. The grey in it was starting to bother him. Why was he getting so much grey lately? He was only thirty-eight. Then again, Dad had been mostly bald by forty, so maybe grey wasn't so bad.

"I'm not with you because of your money. That's not who I am."

"I know," she said. "But it's never bothered you before that I have a slightly higher standard of living."

He raised an eyebrow. "Slightly?"

Her embarrassed yet slightly coy smile was framed by uncharacteristically blushing cheeks. "Touché."

They stared at each other, two people madly in love but being held back by baggage that should have been tossed long ago. Was he afraid that if he finally said yes, he'd be closing that door from his past forever?

"Talk to me," Kate said. "You need time to think about it? Then take it. I know I blindsided you a little . . . okay, a lot."

"I just don't quite get it. Why now?"

"I turned forty back in May."

"It was a great party."

She smiled. "It was."

"So?"

She reached for his hands and took a moment before she looked at him. "I'm forty and I want to have a baby with you."

The look on his face was that of a man who'd been shot and hadn't realized just yet that he was bleeding out.

☙ ❧

Bradley pulled his hand away like he'd just touched something hot, and backed away. He looked at Kate as if she were a stranger. "A baby?" he said, sounding as horrified as he felt. "You want to have a *baby*? You? Do you know what that will do to your career? Are you going to become a stay-at-home mom? I can't afford to keep us in this condo, and my tiny apartment is going to get real cramped real fast with three of us living in it. A baby! Really?"

He started to pace the length of the island like a dog needing to go out for a pee. Or in his case, flee.

"Brad, stop!" She waited until he stood still and looked at her. "No, I'm not going to become a stay-at-home mom. I don't know the first thing about babies, I admit. But there are lots of great nannies out there. I'm not giving up my career, but I'm willing to make concessions. Having a baby with you is the purest sign that I know of to show how much we love each other. And I want our child to have married parents. That's important to me. My parents are still together after fifty-one years."

"And they already have ten grandkids thanks to your brother and sisters."

"But not from me and you," she said. "You know they're very fond of you."

They were great people who'd been good to him. Her entire family was what he thought families should be like: lots of laughter, innocent ribbing, and a ton of love and support. And they had accepted and welcomed him into their stronghold instantly, easing the estrangement from his own family.

But a baby?

At this point in their lives?

Boy, she was full of surprises today. First, she proposed to him, and now she wanted a baby. None of these things had ever crossed his mind before, and he was pretty sure they had never crossed her mind before either. The last thing he'd ever seen himself as was a married man and a father.

And then it hit him, the irony of his predicament. If—and that's a big if—things had worked out all those years ago, he'd probably be married now and odds were that he'd have at least one kid, probably more. Maybe what had happened was a blessing, because he wasn't convinced that he was cut out for either of those.

So, what exactly was he cut out for? What did he want?

What he was cut out for and what he wanted was what his life already was: Program Director of the most popular radio station in Vancouver, and sharing his life with the most wonderful woman he'd been lucky enough to find. That was enough for him.

Apparently, it was no longer enough for her.

"We can't have a baby for your parents' sake."

"That's not why I want one."

"This is coming out of nowhere. You can't return it after it's born, there is no thirty-day money back guarantee. A baby comes out screaming and turns everything upside down. Not unlike the Tasmanian Devil."

"You're comparing our child to the Tasmanian Devil?"

"Our child?" A worried frown wrinkled his forehead. "Are you already pregnant? Because if you—"

"Relax," she said with that tone she used at the office to take control of a situation just before it got out of hand. "Take a breath. I'm not pregnant. Give me some credit here. I'm not trying to trap you into a situation that would be based on a lie. I want you to be as committed to us as I am."

Bradley clenched his jaw and gritted his teeth, a habit he'd developed long ago to control his anger when all he'd wanted to do was take a baseball bat to David after another humiliating prank by his brother. Like then, he now felt trapped and helpless; he loses and someone else wins. He'd really believed that twenty-year-old loser Bradley had been left behind in Ottawa, that finding Kate had been meant to happen all along, that finding her had been the biggest win of his life, a win that big brother David couldn't ever take from him.

But now he feared that if he didn't go along with Kate's plan, he'd lose her. No David to blame. Just himself.

He was so damned tired of being on the losing end.

"I am—"

His cell phone began to play *Time Bomb*, a song that had resonated with him as a teenager and had seemed fitting as his ring tone—the perfect anthem to his chaotic and messy life. Definitely fitting for today.

"Who is it?"

Bradley looked at the number on the screen and his face folded into a questioning frown. "My sister."

Connect with François Houle

www.francoisghoule.com

www.facebook.com/francoishouleauthor

www.bookbub.com/authors/francois-houle

Acknowledgments

My wife and daughter mean the world to me and their support inspires me every day. My daughter is a teenager now and is very artistic, so she's become a wonderful resource for judging my book covers, and we both think the cover for *Beautiful Midnight* is the best one so far.

I'd like to say a special thank you to my editor Ethan James Clarke of SilverJay Editing. He has a wonderful eye and provided awesome suggestions that helped make this story that much stronger.

Most importantly, I want to thank you for coming along on this journey with me. I hope you enjoyed reading *Beautiful Midnight* as much as I did writing it.

Until next time, take care.

Also by François Houle

We Became Us

Broken Hearts

It Happened to Us

The Little Lies We Hide

The Trees Have Buds

About François Houle

François Houle's first novel *It Happened to Us* spent multiple weeks in 2019 as an Amazon top 100 best seller in two categories. His fiction explores themes that are universal such as family and friendships, love and grief, and anything else that makes us all human. Reviews often refer to his books as "beautifully written," "heartbreaking and heartwarming," and "intense and emotional."

François is one of five boys so it's no surprise that family is a strong theme in his books. A lot of the inspiration for his first two novels *It Happened to Us* and *Beautiful Midnight* came from the passing of his father in 2005.

François grew up in a small town outside of Montréal, moved to Toronto when he was ten, and currently lives in Ottawa. An avid reader from a young age, he tried to create a comic book when he was twelve, penned hundreds of song lyrics as a teenager, and wrote his first novel in 1985, a sci-fi influenced by the novel *Dune.* Several horror novels followed, and although none of these books will ever be published, they were important in his development as an author.

In 1985, at the age of 22, he graduated from college with a Programmer/Analyst diploma and then went into the ice cream business with his family, owning three Baskin-Robbins franchises for about 6 years. In 1991, he started his IT career, and from 2003 – 2017, he was a Certified Professional Résumé Writer and operated a part-time business writing résumés, which helped while his wife took a sabbatical from work to stay home and care for their two kids.

If you'd like to stay current with what he's working on, please like his Facebook page and join his Insiders Group at *www.francoisghoule.com*.

Fun Facts About Me

1. I'm a big hockey and football fan.
2. I love alternative music (*The Twilight Sad* is one of my all-time favourite bands).
3. I enjoy woodworking

www.ingramcontent.com/pod-product-compliance
Lightning Source LLC
Chambersburg PA
CBHW070621260626
47161CB00007B/2535

* 9 7 8 1 7 7 5 0 4 9 0 2 9 *